'You will leav[e]'

Francis smiled, but the expression on his face sent a shiver down Charlotte's spine. 'If you are looking for a gentleman to seduce, I am available. You would, I fancy, find my attentions more acceptable than those of a man old enough to be your father.'

He stopped on Charlotte's outraged gasp, as tears of anger and disappointment streamed down her cheeks. 'I thought you a gentleman, but I have misjudged you. I want nothing from either of you except my due as a governess!'

Dear Reader

We have a Regency treat from Petra Nash this month, when ALL OF HEAVEN follows the tribulations of Miss Cecilia Avening. Lord Marcus Inglesham doesn't know what he holds, but the children make sure he finds out! We welcome back Sarah Westleigh, as she moves from medieval to the Devon of 1866, when eighteen-year-old Charlotte Falconer discovers her real father is Sir George Bradgate. We think you will enjoy HERITAGE OF LOVE. Have fun!

The Editor

Sarah Westleigh has enjoyed a varied life. Working as a local government officer in London, she qualified as a chartered quantity surveyor. She assisted her husband in his chartered accountancy practice, at the same time managing an employment agency. Moving to Devon, she finally found time to write, publishing short stories and articles, before discovering historical novels.

Recent titles by the same author:

LOYAL HEARTS
SET FREE MY HEART ⎱ d'Evreux family trilogy
THE INHERITED BRIDE ⎰

HERITAGE
OF LOVE

Sarah Westleigh

First published in Great Britain 1993
by Mills & Boon Limited

© Sarah Westleigh 1993

Australian copyright 1993
Philippine copyright 1993
This edition 1993

ISBN 0 263 78053 8

Masquerade is a trademark published by
Mills & Boon Limited, Eton House,
18–24 Paradise Road, Richmond, Surrey, TW9 1SR.

Set in 10 on 11½ pt Linotron Times
04-9305-73885

Typeset in Great Britain by Centracet, Cambridge
Made and printed in Great Britain

AUTHOR'S NOTE

ALTHOUGH the major events affecting Brixham in the years 1866/67 are historically true, where necessary and where information is scant I have bent their course to my purpose. In the main I have peopled my story with persons who have never existed other than in my mind, and have invented the houses in which they dwelt. Exceptions are Mr Richard W. Wolston, solicitor, businessman and the moving spirit behind the building of the Brixham Branch Line, and his Resident Engineer, Mr S. Stewart. Without mention of these two men no reference to the building of the railway would be historically credible, though of necessity my descriptions of them rely entirely on imagination.

CHAPTER ONE

CHARLOTTE'S knuckles whitened under the fierceness of her grip on the bars of the great gate, a grip which strained apart the stitches of her woollen gloves. The cold of the iron struck straight through, but she did not notice.

She pressed her body against the barrier and squeezed her face between the uprights—just below the place where a heraldic shield had been fixed, depicting a fancy cross and a couple of anchors, the coat of arms of the family who had owned the Hall since the times of Queen Anne. The Bradgates.

Still the outline of the building at the end of the rising avenue of leafless elms remained obscure. Eyes narrowed, absorbed in her scrutiny, she failed to register the approaching sound of horse's hoofs until the rider swung his mount into the sweeping entranceway behind her. Startled, she jumped aside, her muttered sound of apology lost in the clangour of the bell as the rider reached up to flick it with his crop.

The sound jangled harshly on Charlotte's already stretched nerves. She should not be here. She drew her shawl about her and began to sidle away.

But she was not to escape so easily.

'Who are you? What are you doing here?'

The sharp tones, holding some alien accent, rapped out from far above her head. Charlotte raised golden-flecked hazel eyes rimmed with long, dark lashes to the figure sitting with easy, upright grace in the saddle of the huge roan. She swallowed nervously.

'I was just. . .just looking, sir,' she muttered, dipping an automatic bob.

'At the house?' He lifted a finely shaped fair brow over an eye so blue it reminded her of a cloudless summer sky. Frowning, he spoke again, in a clipped tone of authority. 'Are you a stranger hereabouts, then? Have you not seen it before?'

'I live down in Brixham Quay, sir. I seldom come up Town, and I cannot remember ever being out so far as this before.'

She had an attractive Devon burr, but her voice and way of speaking bespoke superior education. Hers was not the thick, almost unintelligible speech of most of the locals with whom he had exchanged words, and he could not fault her grammar. Her manner was that of someone gently bred.

The man eyed her curiously, his gaze rising from the wide hem of her rusty black serge gown, up past her waist — trim despite a lack of whalebone and lacing evidenced by the supple way her body moved — to linger on the enticing swell of full breasts that even the ill-fitting garment and a tightly clutched shawl could not disguise. A gleam of appreciation lit his eyes before they lifted to the unbecoming black bonnet which framed her face but concealed most of her tightly twisted, abundant chestnut hair, tendrils of which had escaped their bonds to shine like polished copper in an elusive shaft of winter sunlight.

His broad shoulders relaxed under the layers of brown suiting and cape which swathed them. Leather creaked as he shifted in his saddle. Muscular thighs, moulded by buff breeches, flexed as his shining boots, slightly dusty from his journey and showing traces of thick mud around the soles, bore down in his stirrups. He lifted his thickly gloved hand and tipped his high beaver hat in her direction, revealing more of thick hair the colour of ripe corn, a shade brighter than the carefully trimmed sideburns which reached down to the angle of his determined jaw.

'A pity,' he drawled softly, his eyes lazily scrutinising the perfect oval of her face, a perfection marred only by an intriguing cleft in her firm little chin. Her full lips, parted now in agitation, hinted enticingly at latent passion. He noted the transparent paleness of her skin, the redness around her unusual eyes, and his own sharpened. 'You are lately bereaved?' he asked abruptly.

Charlotte dropped her gaze, bemused first by the blaze of interest and then the sudden sympathy in the arresting eyes still set boldly upon her.

Resenting his intrusion into her sorrow yet unable to refuse him an answer, she swallowed down the renewal of emotion his words evoked and blinked her lids to deny threatened tears.

'My mother, sir,' she informed him tightly. 'She died last evening.'

His face immediately sobered. He dipped his head in acknowledgement of her grief. 'My condolences,' he offered quietly. 'But should you not be at home? There will be others who need comfort.'

'No doubt, sir,' came her swift, defensive reply. Her shoulders stiffened and her chin lifted challengingly. His implied criticism had hit a tender spot in her conscience. 'But I needed to walk. And my steps brought me here.'

'Only to have your mind plagued with curiosity about Bradgate Hall?' he queried, a hint of humour entering his cultured tones, giving them a softer, musical quality which immediately lightened the strange, almost antagonistic atmosphere which had built up between them.

The smile accompanying his words lit his lean features with irresistible charm.

At that moment a woman panted out of the door to the gatekeeper's lodge, wiping her reddened hands and arms on her white apron and crying aloud her apologies for keeping the young man waiting.

Charlotte was not sorry to have his attention diverted. His questions, his manner, particularly his smile, were having a disturbing effect on her composure. There should have been no thread of awareness between them to cause tension. He should have dismissed her coldly as of no account and she should have accepted his reprimand without any attempt to justify her actions to one so far above her in station.

'I be that sorry, Major Langford, sir. But my Sawyer, he be off to the master's bidding. . .'

'That's all right, Jess. Miss —' he hesitated, giving Charlotte an enquiring glance. When she failed to respond with her name, one corner of his mouth dented in, but he did not press her. Shrugging dismissively, he went on, his tone reverting to his original clipped accents, 'The young lady here has kept me well entertained.'

One half of the great gate swung open. He prepared to pass through into a world so far removed from hers that it might as well have been up on the moon. Polite to the last, he touched the brim of his hat with his crop.

'Good afternoon to you, ma'am. I trust you will soon recover from your grief.'

His parting smile was brief, cool and aloof, yet he had bothered to give it. Something thumped in Charlotte's chest and rose into her throat to prevent her answering. She watched the horse and rider trot along the gravelled drive, her feet rooted to the spot.

Jess swung the heavy gate back into place and locked it. Bradgate Hall was not open to casual visitors.

'Best be on your way, my girl,' she muttered crossly, suppressing a shiver and clamping a hand to her head as a gust of bitter wind flapped her apron about her body and threatened to dislodge her linen cap. 'Bain't no use hanging about here no longer. The Major won't be coming out again today. Anyways,' she observed disparagingly, 'he had no business conversing with the likes of you.'

'Who is he?' asked Charlotte huskily, having recovered the power of speech.

'Francis Langford be the master's stepson, if'n' it be any business of yourn. Grandson of an earl he be, and not properly a major no more, but I keeps forgetting he's handed in his colours since he was wounded in that there civil war over there. So, like I says, bain't no point in you hanging around these parts. He won't want nought to do with the likes of you, can't think why he took the trouble to speak at all. He's a decent young gentleman, is our Major Langford, even though he be from America, like his ma.'

Jess was already halfway back to her snug cottage. Charlotte called her thanks for the information, choosing to ignore the slight the woman had made on her character. She turned away with a distinct feeling of disappointment.

Not because his surprising interest — explained perhaps by his coming from the other side of the Atlantic — had turned back to cool appraisal. Of course not. That had been her own fault. But because the man she had spoken with had been neither Sir George nor Tristram Bradgate. She would have given much to meet either the squire or his son face to face.

Pulling her shawl more tightly around her body

against the cutting wind, she turned her steps away
from the turnpike road, back towards Church Town. A
group of women loitered chatting by the pump in St
Mary's Square as they filled their vessels, and paused
to pass the time of day. Having acknowledged their
greeting, she headed down into the valley before turning aside to ascend Windmill Hill to reach the ropery.
From there it would be an easy walk down to Brixham
Quay, where the younger children awaited her in the
cottage of the man she had always thought of as her
father.

Her feet lagged and tears sprang to her eyes again as
she climbed, oblivious of the view, of the leafless
orchards which in summer clothed the hillsides in green
and in autumn fed the cider pound. How easily the
tears seemed to fall! She, Charlotte Elizabeth Falconer,
who never cried, had done little else since yesterday
evening.

She had pumped rainwater from the cistern in the yard
to warm it in kettle and pans over the old range. Unlike
some of the newer models recently on the market theirs
had no built-in boiler. Then, glad of the excuse to
escape the shrieks of agony from above, if only for a
few minutes, she had put the yoke over her shoulders
and headed for the nearest communal cistern to draw
fresher water, though even that would have to be boiled
before it was fit to drink.

Her mother was brought to child-bed regularly every
year, so at eighteen Charlotte was well versed in the
facts and rituals of giving birth. After a few hours
Elizabeth Falconer was normally smiling and peaceful,
sad if the babe had died, but resigned, and ready to go
through the whole process again next year if God and
her husband so willed. She had borne seventeen chil-

dren, of whom ten still lived. Of recent years most of
the babies had arrived early and dead, and the one who
had lived for more than a few hours, little Jackie, was
sickly and not expected to survive long enough to be
breeched.

But yesterday something had gone dreadfully wrong.
The baby had been stillborn — as expected since he had
tried to enter the world a full two months before his
time — but Elizabeth Falconer had not recovered from
the ordeal with her normal ease.

The midwife had come down to the kitchen unusually
grim, her apron stained with blood, the dead baby in
her hands. A small wooden box had been prepared for
such an eventuality, and she placed the linen-wrapped
scrap inside before she spoke.

'Your ma wants a word wi' you, my lover. You'd
better go on up. She's weak, mind. Don't tire her.'

'Weak?' Charlotte's voice had tightened with anxiety.
'What do you mean? She's usually fine. . .'

'Not this time she bain't. She be bleeding bad, and I
can't stop it — '

'Why didn't you tell me? We must send for Dr Stone
at once! Danny!' She darted through the lean-to scullery with its leaky roof and across the yard to the shed
behind, where her brothers and sisters were playing by
the light of a storm lantern, surrounded by accumulated
junk and stores of rope. 'Danny! Come here!'

The tall lad came reluctantly, at sixteen a truculent
obeyer of orders, especially from her.

'Aw, Lottie, I've only just got back. I'm whacked.
Why pick on me?' he grumbled as he slouched into the
kitchen.

He had been sitting on the ground idly throwing his
five-stones. Charlotte eyed him in the lamplight with a
certain amount of sympathy. He did look weary. He

worked long and hard up at the ropery. Turning that huge wheel for hours on end was not easy, even for a stalwart youngster like Danny. Charlotte suppressed her sympathy and sharpened her tone. 'Danny, this is urgent. Run for Dr Stone at once. Tell him it's Ma. Mrs Regent here can't cope. He's needed immediately!'

'What do I do if he's not there?' frowned Danny, kicking mutinously at a corner of the rag rug set on the flags in front of the range, which had decided to sulk, adding the smell of soot to that of a smoking wick.

'Then I suppose you'll have to go to Beeston, the parish doctor, though I've little faith in his ability to help. But do hurry!' she urged, desperation entering her shaking voice.

Danny looked up. His handsome young face held the first signs of growing apprehension as he began to sense the urgency driving his sister. 'Isn't Ma all right, then?' he asked anxiously.

'No, she's not. Tell Doctor she's bleeding badly. But don't frighten the others yet. Do your level best to fetch Dr Stone — and do be quick!' pleaded Charlotte.

'Didn't think you could afford doctor's fees, my lover,' muttered Maria Regent uncomfortably as Danny, convinced of the urgency of his errand at last, grabbed his cap and shot out. She had washed the blood from her hands in the wooden sink and was drying them on the kitchen towel. 'I knew it weren't worth calling in old Beeston 'cept to sign the death certificate — he's bound to be incapable — but I'd've come down sooner if I'd thought you could pay Stone.'

'We'll find the money somehow. Pa's got a bit put by. You should have asked!' Charlotte didn't want to antagonise the woman, whose broad face was red and flustered enough already. Mrs Regent had proved a good and efficient midwife over the years. So she

quelled her rising annoyance and panic to explain, 'If
necessary, Pa will give up his pipe and drink for a
while. We can save on food.'

Mrs Regent jerked her head and snorted, sending
her plain white cap further awry. 'That'll be the day,
when your pa gives up his pleasures! Where is he,
anyway?'

'Danny left him up at the ropery.' In common with
most men, her father never allowed his wife's confine-
ments to interfere with his life; in fact he always
managed to disappear at the first signs of impending
birth. 'He works hard. He's not as bad as most,' she
defended loyally. 'He sees we're well fed and clothed.
We don't lack for much. I'd send Bertie back up to
fetch Pa, but I don't want to alarm the others yet. Ask
Danny to go as soon as he gets back, will you?'

'If he'll take it from me. There's no more I can do
for the poor soul upstairs,' Mrs Regent said grimly.
'You'd best get on up, since she's asking for you.'

'Yes.' Though Charlotte was longing to see her
mother, her stomach sank at the thought of what lay
ahead. 'You'll send the doctor up the moment he
arrives, won't you?'

Mrs Regent promised. Charlotte mounted the narrow
cupboard stairs with her heart in her mouth. Her
mother couldn't die, she thought desperately, and
began to send urgent pleas heavenwards as she neared
the partially open door of the room her parents shared
with Annie and Jackie.

Her mother lay so still on the iron bedstead, looked
so white, that for a heart-stopping moment Charlotte
thought she was already dead. Swallowing hard on a
suddenly lumpy throat, she crept up to the bed through
an atmosphere filled with the mingled smell of blood
and carbolic and some other, indefinable odour she

couldn't name until she reached her mother's side. Then the sickly smell of weakness filled her nostrils.

Elizabeth Falconer's body was bathed in sweat. As Charlotte grasped the brass knob for support and bent over her, her mother's eyes opened and the ghost of a smile touched her colourless lips.

'Charlotte! Lottie, my darling, I'm glad you're here. I fear I'm done for this time.'

'Oh, Ma! Don't say so! You'll not die! Danny's gone for Dr Stone. He'll soon set you on the road to recovery!' protested Charlotte, though every sense she possessed told her her beloved mother was rapidly passing beyond human help.

Elizabeth gathered her swiftly draining strength and feebly lifted a hand to indicate the chest standing in the corner of the room.

'Top right-hand drawer,' she whispered. 'The wooden box. When I'm gone, it is yours, and the books.'

Charlotte released the hand she had grasped tightly in her own, trying to impart some of her own youthful strength through the contact, and went over to fetch her mother's treasures. She had known of the old box for as long as she could remember, but had never seen inside. Now, knowing her mother was too weak to open it herself, she inched open the warped lid before laying the carved box on the bed beside the sick woman.

'The locket,' breathed Elizabeth.

The box mostly contained papers, marriage lines, birth certificates and the like, but at the very bottom Charlotte saw the glint of gold. The two sovereigns she ignored. The small trinket, hung on a slender chain, was shaped like a heart and had a strange design enchased on its surface — a shield, with a fancy cross in the middle and a couple of small anchors set in the top corners.

'Open it.'

Charlotte struggled to obey her mother's command. The simple operation seemed to take an age, while her mother's strength ebbed. At last the halves sprang apart, and Charlotte gazed at the small, faded photograph it contained.

The face of a youngish man stared blankly back at her, his handsome features set in wooden lines as he sat rigid before the new-fangled camera. He had darkish hair, side-whiskers and a small beard that traced the line of his chin.

Elizabeth reached out to clutch her daughter's arm with sudden strength. 'Your father,' she whispered.

'Pa. . .?' By no stretch of the imagination could this be a younger version of Samuel Falconer. The features were too fine, the hair not dark enough. The muscles of Charlotte's stomach knotted in sudden fear. 'P-Pa is not my father?' she stuttered as the blood drained from her face.

'No. Let me see.'

Charlotte put the trinket in her mother's limp hand, glad to let it go, for it threatened to burn her fingers. Elizabeth gazed at the likeness it contained with dreaming eyes. 'That is George—he's Sir George Bradgate now. I was maid at the Hall for a while after Mother and Father died.'

She struggled for breath and Charlotte gripped her mother's hand in a new attempt to impart her own strength.

'He seduced you?' she demanded.

'Yes—but not in the way you think,' added Elizabeth urgently as Charlotte made an angry noise. 'I was willing — eager to be loved. I admired him greatly. I would have given my life for George,' she murmured.

'So you gave him your virtue!'

Charlotte's voice was unconsciously condemning, for only condemnation of the man could ease the sense of deep shame her mother's confession had imparted. She watched a pained shadow flit across the tired face and immediately regretted her words.

'One day you will understand,' whispered Elizabeth. 'Do not judge us too harshly. We were so much in love. . .it was impossible, of course. . .I married Samuel Falconer. . .you were born. . .your coming made everything worthwhile. . .'

'Oh, Ma!' choked Charlotte. 'Why did you never tell me? Does P-Pa know?'

'Yes, he knows. He is a good man, Lottie. I hoped never to have to tell you, that it wouldn't matter. But now. . .I can't be certain. You are not settled as I would have hoped. . .' Her voice was becoming weaker by the moment. Charlotte had to bend close to catch the faint whisper coming from her mother's lips. 'And you have a right to know of your heritage. Your father comes of an ancient and respected family. You must not throw your life away,' she urged with a sudden resurgence of strength. 'If you are in need at any time, go to him. Take the locket. He will not turn you away.'

Her voice faded and her eyes closed tiredly. Charlotte stroked the hair from her damp forehead.

'Don't worry about me, Ma,' she murmured hoarsely. 'I'll be fine. I'm sorry I've disappointed you, but I'm in no hurry to wed, and there was my teaching, and you needed help. . .' She drew a sudden, sharp breath. 'But you must get better!'

Elizabeth's body relaxed. Charlotte held tightly to her hands, willing life back into the limp form. She saw

the faintest of smiles curve her mother's colourless lips.
A small sigh, the merest breath, passed through them.

'George. . .'

'Ma?'

Charlotte bent low over the bed, but even as she
heard sounds from below and heavy footsteps on the
stairs she saw her mother slip away. Tears slid unbidden
down her cheeks as she sat, shocked into immobility,
still holding the locket and the lifeless hands.

'You are too late,' she said dully as the doctor
entered the room.

She picked up the precious wooden box, her mother's
legacy, and allowed Mrs Regent to lead her downstairs
while the doctor did what was necessary.

'I must get the children's supper,' she said in that
same, toneless voice. 'They'll be hungry.'

Maria Regent did not attempt to stop her. Charlotte
needed something to occupy her hands.

A subdued party gathered in the kitchen for the
bread and dripping Charlotte produced. Sam Falconer
had hurried back from the ropery to find his wife
already dead. He sat by the range, now burning steadily
in the cosy, spotless kitchen, a dark, taut man in his
mid-forties, staring angrily into the fire as he puffed on
his pipe. Rose, her eldest sister, a budding beauty at
thirteen who worked down on the quay gutting fish, sat
in their mother's rocking-chair nursing Jackie, who was
grizzling quietly, his persistent cries getting on everyone's nerves. Albert, who at fourteen had already been
working at the ropery with his father and older brother
for four years, crouched disconsolately next to Danny
on the rug. Both boys were normally ravenous and full
of high spirits, even if physically tired.

Lizzie was tearful, Willie sombre, but George and
Annie sat expectantly at the oilcloth-covered table,

their young appetites as yet unaffected by the loss of their mother. The news had not really sunk in.

Willie and Georgie, ten and eight respectively, Willie due to start work very soon, squabbled half-heartedly over the crust, while eleven-year-old Lizzie, sobbing at irregular intervals, helped Annie, seven, to spread her mutton dripping and add pepper and salt. Only Sammy, the eldest boy, out at sea on a trawler, was not there, did not yet know that his mother was dead.

Charlotte, pouring boiling water on the tea-leaves, knew food would choke her. The reality of the situation had yet to sink in, even for her, but life could never be the same again. The locket hung around her neck, hidden under the high collar of her green gown. Tomorrow she would have to search out her mother's black dress. And organise the children's mourning. . .

And keep house and cook for all of them. It was her place, as eldest daughter. It seemed as though her high hopes of becoming someone — a proper schoolmistress perhaps — were to be dashed.

She went over to the rigid figure by the stove and laid a hand on his shoulder.

'Don't worry about the little ones, Pa. I'll see to them.'

Sam stirred. He stared up at her, a strange expression in his rather bloodshot, slate-grey eyes. Charlotte knew he was wondering if she had been told. . . 'Aye,' he muttered. 'You're a good lass. It'll be hard on you.'

'On us all, Pa. But we'll manage.'

'Aye.'

She had not slept much, her thoughts too troubled. She needed to sort them out. So, after a bowl of midday stew, she had set out to walk, choosing first to wend her way through the jostling shoppers and tradesmen in Fore Street, dodging horse drays and donkey carts with

practised skill. At Bolton Cross she glanced across at
the huge tank, the size of a small lake, its sides almost
as tall as a man, from which the Royal Navy drew its
water supplies. Its presence made this part of the town
seem open and spacious compared with the clutter of
cottages nearer the harbour, with the gasometer rising
in their midst.

From the reservoir she turned left, allowing her steps
to take her towards the original settlement of Brixham,
a large church surrounded by a graveyard and a cluster
of cottages, set on a hill well above the creek, for it had
been built in the days when it had been safer to live a
mile or so from the shore. She paused to view the old
church with its impressive tower, dreading the day soon
to come when she would take this same walk behind
her mother's coffin.

But she had not come to gawp at a church. She
pressed on, past the cider pound and on and on to
Bradgate Hall.

She had scarcely known where she was headed when
she set out, but the compulsion to see her natural
father's home had grown with every step. She'd had no
purpose in going there; she could not appeal to Sir
George for help, could not readily leave home. Sam
Falconer needed her as never before, and she owed
him eighteen years of rough affection and support.

That thought was uppermost in her mind as she
approached the ropery on her way home.

It was busy. Sir George Bradgate owned the walk,
Sam Falconer rented it from him. She wondered now
whether that was just chance.

Sam specialised in making the rope, twine and nets
used by the fishermen. It was no uncommon sight to
see whole families sitting outside their doors in fine

weather making or mending nets, and Sam Falconer's
was no exception. Charlotte had been able to braid a
net for as long as she could remember. But some busy
fishermen bought theirs ready-made.

She paused between two of the stone pillars which
supported one of the eaves of the heavily timbered
roof. One of her grandfather's books contained an
engraving of a monastic cloister, and the open-sided
walk always reminded her of it, though here the arches
were flat and the solid wall facing her was festooned
with twine, and coils of finished rope lay tidily stacked
against it. A sturdy wooden framework ran the entire
length of the long covered way, supporting skirders —
horizontal slats of wood with upright spikes stuck into
them — which, set well above ground level, prevented
the paid-out yarn from dragging the floor. The spikes
kept the sets of twine, three, sometimes four strands,
apart. Without the skirders the twine would end up in
a hopeless tangle.

At the far end stood the jack with the hooks to which
each set of yarn had been tied. These were being turned
at high speed by way of gears and Danny's energetic
use of the crank handle. At the nearer end, all the
strands of yarn had been tied to a single swivelling hook
attached to a weight and pulley so that the hook would
be pulled forward as the individual sets twisted
together, shortening their lengths. As they did so Sam
moved slowly along beside the hook, the grooved,
wooden top separating the groups of twine held firmly
in his hands. Despite his deep concentration he spared
her a nod of greeting.

This was where Pa's skill came in. Charlotte had
often watched the magic of making an immensely strong
rope from so many thin strands of twine, but the sight
never ceased to fascinate her. Even today she found

herself waiting and watching for the crucial moment when any more twisting would create kinks. Sam judged it exactly, and began to move the top forward between the twisted sets at precisely the right instant. Behind him the swivelling hook began to spin, making the rope as though of its own accord! Sometimes Bertie was needed to turn a handle fixed to the swivelling hook, and Sam walked forward more slowly. That was when they were making a hard-laid rope.

Charlotte decided not to disturb them by more than a wave. She hoped the boys were warm enough, that Danny wouldn't catch a chill when he stopped work and the sweat began to dry. The wind had got up strong and was beginning to whistle between the pillars. As she passed by the old windmill, crested the hill and began the downward trek towards the harbour, she noticed dozens of brigs and schooners had taken refuge in Tor Bay, most within Brixham's outer harbour, protected by the Breakwater—many more than were normally moored there. Some had bare poles swaying with the increasingly choppy sea, others had some of their sails still set on the yards to dry in the stiffening breeze.

A crowded forest of masts suggested that craft already packed the sheltered inner harbour, though many local fishermen were still hooking or trawling out on the horizon, judging by the sails dimly visible against the lowering sky. Sammy must be out there somewhere, she supposed, unless his skipper had decided to return early because, like other mariners, he had scented a storm. Ice imported from Norway meant that the catch could be kept fresh at sea for several days, but his trawler was due back in time for the market next morning.

She looked up. The sky was an almost uniform,

ominous grey. Where was the silver lining, the patch of blue large enough to make a pair of trousers? No, the weather was not clearing and wouldn't now, before dark. Charlotte prayed that those still at sea got home before the threatened storm. Sammy was not the only one for whom she felt concern. Many of the skippers and hands were friends and neighbours.

She hurried across the common of Rae Hill, greeting the women busy taking in washing spread there to dry, finally running down the steps at the rear of their cottage and in through the yard. Rose would not be finishing work yet, but the younger children would soon be home from school. Thank goodness the Christmas holidays were over. Lizzie had missed lessons to look after Jackie. She should not have left her so long on her own; there was no knowing what the child would do. She might decide to run off and leave the baby——

Charlotte firmly dismissed her anxious fears. Lizzie was quite an obedient and responsible girl for her eleven years.

All the same, she should not have gone out and left them. But she'd just had to get out of the house, to be alone for a while.

And she'd caught a glimpse of the place where she had been conceived. Where she truly belonged.

CHAPTER TWO

No! CHARLOTTE opened the kitchen door to breathe in the familiar mixture of scents that meant home, giving Lizzie a relieved smile when she saw the child playing on the rug with the baby. No! This was where she belonged! Here, in this stone cottage her mother had kept so neat and scrubbed, here with her foster-father and half-brothers and sisters.

If she was to look after them properly, she thought as she flung off her shawl and tied her apron strings, she would have to give up her job as part-time assistant at the National School. Ma had been so keen on her bettering herself, on her making use of the education she had so determinedly engineered for her. Not only had she found the penny a week necessary to send her to school, but had spent hours teaching her herself.

Ma's father had been a clergyman, and before his untimely death had instilled much of his knowledge into his daughter, who had been keenly insistent on passing that learning on to her firstborn. She had seen that all her other children received an education, for she deeply loved them all. But Charlotte had known herself to be singled out for special attention, had often wondered why her assimilation of knowledge had been of such great importance to her mother.

Now she knew. Ma had tried to fit her to take her place in the world of her natural father.

Which had been silly. Her glimpse of that enormous house, her meeting with the squire's stepson — what was

his name — Francis Langford, was it? — had soon convinced her that she had no place at all in that world.

Francis Langford's face, at its charming friendliest,
swam before her eyes as she poked the grate vigorously
to stir it into new life before emptying the scuttle on the
revived coals.

'Where've you been, Lottie?' asked Lizzie queru-
lously, moving out of range of the activity. 'I could've
been out earning a penny or two down at the quay if
you'd been here!'

'I'll give you a penny, when Pa gives me the housekeeping,' promised Charlotte with as much of a smile
as she could manage. She gave her small sister a quick
hug. 'You have been a great help today, Lizzie, and
I'm grateful.'

She loved her brothers and sisters. It would be no
hardship to look after them for a few years, until they
were old enough to fend for themselves, or until Rose
or Lizzie could take over.

And then? Strangely, Francis Langford's face swam
into view again. No other man had ever made such an
impression on her, and she'd seen plenty of gentry one
way and another, either in the town or in church, so it
wasn't that. There had been something about him — a
masculine virility and charm some part of her had
responded to quite spontaneously. She shuddered at
the memory. It had been a strange sensation. She'd felt
nothing like it before.

She resolutely turned her thoughts away from that
disturbing encounter to consider her future. Thanks to
her mother she was reasonably well educated and quite
widely read. That collection of books locked away in a
cupboard, books that had belonged to her clergyman
grandfather, were now hers. Her mother had treasured
them and encouraged her to study. And — her spirits

lifted on the realisation — she, Charlotte Elizabeth
Falconer, was of gentle birth, even though her present
circumstances did not make the fact obvious.

But if the truth came out society would shun her,
treat her as a no-account bastard, make her suffer for
what it considered to be the sin of her mother.

So she must guard her secret well. And since she
could not contemplate marriage to a man who did not
know the true facts of her birth she would be unlikely
to wed. Unless she met just the right man, she thought
wistfully, one who would not let the truth be a barrier
between them.

But that was an unrealistic hope, given society's
condemnation of those whose parentage did not bear
close scrutiny. She put it firmly from her mind.

She could teach, so she would. As a schoolmistress
or as a governess. Perhaps one day she would be able
to establish her own school. . . A smile lightened the
sombre expression of her face, the first since her mother
had died. She would make a good teacher. Miss
Harper, the schoolmistress she assisted, said she had a
flair for making things interesting for the children.

Life would not be easy without a husband to keep
her, but satisfying and modestly comfortable, infinitely
better than pandering to a man's needs just to secure a
roof over her head. Miss Harper managed quite
comfortably and she was well past marriageable age.
Like Miss Harper, she would be tolerably free — and
therefore, she told herself stoutly, happy.

Charlotte kept up late that night. She knew it would be
useless to go to bed with the wind howling around the
chimney-pots and the rattle and slap of rigging echoing
across from ships anchored in the harbour. Their cottage was sheltered from the worst of the storm, tucked

in as it was behind another row of houses which was taking the brunt of the gale, but even so the noise sounded fearsome.

Slates clattered off a roof near by and crashed to the ground. Jackie protested in his sleep, disturbing Annie, who was sharing his cot. She'd had to bring the youngest children in with her and Rosie and Lizzie — she couldn't leave them with Pa — and Jackie was too small to be put in with the younger boys as yet. It made the bedroom crowded, the big bed she shared with her sisters took up most of the floor, but they managed somehow. Pa, of course, was well off for space now, with the biggest bedroom of all to himself, but probably Sammy would move in with his father. When he was at home he often slept on the kitchen settle rather than crowd into the narrow bed he was supposed to share with Danny and Bertie. With four bedrooms they were better off than most, but two of them were quite small and it was still a squeeze.

Gently, Charlotte tucked the covers around the sleeping children and spoke to Rose, who, like her, was still fully dressed.

'I'm going out to find Pa and the boys. Look after things here, will you, Rosie?'

'The snow's turned to rain. It'll be slushy underfoot and you'll get wet through,' her sister warned as she swung round from staring from the streaming window.

The black sky was unrelieved by any sign of moon or stars, though a puzzling orange glow had appeared over the roof-tops.

'I'll wrap up, I've got my thick cape. But something's up. That looks like a fire, and the town's all abuzz. I simply must find out what's happening. Sammy's still out there somewhere. Pray the dear Lord to keep him safe!'

Sammy, the eldest son, the restless one, who had defied his father and worried his mother by going to sea instead of remaining ashore to help at the ropery. Sammy, who came romping home every few days smelling of salt spray and fish to bring a breath of freedom and fresh air into their more mundane lives.

Rose followed her downstairs. The open range had been banked down for the night, but the kettle hanging over it was warm enough to sing.

'Have a cup of cocoa to keep the cold out,' suggested Rose, pinching out the candle she had been carrying and turning up the wick on the oil lamp. She stood on her toes to reach a shelf and got down the cocoa and condensed milk. The boys loved the thick, sweet stuff from the tin, but Charlotte preferred fresh cow's milk, and there wouldn't be any more of that until the milk float came round the next day.

'No, thanks.' She gave her sister a smile to cushion her refusal. 'I'd best be off. I'll try not to be long; keep the kettle hot. We'll all be cold when we come in.'

Sam and the two older boys had been gone some time, adding to her concern. Sam's still handsome face, shadowed by a pain of loss Charlotte had somehow not expected, had looked grim as he prepared to go out.

'I be going round the harbour t'see what's up; everyone's making for there—I've been watching,' he had announced as he fought his way into oilskins. 'Mebbe me and the lads can help if there's trouble.'

'You'll see if the *Bonnie Maid* is in?'

'What do you think, girl?' he growled irritably. 'But I mayn't be able. The wind's backing fast; it be coming from the north-east now, straight into the bay. I reckon there'll be some damage done tonight.'

'Oh, Pa, I do hope Sammy will be all right!'

'Aye, girl, so do I.' Sam spoke gruffly, hiding his

feelings under a resolute exterior. He had put on a pair of thick boots, and now he proceeded to fasten his oilskins close about his body, for the rain lashed at the windows, emphasising the wildness of the night. 'Anyhow,' he'd added, 'we'd best be doing summat. Can't sit about idle while seamen are in trouble.'

'Take care, Pa. And you too, Danny. Do your buttons and ties up tight! And look after Bertie.'

'I can look after myself!'

Excitement glowed in both boys' eyes under their sou'westers. They were straining at the leash, eager to be off into the storm to do deeds of bravery and derring-do. Charlotte watched them go with an anxious heart.

Time had passed, but they had not returned. She could stand the suspense no longer. She had to find out what was going on. Sick with anxiety, she pulled on her stoutest boots, wrapped herself in the thick wool cloak and drew the hood over her head.

A blast of wind and rain hit her as she emerged from the yard and the shelter of the cottage, taking her breath. Some scraps of paper, scoured from some dark, dry corner, swirled and lifted like a flock of birds, came to rest and were immediately plastered to the sodden ground. She fought her way round the corner to The Beach, though the cobbled slipway and shelving stone bulwark built across the creek to reinforce the silt which had long ago closed off the end of the harbour was hardly entitled to that name, for at low tide it ran straight down to mud.

There, she met the full force of the gale and was almost buffeted off her feet. Bobbing storm-lanterns carried by dark, shadowy people seemed to be everywhere. Straining her eyes in the darkness, Charlotte could see the boats crowded into the inner harbour, their towering masts silhouetted against the glow of a great fire blazing on the end of the New Pier, which enclosed the haven. The vessels looked largely in place and undamaged, even if lying askance and rocking wildly on the mud lying a foot or two below the surface of the water.

'Mrs Regent!' Charlotte recognised the midwife and caught at her arm as she hurried past. 'Mrs Regent!' She glimpsed the woman's face and caught her breath in alarm. Maria looked absolutely dreadful in the light of the new gas lamp. 'What is it?' she asked fearfully.

''Tis a dreadful sight!' gasped Maria Regent. 'The end of the Breakwater be swept away! They've lit the brazier on the end of the pier to signal the vessels in, but they be helpless afore all this wind! They're being driven against the side of it! You bain't never seen nothing like it, my lover! Spars and yards and blocks and rigging torn to pieces and flying in all directions! Hear them screams?' Charlotte wasn't sure that she could, but Mrs Regent seemed able to distinguish the cries of the unfortunate seamen above the howl and bluster of the wind and the slap of nearby rigging. 'Men are being crushed and mangled by the wreckage!'

'Dear lord!' exclaimed Charlotte, aghast. 'Are many dead? Is Pa there?'

'He be that; so's my Zac—he came in this afternoon, thank God, Tony too. As for dead, I bain't sure. I'm for home to get blankets and bandages, some of me medicines and a pot of soup. Most women are on The Quay helping all they can, either ministering to the rescued men there or taking them back home wi' them. Those poor souls, they be freezing to death in the water!'

'Sammy's not home yet,' shivered Charlotte. Her teeth had begun to chatter, not so much with the cold, though it was bitter, but with fright. 'I must go and help!'

Skirting the harbour, she fought her way along the road they called The Quay towards the New Pier, thrusting her way through the jostling, noisy throng of saviours and saved, looking for Sam and the boys, automatically acknowledging the greetings falling about her ears.

"Lo, Lottie!"

'Wondered where you be, my lover! Glad to see you here; we need every helping hand.'

'If you're looking for your pa, he be on the pier wi' the boys, m'handsome! Lend a hand here a minute, will you?'

Charlotte paused to help lift an unconscious seaman on to a makeshift stretcher, but quickly abandoned him to the care of others and continued on to the pier, where the local men stood lining the seaward wall, hauling in and catching the wrecked sailors as they clambered up the rigging and slid down the yards to safety.

Now the agonised cries and screams of the injured seamen could be clearly heard above the uproar. Their uninjured mates on the smashed decks heaving low down beside the wall of the pier—the tide had turned but the water had not yet risen much—were tying lines around their less fortunate shipmates so that the Brixham men could haul them up.

Charlotte breathed a sigh of relief as she spotted Danny and Bertie throwing more timber into the brazier. They had been given the job of keeping the beacon fire blazing, and there were plenty of smashed spars and planks to feed it—not even wet wood and lashing rain could quench the inferno they had stoked.

Then she heard Sam's voice.

'Haul hard, my lover! Haul hard! But gently now!'

She almost reached his side before stopping abruptly. He was guiding up an injured man, the line holding him being hauled in by someone seemingly quite out of place here. Francis Langford had not seen her yet, and probably wouldn't recognise her if he did. But she would never forget his face, and in the pool of light from a lantern held aloft by a young lad she could see the astonished amusement which overlay the harsh-breathing effort in the glance he threw Sam.

A sense of relief at sight of Pa and the boys, a cautious relaxation of tension, a surge of bubbling excitement, of stimulation in the face of confusion and danger, gave her a desire to giggle, though she quickly suppressed the alien urge. Did Mr Langford not know that everyone here called everyone else, man or woman, my dear, my lover or my handsome? If not, he could not have been in Devon long!

And what was he doing down Quay mucking in with the locals? He wasn't dressed for it. His thick cloak dripped and clung, heavy with water, his hair hung sodden about his face. If he had once worn a hat it was missing now. His fine leather boots would be the despair of his man, impossible to reclaim.

She could see no sign of Tristram Bradgate. His presence she would have understood more readily; he was reputedly quite friendly with some of the skippers who put in here, especially those engaged in smuggling. But Sir George — her father! Incredible thought! — would keep well clear and send a servant down tomorrow to see if there was anything he could do. She would have expected the same from Francis Langford. His being there came as a complete surprise.

He was using his powerful muscles to good purpose, though the man he was lifting was slight enough for him to manage without help. Sam was guiding the burden, preventing further damage to skin and bone from abrasion and knocks, and eventually eased the limp, dripping body over the lip of the stonework and laid it in a space clear of threatening boots. He looked around and spotted Charlotte.

'Lottie! You here? Stop standing around doing nothing, girl! See what you can do for this poor lad.'

Charlotte started and stepped forward. Francis Langford looked up from bending over the man he had helped to rescue. Charlotte saw recognition leap into his eyes. For an instant they could have been alone on that chaotic pier. Her hood had blown off and her hair escaped its coils to cling to her head and neck in flat, wet swaths. She put up a hand to wipe stray tendrils from her face, conscious as never before of her appearance.

'Hello again,' said Francis Langford quietly.

She acknowledged his greeting with a nod. Then she tore her eyes away to gaze down on the young boy Francis had hauled to safety.

'What's the matter with him?' she managed gruffly.

Francis returned his attention to the lad at his feet. 'He's knocked out, I think, and is so cold he's barely alive. He must have been in the water for some time before his shipmate got him out. I'll carry him to one of the inns; they've thrown open their doors. He needs warmth above all else.'

Charlotte began to chafe one of the ice-cold hands. 'Can you manage him?'

'I think so.'

The reply was brief as Francis Langford bent down to lift the lad into his arms. The young face looked blue in the distant light from a lantern.

'Support his head, will you?'

Charlotte bridled at his tone. That had not been a request but an order, and she was not used to obeying such brusque commands from anyone other than Pa. Should she go with him or remain on the pier? Pa had ordered her to do what she could for the boy. And something in Francis Langford's manner impelled her to obey.

'Very well.' Her own tone was stiff with quite unwarranted resentment. For after all he was only demanding help and efficiency in a difficult situation. She could not imagine quite why she had taken such offence. She put her hand under the boy's sagging head and immediately his breathing eased.

Francis Langford acknowledged her aid with a nod of approval. Having ensured that the patient was as comfortable as he could make him, he strode towards The Quay as though his burden were half the weight Charlotte knew it must be. Keeping close despite the jostling throng, ignoring the new commotion as another vessel was driven hard against the other wrecks piled up against the pier wall, the force of the gale now aided and abetted by the fast-incoming tide, Charlotte followed as he made his way to the warmth of the Victory's taproom.

It was so crowded that she wondered whether there would be room for them, and so stuffy that she doubted if there would be enough air to breathe. However, people shuffled up and made a space for Mr Langford to set the lad down on the floor.

'Get him out of them clothes,' suggested one of the helpers.

'Do you have a blanket?'

'Mebbe, somewhere. . .'

Ranks of men were already laid out wrapped in an assortment of blankets. Mrs Regent had not yet returned with her contribution, unless she'd taken it to the Dolphin next door, or the Rising Sun further along The Quay.

'He'd do better in warm, dry clothes,' Charlotte whispered as Langford began to unbutton the boy's coat. 'He's about the same size as my brother. I could go and get some. . .'

'How far?' he demanded briskly.

'Just the other side of the harbour, sir. It won't take me many minutes——'

'My name is Langford, Francis Langford,' he introduced himself, glancing up. His hair looked dark now, being so wet. 'May I know yours?'

'Charlotte Falconer,' admitted Charlotte reluctantly. Giving him her name seemed somehow to commit herself to something, though she could not imagine what.

He smiled briefly, a warm smile that lit his eyes and sent strange quivers along Charlotte's nerves.

'Could you offer him a bed, Miss Falconer?' he asked. The colour rose in Charlotte's cheeks. Miss Falconer! When had she last been called that, except by the children in school? 'He needs better care than he'll receive here,' Francis Langford went on. 'I'd take him back to Bradgate Hall, but I doubt he'd weather the journey.'

He appeared to be feeling a personal responsibility for the life he had helped to save. Charlotte frowned in thought. A bed, no, unless she dared to use Pa's or the boys', and they'd need theirs later. But the settle in the kitchen would be warm and safe — provided they could carry him there.

'He'd be welcome to the settle in the kitchen,' she offered, 'except that I don't think he's capable of walking, and although it's not far it's still a good distance to carry him.'

The boy was stirring now, recovering consciousness after the blow to his head, but shivering violently and retching. Between the spasms of sickness he looked puzzled and confused. The only sounds to come from him were unintelligible and he was making weak, plucking movements with his hands.

'I'll manage.' Francis Langford sounded confident of his own capabilities. 'I'd put him up on my hack, but I left the horse in stables up Fore Street. While I was fetching it, we would be there.'

He bent to his burden again, and Charlotte had to admire the ease with which he lifted the dead weight. The man was no weakling, despite his expensive clothes and refined ways. This time he had the boy's arm around his neck and was holding him upright against his own length.

'Pull my cloak around him.'

Charlotte complied, her fingers trembling slightly as she touched his sodden garment. He had been relatively dry beneath its protection, but the young seaman's clothes were already soaking his shooting-coat and breeches. It seemed a shame to ruin such fine suiting.

They pushed out of the crowded, steamy room with its overpowering smells of damp wool and stale beer, the boy doing his best to walk, but succeeding only in dragging his feet at Francis's side. Charlotte led the way, forging a determined path through the crowds by making good use of her familiarity with most of the people. Francis Langford followed in her wake, his own impressive presence doing nothing to hinder their progress. In fact Charlotte suspected that had she not been there the way would have opened effortlessly before him.

She bit her lip as they neared the house. She did not really want Mr Langford in the cottage. Not that she was ashamed of her home, but it contrasted so strongly with the sort of surroundings he must be used to. It would point up the difference in their stations in a way he could not ignore. But then, how could that possibly matter? She was being silly, and had no choice in any case.

Yet at the front door still she hesitated. She couldn't take him in the back way, round the alley, through the yard and past the privy. That would be too demeaning. But. . .

'My mother,' she said thickly. 'Her coffin is in the parlour. We shall have to pass it.'

She saw his head move in the darkness as he nodded. 'I feel sure she would not mind being disturbed for this errand,' he said quietly.

'No.'

She opened the door, which blew out of her hand to knock back against the wall, and stood aside for them to enter. As she followed and put her weight against the wood to close it behind her, the kitchen door opened, throwing a shaft of light across the room. She saw Francis Langford glance at the coffin and bow his head in respect as he walked through to where Rose stood awaiting them.

'Rose,' said Charlotte quickly, before her sister could enquire, 'this is Mr Francis Langford, from Bradgate Hall. Mr Langford helped Pa to rescue this boy, and we thought it best to bring him here. His head needs bathing and binding, and he needs warmth, a hot drink and dry clothes. I thought some of Danny's might fit —'

She was babbling in her nervousness and Rose looked at her in amusement. It wasn't often Charlotte became agitated, and Rose examined the cause of her sister's jumpiness with curiosity.

'Good evening, Miss Rose.' The man smiled briefly, nodding a greeting before addressing Charlotte. 'Where may he lie?'

'Oh! Here!' She indicated the settle and as Francis eased his burden on to its cushioned seat she turned back to her wide-eyed sister. At thirteen, Rose could be counted on to be dazzled by such unusual courtesy. 'Rosie, go and fetch some things, will you? Anything you think will fit, and the thickest jersey you can find.'

Rose departed reluctantly, her curiosity still rampant. Both Charlotte and Francis threw off their cloaks, which began to steam gently in the warmth of the kitchen. Rose had poked up the fire and it sent a cheerful glow to illuminate their faces. Charlotte took clean towels from a pile of ironing in the corner and handed one to Francis, using the other to rub the worst of the moisture from her hair.

He used his on the boy. 'I must strip him,' he said briskly as he dried the blue face and black hair, being careful not to touch the ugly grazed bruise on the forehead. 'If you wish to leave —— '

'Oh, no. I have often tended my brothers. . . But perhaps Rose should not be here.'

Though why not she couldn't think. Rose, too, had bathed her brothers. But the younger ones, not Sammy, Danny or Bertie. And the lad must be Sammy's age, though smaller. No, it wouldn't be right for Rose to see him naked.

So when Rose returned with the clothes, to her disgust she was sent to bed.

'It's nearly three,' Charlotte pointed out. 'You'll be fit for nothing tomorrow morning —— '

'There won't be any fish to clean, that's for sure,' grumbled Rose. 'Let me make the drink——'

'No, Rosie,' said Charlotte gently. 'Thanks for waiting up for me, but I can take over now. You're dropping off on your feet. Please don't argue.'

Rose, struggling to keep her eyelids from drooping, pouted but obeyed. Since their mother's death Charlotte had assumed a new air of authority, and Rose for one was not prepared to challenge her older sister's right to order the household.

Charlotte put the clothes by the settle together with the blankets Sammy normally used and went to dampen a clean piece of flannel with the water from the kettle, which she replaced over the hottest part of the fire so that it would boil quickly for the drinks.

'Shall I sponge his forehead?' she asked Francis, who had the semi-conscious boy stripped to his underclothes.

'Let me get him into something warm first.'

Francis finished removing the boy's last pieces of clothing and gave his shivering flesh a brisk rub down before dressing him in the dry clothes. As a thick flannel vest went over his head the kettle boiled.

'There's no fresh milk, I'm afraid,' Charlotte apologised. 'Will condensed do?'

'Hot, strong and sweet is just how it should be,' grinned Francis, easing their charge into a pair of Danny's thickest trousers. 'I remember that on a cold night on campaign there was nothing to beat hot, strong, sweet tea to cheer the men!'

'You would prefer tea to cocoa?'

'If you have some?'

'Of course.' They were not so poor that they could not afford to buy tea.

Her conversation sounded stilted, even ungracious,

but having two strange men in the kitchen and one of them gentry had put a constraint on her tongue. Had it been almost anyone else it would not have been so bad. But after that one brief exchange earlier she'd let Francis Langford take a hold on her imagination, and now she couldn't remember when she'd felt so embarrassed. And she didn't like hot, strong, sweet tea. It would probably make her sick.

To hide her discomfort, she said the first thing that came into her head.

'You are American.'

He stopped in his work for a moment to give her a sidelong glance. 'Does my accent give me away or did Jess inform you?'

'I —' She swallowed. 'Yes,' she admitted, 'she did.'

'So you probably already knew my name.'

'Yes, sir.'

'And that my mother married Sir George some years ago and that I'm here to visit her?'

She nodded.

He grinned suddenly. 'You know far more about me than I know about you. I gather that was your father I was working with?'

She couldn't bring herself to actually tell the lie, though she flushed uncomfortably as she nodded again.

Francis frowned. Was the girl ashamed of her parentage? She had no need to be.

'He is a brave man,' he told her sharply. 'He'd been down that rope himself earlier, to bring up a man with a broken leg. Almost got knocked out by a block flying about in the rigging. He'll have a few knocks and bruises to mend before morning.'

Charlotte poured boiling water on the leaves in the pot and stirred with great concentration.

'I know. He used to be a fisherman, but gave the sea

up after he married. My mother wanted him ashore —
she hated the water. So he took over the ropery up by
the windmill. He makes a good living, and we don't
want for much,' she added, repeating the defence of
her foster-father she had made to Mrs Regent before
she knew the truth.

She risked a glance from under her thick lashes to
see Francis wince as he tugged the rough oiled wool of
one of Sammy's jerseys over the boy's head.

'Oh! Mr Langford, your hands!' she exclaimed.

Francis finished his task, laid the boy back on the
settle and regarded his raw palms with a wry grimace.
'Not used to hauling on ropes, I'm afraid,' he admitted,
flexing his fingers. 'But they'll mend in a day or two.'

'You'd better treat them with salve and bandage
them,' Charlotte told him anxiously. 'Without treatment those rope-burns could turn nasty — here! But
wash them first!'

She handed him a pot of ointment and a length of
prepared bandage, which he accepted with wry reluctance. She pumped some water into a basin and pre-
sented him with a bar of soap. He winced again as he
washed, and Charlotte was moved to remark, 'They're
pretty bad, aren't they? I don't know how you managed
that last haul! What happened to your gloves?'

He laughed ruefully. 'I took them off to do something
earlier, and lost track of them. But others are worse off
than me! And I've suffered worse myself.' Almost
absently, he lifted a wet finger to touch a scar on his
forehead, which still throbbed from time to time and
was inclined to do so now. It was almost hidden in his
hair, and Charlotte had not noticed it before.

'Oh!' she exclaimed. 'Were you wounded? In the
Civil War?'

'Just a graze, really. A musket-ball — an inch lower

and I'd have been a goner. But——' he grinned, an engaging grin that quite transformed his face '—here I am, safe and well and grumbling about skinned palms! Where's that ointment? The boy could do with some, too.'

Reminded of their charge's wound, Charlotte hastened to bathe it and smear on some of the salve.

'Better?' she asked with a smile.

The young seaman had gathered some of his wits by now. 'Much, ta, but I'm that cold still. . .' He smiled back, a shy, grateful smile that touched Charlotte's heart. He was so like Sammy!

Sammy! The tears gathered as she wrapped the youngster in one of the blankets.

'There!' she told him, though her voice was choked. 'You'll soon warm up. What's your name?'

'Bill, ma'am. Bill Jackson, off the barque *Wild Rose*.'

'Well, Bill, you're safe now.' If only she knew the same was true of Sammy! 'I'll pour you some hot tea.'

'What is it?'

Francis Langford's soft voice caught her unawares. Her hand shook as she poured and tea slopped into the saucer. She put the pot down with a stifled sob and hid her face in her hands.

CHAPTER THREE

FRANCIS LANGFORD'S touch on her shoulder made Charlotte tremble. She turned from his reach, searched out her handkerchief and controlled her tears with a determined effort. He would think her weak and foolish!

'I'm sorry.' She lifted a defiant face, sniffed hard and got on with her task. 'It is just that Sammy is still at sea. I'm worried about him.'

'My dear, I'm sorry. I had not realised you had anyone. . .'

'How should you?' That endearment had not been part of customary local parlance! Her discomfort in Francis Langford's presence grew.

She handed out the tea in silence. It didn't taste nearly as bad as she had thought it would. In fact the hot, sweet brew had a calming effect on her nerves, and Francis downed his with obvious relish. Bill began to recover some colour in his cheeks.

They all sat in somnolent silence while the storm raged outside. The kitchen was warm, clean and cosy. Francis sat in Pa's chair, his hair dry by now and burnished red-gold by the firelight. She rocked herself in what had been her mother's chair, the shawl draped round the back keeping out any draughts. She began to nod and soon dropped into a doze.

Francis studied her as her lids drooped, certain she was not aware of his scrutiny. Her gorgeous chestnut hair tumbled about her shoulders in tangled disarray. She still wore the ill-fitting black dress, which had been

wet to the knees and was drying off in a gentle haze of
steam. It could not conceal the lush contours of a body
which could not in the slightest degree be described as
plump, yet the bones were well and softly padded,
presenting a temptation to any man's hands. Her thick
lashes, a darkish browny black, rested on flushed
cheeks; shadows cast by the fire and lamp highlighted
wide cheekbones, the slight cleft in her chin which had
intrigued him before — and her mouth, soft and relaxed
in sleep, asking to be kissed into ripe surrender. . .

He pulled his imagination up sharply. Such thoughts
were out of place here. Yet he'd been unable to forget
his encounter with the girl at the gates. There had been
something about her which had instantly aroused his
interest. At the same time he had known she was not
of his world, and had not expected to see her again.
Or — had the hope contributed to his decision to come
down to Brixham Quay to discover what was
happening?

If so, it had not been consciously. He had seen the
beacon-glow of the fiercely burning brazier and thought
the town on fire. Agonising memories of war, the firing
of towns and cities and the devastation, the terror and
anguish, had made him saddle his horse and hurry
down to see if he could help. Under orders, he'd been
denied the chance to alleviate suffering in the chaos of
war — he would never forget his feeling of helplessness
as he watched Atlanta burn — but now. . . Now, perhaps, he could atone.

He had discovered not a blazing town, but another
kind of disaster, and done his best to lend a helping
hand.

And in so doing had met Charlotte Falconer again.

He rested his bandaged palms on the arms of the
chair, laid his head back and continued his scrutiny

through his thick, sweeping lashes. This was her home,
yet there was something about her screaming the message that she did not belong in these surroundings. She
had a quality he could not name, could not define. But
it was one that intrigued and attracted him sufficiently
for him to determine that they should meet again after
this night.

Bill was curled up on the settle sleeping, comfortably
warm at last. Francis knew he should take his leave, his
usefulness past. But he did not. Instead, he shifted his
hands to a more comfortable position, shut his eyes and
tried to snatch a few moments of sleep himself.

A gust of cold air swept in from the lean-to as the boys
barged through into the kitchen, startling them all back
to wakefulness. Charlotte glanced at the clock on the
mantel and gasped her surprise. Half-past five already!
How long had she slept? And with Francis Langford
sitting there!

He rose to his feet in a fluid, easy movement, greeting
the newcomers with a slight smile.

'Danny! Leave those oilskins outside!' cried
Charlotte, seeing the kitchen floor awash with water
before long if they were allowed to drip all over it.

They made a noisy exit. Charlotte noticed that the
lamp had burned low and took the glass chimney off to
trim the wick before she turned it up. Francis stood
warming his backside in front of the fire, watching. She
wished he would not. By the time she had finished the
boys were back, and she was glad to see they'd
remained dry beneath the oilskins.

'Any news of Sammy?' she asked anxiously.

'Not yet,' replied Danny. 'It's still dark; we can't see
much out there. There are plenty of vessels in the outer

harbour, though, anchored safe and sound. His is probably one of them.'

'I certainly hope so!' Her worry did not communicate itself to them. They would be sorry enough if anything happened to their brother, but could not imagine disaster in advance. It was nice to be young.

Francis wondered who Sammy was. Her young man? He shouldn't be surprised if she had one, a girl like her, but the thought did not please him. He rested his arm on the mantel and frowned into the glowing coals.

'Got anything to eat, Lottie?' Bertie demanded, accepting the presence of strangers with no more than a curious glance and tentative smile.

Charlotte visualised the loaf and crust left in the crock. 'There's bread and jam,' she offered. 'This, by the way, is Mr Francis Langford. He helped Pa to save Bill Jackson here earlier.' She swept a hand to indicate the boy on the settle, and the three youngsters exchanged grins and hellos before her siblings turned back to Francis Langford. 'These are two of my brothers, Danny and Bertie,' she told him. 'Say how do you do to the gentleman,' she ordered.

They complied and Francis gravely shook hands with each one in turn.

'Where is Pa?' asked Charlotte.

'Gone along to Churston Cove; there's been a wreck there,' Danny told her. 'He wouldn't let us go; he sent us home. Said we'd done enough for one night,' he grumbled glumly, but soon brightened again, eager to impart his news. 'There're wrecks all round the bay. We heard the *Salem* went ashore at Oxen Cove, but all four hands managed to swing to safety and were hauled up the cliff.'

'Thank goodness for that! Was—was anyone killed by the pier?'

'No! We got 'em all up alive! Pa says it was a miracle no one was hurt worse than they were. Haven't you got anything besides bread and jam?' he suddenly demanded, his mind shooting off at a tangent.

Bertie quickly followed his brother's lead. 'I'm famished, Lottie!' He rolled his eyes and rubbed his stomach soulfully. He always was a bit of a clown.

Charlotte found she could laugh. 'All right, I'll see what I can find!'

She went to the food-safe in the chilly scullery and surveyed the contents. A couple of rashers of fat bacon, a bowl of eggs and half a basin of lard looked promising.

'Bacon, egg and fried bread?' she enquired, returning with her arms full.

Enthusiastic nods greeted this suggestion.

'You'd better wash your hands, then.'

As the boys descended on the sink, Charlotte put both frying-pans on the hob.

'How many brothers do you have?' enquired Francis as she spooned in lard and laid one bacon rasher in each. His mouth began to water just seeing the food; he had not realised he was so hungry. 'Could you spare some of that for me?' he asked with a persuasive smile. He really shouldn't take their food. He would repay her later. He had no wish to impose, but he did have an instinctive and strong desire to remain for a while longer.

'Of course!' Charlotte had found his smile quite devastating and gave him a quick, rather nervous one in return. Providing food for all and sundry would stretch her housekeeping budget, but she could not even think of refusing. Though why he had not taken his leave long ago she couldn't fathom. Still, his presence was in some undefined way comforting, although it was also unsettling. 'And for Bill, if he wants it. Do you?' she asked the youngster.

'Please, mum, ta!'

'There won't be much bacon,' she warned them.

'Whatever you've got will do me fine,' Francis assured her, watching while her capable, work-roughened hands cut thick slices from the loaf with quick, neat movements. Two of her fingers were swollen and red with chilblains, he noticed with a frown of concern. The ladies of his acquaintance scarcely ever suffered from such a painful affliction. 'But you didn't answer my question,' he pressed her. 'You have other brothers?'

'And sisters,' Charlotte told him quietly. 'There are ten of us altogether. Six boys and four girls. I'm the eldest.'

'And now your mother is dead you are responsible for their welfare?' he asked in shocked tones. 'You are far too young for such a responsibility!'

'I am eighteen, sir! And fully capable of doing my duty! My mother died trying to bring yet another baby into the world. It is not always a blessing to be so fertile.' Her voice had become unconsciously bitter.

'I see. I'm sorry,' he said quietly.

His sympathy was genuine, but she did not want it. He was a man. He would think nothing of subjecting his wife, if he had one — did he? she suddenly wondered as the knife slipped because her hand had jerked on the thought — to a similar fate. Besides, her life, her problems were her own, and he had no part in them. She piled the slices of bread on a plate with controlled energy and, glad of the excuse to turn away, took them over to the stove and left them there while she made another pot of tea.

The boys chattered on, drawing Bill into their conversation. Francis sat relaxed on a hard chair at the table, making himself quite at home and offering a remark here and there. She was aware of him watching her again as she worked, soaking the bread in the fat and putting the slices on one side, cracking the eggs into the pans, cooking them and lifting them on to warmed plates to wait while she put the bread back and browned it. He made her nervous, and she broke the yolk of one of the eggs. Danny would not mind having that one.

He was good with boys, Charlotte realised, and remembered that he had served in an army, as an officer. She wondered for which side he had fought.

The smell of frying made even her mouth water. After she had got out the cutlery and dished up the others' breakfasts, dividing the bacon into four to make it go round, she put more fat in one of the pans and added an egg and a slice of bread. It cooked while she poured the tea.

'Come and sit down,' commanded Francis quietly as she put a steaming cup in front of him. 'Where is your breakfast? You need to eat, too.'

'I'm going to.' She pressed the bread down against the hot pan with the back of the fish-slice to encourage it to brown. 'It's just ready.'

She wasn't sure whether to resent his interference or be flattered by his concern. It was nice to be the object of a little consideration. How her mother would have appreciated such a gesture from her husband! But Sam had been brought up in a school where such solicitude would be seen as a sign of weakness. She sat down with heightened colour—from bending over the stove, of course—and began to eat just as the boys clattered their knives and forks down on empty plates.

'Can we have some bread and jam now?' demanded Danny.

'I'll cut you some.'

She was halfway to her feet, her own meal almost untouched, when Francis intervened.

'Can't you cut it yourself?' he enquired of the boy, his expression critical. 'Your sister is eating.'

'Oh!' Danny took the reprimand in good part, to Charlotte's astonishment. 'Sorry, Lot, didn't think.'

Charlotte subsided as Danny began to slice thick wedges off the remains of the loaf. He was not particularly adept, for he had had little practice at that particular chore. Although their mother had allotted all the children their share of the household tasks as soon as they were old enough, food had been the province of the older girls. 'Leave enough for Pa and the others,' she warned faintly.

'The baker's will be open before they need any.'

'I hope you're right, or you'll get the sharp edge of Pa's tongue!'

'Rose can go for some when she gets up. Pa'll like it fresh.'

'Rose didn't get to bed until late; she should sleep in. What a night! You must go and get some rest when you've finished eating. You, too, Bertie. There'll be no work for you today. And maybe they haven't done any baking tonight, with all this to-do,' she added as an afterthought.

'Someone will surely have a loaf to sell. What time do they open?' asked Francis.

Charlotte glanced at the clock on the mantel. Time had flown! It was six-thirty already.

'They should be open by now.'

He rose to his feet. 'Then I'll go and see what I can find. I'll not be long.'

'Mr Langford, I cannot allow you ——'

He cut her off. 'Miss Falconer, you cannot stop me! I believe the rain has eased, but I shall need my cloak. See to your family!'

He gave her a smile that melted her insides. This was ridiculous! She could not allow her emotions to become involved with this man! He might seek her company for a while, might even want. . . Her mind balked on the thought. But once his carnal lust was satisfied he would go away and forget all about her and where would she be then?

But she smiled back. She couldn't suppress or contain the warmth she felt at that moment.

The boys had gone up to bed and Rose had come down by the time he returned with three large loaves emitting the mouth-watering aroma of freshly baked bread, a pile of bacon rashers, a pound slab of butter, a packet of tea and a large paper bag.

'Eggs,' he informed her as he set the last item down carefully. 'All the shops seem to have opened their doors and I thought you might be running short of a few things.'

'Thank you, but there was no need ——' began Charlotte uncomfortably, only to be cut off by an airy wave of his hand.

'Forget it. Accept the things as my thanks for the breakfast.'

Charlotte decided there was no point in making a fuss. In any case, with the rising price of bread threatening to provoke riots, she could scarcely afford to reject his generosity. She nodded graciously. 'You are most kind. How are things outside?'

'Quieter. I looked out over the harbour; there is still a lot of activity, but I think the worst is over.'

'I must go out and see if I can find news of Sammy.

I'd best go along to the Breakwater. It will be light enough to see soon, and you get a view right round the bay from there.'

'May I escort you?'

'There is really no need.' The prospect of his accompanying her was seductive, but dangerous. She cast around for an excuse to put him off. 'Won't your mother be wondering where you are?'

For the first time that night a slight frigidity entered his tone. 'I cast off the leading-strings many years ago. She knows I can take care of myself.' And my relationship with my mother is no business of yours, his tone informed her. Suddenly his attitude softened again. He smiled. 'Are you ready?'

'Really——'

'Don't be silly, Lottie,' put in Rose with youthful forthrightness. She had risen at her normal time despite her late night. 'If Mr Langford wants to go with you, let him. You'll be glad of someone's support if anything *has* happened to Sammy. Do you think it has?' she added anxiously.

'I don't know, Rosie. But surely God could not be so unkind. We have only just lost Mother. I don't dare think of it.'

Rose's eyes filled with tears. 'Neither do I. He's me favourite,' she sniffed, forgetting her grammar under stress. 'I wish I could come with you!'

'You must stay here and see to the younger ones, Rose. Get them off to school, though you'd better go with them, because you may have to bring them back again if there isn't any class today.'

'Sammy is your brother?' asked Francis as he helped Charlotte into her cloak.

Charlotte looked at him in surprise. 'Of course. Who did you think he was?' She evaded his touch quickly.

His hands had not lingered on her shoulders, yet they had seemed to caress.

'I did not know.' He hid his surprising feeling of relief under a brisk enquiry which was more of a command. 'Shall we go?'

There seemed to be no way of getting rid of him without being rude. Charlotte lifted one shoulder in a helpless gesture. 'If you insist.'

The gale had not abated much, and the road reared unprotected along the cliff-edge above the harbour. As they passed above the shipbuilding yards down on the harbour side they were walking into the teeth of it. At times the wind brought Charlotte to a standstill, even forced her to take a backward step or two. Then she was glad of Francis Langford's steadying hand on her back.

The sky was lightening fast, and by the time they reached King's Quay, where the Royal Navy watered its ships from pipes connected to the reservoir, and which, with the New Pier, formed the jaws of the inner harbour, they found that the tangled mass of broken wreckage had spread to form a causeway between the two. Everywhere the eye could see the surface of the water was strewn with splintered timbers and every kind of article broken free from the vessels.

As they walked on Charlotte strained to make out the ships anchored in the outer harbour among all this wreckage, but it was still impossible to distinguish anything distant clearly. Only as they left King Street behind and progressed towards Berry Head could they see signs of the devastation at the far end of the Breakwater. Although seventeen years had passed since construction began, the Breakwater still fell far short of its planned length. At something around fourteen thousand feet work had stopped for lack of funds, and therefore even before the end had been swept away it had given scant shelter, virtually none from the northeast.

Before descending the cliff Charlotte stopped again, braving the exposed position and the gusting wind to scan the scene. Wrecks could be seen piled up against this devastated barrier, just as they were against the inshore pier. In the cold grey light of dawn their spars and rigging stood out against sea and sky like ghostly, broken skeletons.

It was still too dark, too damply grey for much of Tor Bay's coastline to be visible as yet. The shipyard on the beach just beyond the Breakwater had survived without much damage, as far as she could make out, the hull on the stocks still secure, as it had been left after yesterday's work. But anything loose had been lifted and tossed, to be deposited again in pathetic, crumpled heaps hard up against any obstruction. And the tragic line of jetsam littering the pebbles behind the outgoing tide was already being squabbled over by gulls and a group of scavenging women.

A sob tore her throat as she hastily averted her eyes from the sight and sped on down. The retreating sea, fighting an uneven battle with the stronger gale, which was still driving ships to their doom on rocks further round the bay, had become a seething cauldron in which the flotsam released from smashed hulls was being washed hither and yon in angry, aimless surges. There would be plenty of rich pickings on the beaches later on, but for the moment all decent men and women were too busy hurrying to and fro to the work of rescue and revival to think much of gleaning.

Charlotte picked her way down the track on sure feet, aware of Francis Langford's firm tread crunching behind. She made straight for a knot of fishermen and

boatyard workers gathered on the fringe of the sea
within the harbour, near a brig which had been driven
hard on the beach, though without suffering much
apparent damage.

'Jem!' she gasped. 'The *Bonnie Maid*—have you
news?'

'Aye, my dear, she be out there safe and sound; can't
you see?'

'Oh, Jem!' In a burst of relief she threw her arms
around the grizzled, weathered old salt and hugged him
hard. 'What about the men off those wrecks piled up
against the Breakwater? Were they saved?'

'Some, my lover, but not all, though us did our
best—those as could swim went out with lines and
brought 'em in. They be gone home to warm up and
change now. There bain't much more us can do.'

'Look!' cried someone else. 'They be coming ashore!'

'Who?' asked Charlotte, eagerly scanning the harbour for signs of activity.

'The crew of the *Bonnie Maid*. They be lowering
their sculler.'

'Isn't that risky?' demanded Francis.

The gathered men accepted his presence without
comment, affording his remark the consideration it
deserved.

'The master knows what he be doing, zurr.' Jem had
recognised quality and given it his respect. 'It be calmer
behind the Breakwater, and he be anxious to get some
of his catch to market, no doubt.' He grinned at
Charlotte. 'You'll soon have young Sammy home now.'

Everyone watched as the boat was lowered. A man
went down, followed by several baskets of fish and two
further hands. One put the oar over the stern and
Sammy—Charlotte was sure it was Sammy even at that

distance — waved as he released the line attached to the trawler.

The sea chose that moment to let loose one of its most violent surges. The tiny cockle-shell of a boat was swept willy-nilly to one side. All would still have been well had it not fouled the swing-chains of a neighbouring trawler. As it was the sculler was driven across the taut metal so hard that it jumped clean out of the water, was tossed high into the air, spewed out its crew and their catch and landed with a crash that shattered it to matchwood.

The urgent cries of alarm among the watchers died into stunned silence as what sounded like the crack of doom met their ears and they saw the boat disintegrate.

A horrified shriek echoed across the harbour.

'Sammy!'

Charlotte darted into the water. She was up to her knees in the icy waves before anyone could stop her.

Jem hauled her back.

'Bain't no good, my lover. You'd never reach him, 'specially in all them skirts. You'd drown, an' all.'

'Let me go!'

Charlotte struggled desperately against his hold, her eyes wide and her ears stretched to catch the faintest glimpse or sound of the men who had been so needlessly lost.

'There be nothing any of us can do, my dear. All the swimmers be gone home to dry off and rest.'

'I can swim. Help me off with these boots.'

Francis's clipped tones gained immediate attention. His cloak and coat were already cast aside. The wind cut across his back, plastering his thin shirt to broad, muscular shoulders. He sat on the nearest upturned boat and held out his foot. One of the men jumped to pull at the ruined leather, while another secured a line about his body.

'Not that there be much hope,' he was warned. 'They was most likely knocked silly when they hit t'water. They'd be drowned within a minute.'

As he plunged into the icy sea Francis knew why he had felt compelled to accompany Charlotte on her mission. Some sixth sense had told him he would be needed, though he had not known how or why. But if there was a chance to rescue her brother he had to take it. He might come across one of the other men first, and that would be that—he could not leave him, whoever he was, if he showed any sign of life. But he would have done his best to save someone she loved, and the idea of another tragedy hitting her and her family caused him unexpectedly sharp pain.

The freezing water had taken his breath, and his muscles immediately began to stiffen with the cold. He struggled on, the line a reassuring drag as he was swept along on the tide, less vulnerable to the attentions of the contrary wind since he was fully immersed. He did see a body floating face down in the water among all the other flotsam—some of which could prove dangerous were he not to have a care, he realised—but the hair was grey. He passed it by, knowing the man could not still be alive.

It seemed an age of freezing, lung-defeating effort had passed before he spotted the navy blue-clad figure caught up by the very chain which had caused the disaster. Fair hair crowned a half-immersed face. He headed for the body.

It must be Sammy: the face was young and had something of Charlotte's look about it. Whether the lad was alive or not he couldn't tell, though if he were the signs were lacking. He'd taken a nasty blow on the head.

Francis freed the body from its unscheduled mooring, cupped a hand under the chin and lifted an arm to signal the shore. A welcome tug on the line told him the men had begun to haul him and his burden in. In the struggle to keep the boy's head above water and to avoid the hazards of floating debris, Francis swallowed a deal of sea himself, and reached the beach in a state of sick exhaustion. He knew he should, but he could not drag himself back into the water to search for the other men. His tired and frozen muscles would not answer. He had never felt more incapable in his life.

He was, however, fully alive and simply in need of time to recover. After straining arms had heaved them both out of the water and a chorus of admiring thanks had been thrown his way, together with his relatively dry coat and cloak, the men left him to his own devices while they gathered around Sammy's still body and began their work of revival.

Charlotte knelt by her brother's side, her face blanched, her arms wrapped across her chest, her hands clenched under her armpits, holding herself together when she felt like falling apart, rocking backwards and forwards in her agony. These men had seen drowning and near-drowning before. From the grim looks on their faces they had little hope of success. When they turned him over water surged from Sammy's lungs, but they had been waterlogged for too long. No spark of life returned to his inert body whatever they tried.

After her first wild reaction Charlotte had remained outwardly calm. She knew, before Jem turned to tell her, that Sammy was dead. The world about her receded. Nothing was real except the insistent pounding in her head. Not Sammy's body, not Jem, not the knot of men gathered about him. She heard Jem tell her that they would make a stretcher from old sailcloth and spars and carry Sammy home. They had made several already that night, and another would be quickly done.

Still she knelt beside his body. Not until he was lifted on to the makeshift stretcher did she attempt to rise stiffly to her feet. Someone helped her, but faces meant nothing to her now, seen dimly through a haze of anguish. She saw only one face, so still, so serene in death — that of Sammy, her beloved brother, who would never again come home to give joy by his presence.

Ignoring the pain which threatened to split her head open, keeping upright by sheer will-power when every instinct told her to lie down and let oblivion take her, she walked beside the stretcher as the sombre procession made its way back down King Street to home.

Francis followed a yard or so behind. His sodden boots pinched, he was wet, cold and weary to the bone and a deep sense of loss had settled over him.

He had failed. But, more than that, as he had helped her to her feet Charlotte had looked straight through him, as though she had never seen him before, as though they had never shared a night of high drama and joy in the saving of a young life. What, to him, had seemed like a welcome into the warmth of a loving family had, to her, been nothing of the sort. Merely a courtesy extended to an unwelcome guest. He had sensed her reluctance, her withdrawal even, but had been sure it was due to nothing more than the strangeness of the situation, that given time it would pass.

As he trailed along behind the stretcher party he could deceive himself no longer. The unusual warmth she extended to her family had not reached out to encompass him, as he had hoped.

He made no attempt to go inside the Falconers' cottage. She would not need him, and besides he must get back to the Hall to change. He squared his tired shoulders and limped round to the Globe, where he called for the ostler to bring his horse and then for a large brandy, which he tossed down in a single swallow. The warmth curled around his insides and he began to feel marginally better.

Once the horse was ready he mounted and urged the huge roan into swift motion, eager now to be home — Except that Bradgate Hall was not home, had never been home and was unlikely ever to become so. Whatever home he had was on the other side of the Atlantic, near Washington, a huge, empty shell of a house set in vast grounds. Of course he had servants, but they could never take the place of family. He had been an only child, deprived of a father at fifteen and a mother at seventeen, when she had taken it into her head to come to England and never returned. The enforced years in the army had provided comradeship, but not the warmth he had sensed in the Falconers' home.

It seemed, however, that he would have to continue to do without the comfort of a welcoming hearth. The girl had no use for him, and he had too much pride to thrust himself where he was not wanted, particularly as she was out of his class.

Perhaps, though, that was what had attracted him to her. The women of his own world appeared so superficial, concerned only with money and clothes and their position in society. And with making fools of men while they searched for a gullible husband, he thought cynically. Felicity was a prime example. Such women held little or no interest for him.

It was as well she had decided to cut him off in her grief, he decided. He could have become too fond of

Charlotte Falconer and, however much he might be tempted to wish it otherwise, it was only sensible to forget her and her family. There could be no future in such a relationship. They were worlds apart in more ways than one. He would be returning to America before long.

He dug his heels into his horse's flanks and covered the last stretch at a fast canter, wryly anticipating the sensation he was bound to cause by turning up at the gates in his present bedraggled state.

CHAPTER FOUR

NO ONE would easily forget Wednesday the eleventh of January, 1866, or the night which preceded it. The gale, which reached hurricane force in the early hours, continued almost unabated until noon, by which time the cost in wreckage and human lives had scarce even begun to be counted.

For the remainder of that day Charlotte was aware of little other than her own grief. She walked, talked, cooked and cleaned with automatic precision while her mind struggled to accept this second loss.

Sam, fetched home by an urgent, distraught Bertie, took charge of the additional funeral arrangements. Lucky to acquire a coffin at all, such was the demand, he accepted what was available. The plain deal box containing his son was set down in the parlour beside the more ornate, carved casket in which his wife and the dead babe lay. They would all be buried together.

Only Jackie's incessant grizzling broke the hushed silence which had fallen over the bereaved household. Even Billy, Georgie and Annie had become aware that catastrophe had hit the family and felt compelled to creep about in the presence of so many dead bodies. They had loved their mother and worshipped Sammy. It had begun to dawn on them that they would never see either again.

Sam left them all to go for his usual jug of ale in the Blue Anchor that evening. The younger children were in bed when he returned.

'Over forty ships,' he muttered, shaking his head in

disbelief. 'Over forty ships lost! And we reckon more'n a hundred must be dead.'

'Brixham men?' queried Danny, who had been sitting whittling a stick and making shavings all over the kitchen floor.

'Some,' Sam answered his son wearily. He had had no sleep for nigh on two days, and put on top of his double loss the strain was beginning to tell, even on him. 'They've been out all day patrolling the beaches, helping stranded men ashore and recovering bodies, though they'll never find 'em all. Mostly, they be strangers off the traders. But there be plenty in Brixham like us, mourning their dead tonight.'

Charlotte's numbness had begun to wear off. She swept up Danny's mess and threw it on the fire, wondering how she would survive the coming weekend and the funeral, set for Monday morning before they knew of Sammy's death. Her mother and her brother both gone. How could she bear it?

At the table, Rose had her head hidden in her arms. Having worn herself out with crying, the child had dropped into an uneasy doze. Weary to the bone herself, Charlotte touched her sister's shoulder.

'We should go to bed, Rosie. Come along. You too, you boys. We all need sleep. Goodnight, Pa.'

Sam wiped a hand down his face, rasping his beard, and grunted. Bertie got to his feet. Danny sat where he was.

'I'll come when I'm ready, Lottie. I'll sit with Pa for a while.'

He was asserting his new position as eldest son, Charlotte acknowledged with a sigh as she mounted the stairs behind the other two, glad that the endless day was over at last and that even if she could not sleep she could rest her aching limbs.

*   *   *

The straggling funeral procession wound up the hill to St Mary's churchyard, following the hearse bearing its double load. Elizabeth Falconer had been well liked in the town and the fishing community had turned out in force to pay their last respects to Sammy, making the first of a number of similar journeys which would be necessary over the next few days.

Bill Jackson was not with them, or any of the other eighty-five or so rescued mariners out of distant ports. He, with several others, had already been conveyed to Churston and put on a train to London. The Assembly Rooms had been converted into a temporary hostel to house the remainder until they, too, could be sent home.

After the burial Charlotte stood beside the deep grave shivering slightly — for the bitter weather still held — thinking how well the leaden sky suited her mood.

The new coat did not seem as thick as her old cape. Or was it just that she was cold and dead inside? A local draper had fitted her out with a black gown to wear under a wide-sleeved coat which reached to mid-calf. The full skirts of the gown just cleared the damp ground, allowing a glimpse of the elastic-sided boots she kept for best. A new and becoming capote hat sat perched on her abundant hair, kept in place by long, wide ribbons tied under her chin. Pa had been unusually generous.

He was speaking to a tall gentleman who stood with his back towards her, partly obscured by others in the crowd of mourners now moving from the graveside. She couldn't help noticing how strange Pa looked in a black overcoat and with a tall silk hat swathed by a flowing mourning band on his head instead of his normal cap. As people moved on and her view became clear, her heart, which she had thought dead inside her, began to thud with a new and urgent beat.

Mr Francis Langford had attended the burial! She had not expected him, had scarcely given him a thought over the last days, except to feel regret that she had not thanked him for his effort to save Sammy. He had risked his life, and she had not had the courtesy to acknowledge his bravery.

Of course, she had not been herself. Perhaps he would realise that, if she thanked him now. He had turned to greet Danny and Bertie, and was commiserating with a tearful Rose. Charlotte moved towards him.

Francis did not appear aware of her presence. She was able to stand and study his impressive figure, now clothed in black trousers and a grey greatcoat with a black armband. Not until he had finished talking with Rose did he look up to see her standing there. His expression at once became guarded. Charlotte's mouth went dry.

He lifted his black silk hat.

'Mr Langford.' She essayed a smile but had to pass a nervous tongue over her parched lips, because they threatened to crack. 'How do you do?'

She held out a hand gloved in black kid, which he took briefly in his own. It was as though she had touched crackling silk. The sensation shot up her arm and caused her heart to lurch. She hastily clenched her retrieved fingers round the strings of her purse, feeling embarrassed and foolish.

He inclined his head. 'I am quite well, I thank you, Miss Falconer.'

His tone held no warmth. She might have been a stranger. Acutely uncomfortable but determined to make her apology, Charlotte pressed on.

'You felt no ill effects from your courageous swim?'

He offered no comment except a brief negative shake of his head.

'I am so glad,' she told him breathlessly. 'I fear I was in no state to thank you at the time, but I do so now, with all my heart. Please forgive my discourtesy.'

In her agitation her expression had become unconsciously pleading. His, in turn, relaxed into a half-smile, for once having seen the girl again he found it impossible to maintain the distant courtesy he had determined to show in the face of her rejection and his own better judgement.

Why the devil had he attended this funeral? he asked himself. The answer came back all too clearly. Because of a desire to see this female again.

Her pale face, composed despite the strains of the occasion, the quiet courage implicit in her bearing, moved him to feelings quite out of keeping with the gulf stretching between them. Damned fool! The smile faded as renewed determination to keep his distance tightened his lips.

'Of course!' he murmured politely. 'There is no apology necessary.'

'Oh, but there is!' Her face had lit up at sight of his smile. 'You risked your life to save Sammy, and I can never thank you enough!'

'Then perhaps you will do me the honour of dining with me one evening?'

The invitation emerged without conscious thought. Standing there before him in her new finery, she looked infinitely appealing with that sudden glow in her eyes. Before such charm his determination crumpled. Why not enjoy her company while he could?

The colour flooded Charlotte's pale cheeks. He was treating her like some cheap piece he might pick up in a music hall! The insult was the greater because his attitude had been quite different the other night — he had spoken to her as a friend. Almost as a lady born.

And so she was! And even if she were not she would never demean herself by accepting such an invitation!

'Sir,' she said, very low, her voice trembling with indignation and disappointment, 'you do me no honour by such an invitation. I bid you good morning!'

Damnation! Francis watched her stiff, retreating back and knew he had made a gross error. He should have realised she would misinterpret his invitation. He had meant no harm, no more than a pleasant evening spent in each other's company. Yet — had she proved willing, he would not have hesitated to seduce her, he admitted to himself, while shame sat uncomfortably on his normally sanguine conscience. And in that moment of her dignified retreat he had never admired or wanted a woman more.

She tried to forget him, but he was frequently to be seen about the Quay, sometimes with his stepbrother, Tristram, occasionally with Tristram's sister, Felicity. There was Victoria, too. He often carried the child on his arm, as though he enjoyed having the dainty little girl clinging to his neck asking questions about the ships lying at anchor in the harbour.

Charlotte tensed up when she saw him in the distance and turned aside if she could. If necessary, she about-faced or dived into a shop. She would not admit, even to herself, to being afraid of his companions' curious, disdainful glances were Francis Langford forced to acknowledge acquaintanceship with a girl from the Quay. Or to the devastation she would experience were he to ignore her. Or to the panic which seized her at the prospect of having to speak to him at all.

She managed to avoid him quite successfully until one day he followed her into the shoe shop in Fore Street where she had taken cover. Or she supposed he followed her, for from a lowered, sidelong glance she knew that he did not look at boots, only at her, as he came through the door.

Murmuring an apology to the proprietor, she made to brush past him and escape with no more than a nod of recognition.

However, he would have none of it. Turning, he escorted her from the premises. In the road, he laid a detaining hand upon her arm.

'Miss Falconer, please allow me to apologise for upsetting you the last time we met. I meant no disrespect by my invitation, though I realise it may have seemed otherwise. I merely wished to further our acquaintance.'

Charlotte drew herself up, afraid to throw off his hand yet acutely conscious of his touch. Her heart fluttered. She longed to throw caution to the winds and bask in Francis Langford's interest, but her upbringing, the remembrance of her mother's unhappy experience, prevented her from responding to his overture.

'To what purpose, sir?' she demanded stiffly. 'Our paths crossed for a short time during the storm, but I do not think there is reason for them to do so again.'

'Neither is there reason for you to avoid me, Miss Falconer,' he responded softly. 'Can we not at least exchange greetings when we meet?'

'I —' Charlotte struggled to find a reason for avoiding painful encounters. 'People will think it strange,' she murmured at last.

'Personally, I do not care what people think —'

'But I shall have to live here after you have returned to America!' shot Charlotte desperately. 'You cannot imagine how gossip distorts the most innocent of exchanges!'

'What could people possibly make of our greeting each other in the street?' he enquired with a wry lift of one fair brow. 'Come, Miss Falconer, I will not be deprived of your acquaintance simply because of what your friends and neighbours may think!'

His smile warmed Charlotte to her toes and colour flooded her cheeks. 'Oh!' she cried in total confusion. 'Why are things not different?' Her eyes were enormous and held emotions he was unable to read. And the next moment she was gone.

He realised suddenly that speaking to him had caused her distress, though why this should be so he had no idea. Most females sought his attention with an eagerness he found vaguely embarrassing. But then, he had recognised from the start that Charlotte Falconer was no ordinary young woman.

Why he still wished to pursue the acquaintance he could not entirely fathom, had in fact been battling the desire since his disastrous impulse at the funeral. But her constant and obvious evasions had prodded him into forcing a confrontation.

Much good it had done either of them, he thought sourly. She had been upset, and he found himself strangely disturbed by the encounter.

But he could not regret his action. He was not used to being ignored, and had at least forced her to acknowledge him.

Gradually, the horrors of the January disaster faded into memory. With the surplus funds raised for the relief of the shipwrecked sailors and bereaved families, a memorial was raised in St Mary's churchyard commemorating those who had been lost that day and buried there, including over twenty unidentified bodies, as well as those the sea had swallowed up without trace. But fate had not finished with Brixham that year. During the heat of the summer cholera broke out in the town, and the mournful processions to St Mary's began again.

Sam's brother, David, caught the disease and passed it on to his two sons, who worked with him to fashion the lobster-pots he sold for a living. Charlotte did what she could to help her aunt Ada, who was too distraught, too busy tending her sick family, to have time to cook for herself.

It was as she emerged from the cottage in one of the crowded, evil-smelling alleys which had sprung up where once the creek and more recently the withy beds and the mill-pond had been, that she ran head-on into Francis Langford. There was absolutely no avoiding him, for she had almost bumped into him as she came out of the door.

He put out a hand to steady her as she rocked back on her heels.

'Mr Langford!'

The surprise was the greater since she would not have expected to see him in the crowded back alleys of the town. He normally kept to the main streets, where the shops and inns were to be found.

'Miss Falconer!' She had just come out of one of the cottages, and carried an empty jug. The implication was clear. 'You have been visiting someone who is sick?'

The sun's rays had managed to penetrate the narrow alley. As he lifted his hat in greeting they struck gold from his hair. Mill Tye had never appeared so bright. Charlotte gathered her wits and schooled her voice. She nodded.

'My uncle David and two cousins. They have been struck down with the cholera and are approaching a crisis. Poor Aunt Ada is at her wits' end. But what are you doing here, sir?'

'Visiting, like you — a man I have come to know through the construction of the new railway.'

'You are acquainted with people working there?'

'I am deeply interested in the venture, and Mr Wolston and his engineer are most obliging. I am charting its progress. That is the chief reason for my prolonged stay in England.'

'I see. But I still do not understand why you should be here in town. I thought all the navvies working on Mr Wolston's little line were from other parts.'

'Those in the navvy gang are. John Gillard is a carpenter.'

'John Gillard? He has the cholera? Oh, no! His poor wife!' cried Charlotte in distress.

'Unfortunately, yes,' said Francis gently, touched by her concern. 'Though happily I believe he has passed his crisis and will recover. One cannot but wonder that more are not suffering, with the conditions here.'

His nose twitched uneasily at the stench rising from the gutters, and he scowled ferociously at a scavenging dog, at the same time offering her his arm. Charlotte timidly placed her hand in its crook. She was quite unused to walking on a gentleman's arm. Together, they made their way through to Paradise Alley and walked towards Beach Alley and the harbour.

'The men are better off up in the navvy camp on Churston Common,' he remarked as they progressed.

'I do not doubt it,' came the sharp response, 'but the state of the town is not our fault! It must be four years since the government inspector said how badly we needed sewers and drainage to the houses, but practi-

cally nothing has been done! Thank God *we* are not
obliged to live in this warren; the air is a little cleaner
at home, but the harbour stinks at low tide, the gullies
discharge into it — it is seldom clear of rotting fish — and
people have nowhere else to empty their soil-buckets.'

'I know! My dear Miss Falconer, I am not criticising
you or anyone else, just stating a fact. The cities are far
worse, I am told. But do you not fear to catch the
disease yourself, and to pass it on to your brothers and
sisters?'

'The risk is small, I believe.' Her heart jumped. He
had called her 'my dear' again! Yet there was not the
slightest sign of anything improper in his manner. It
was as though they were back in the kitchen on the
night of the storm. His arm felt strong and warm under
her hand. Charlotte started to take a deep breath and
thought better of it because of the stench. She went on
quickly, before she made a fool of herself and burst
into weak tears, 'There have been outbreaks before,
and the family have not suffered. I am careful not to
touch the sick, and I wash my hands as soon as I return
home and boil every scrap of water we drink. But I
must help Aunt Ada; I would not feel easy in my
conscience if I did not.'

'I understand.'

His smile was warm, appreciative, precipitating
Charlotte into further speech to cover the wild beating
of her heart. 'I keep the younger ones isolated as far as
possible, though Rosie must go to her work. Pa and the
boys are fine up at the ropery all day; the air is quite
fresh there.' She drew a carefully shallow but steadying
breath. 'But what of you? Are you not afraid?'

'Oh, I am tough!' He grinned down at her, his eyes
dancing. This unexpected meeting had come like a fresh
breeze on a stifling summer's day and his resolve was

not proof against her charm. 'I survived an epidemic when I was serving in the army, so I think I must be immune,' he explained blandly, fully aware of the shiver that ran right through her body when he smiled, and the accompanying twitch of her hand on his arm. When she went to remove it he placed his free one over her fingers to prevent her. He was enchanted by her obvious response to his nearness while mourning the fact that his conscience would not allow him to take advantage of it.

Charlotte cast around desperately for something else to say. 'This epidemic is unlikely to spread to Bradgate Hall. Your little sister will be safe enough.'

'Victoria? Yes. You have seen her? I will introduce you one day. But I shall not bring her down here while the sickness remains.'

'Oh, no, you must not!' Now she really was breathless. He was behaving as though he truly desired her friendship! Yet to give it would be dangerous; she had realised that from the beginning. She must not encourage him, or he would be bound to take advantage. Yet his attention was so flattering, so welcome, so tempting! And she had dreamed of him so often since that day he had sought her in the shoe shop.

Mercifully it was high tide, so the harbour did not stink too badly. As they emerged by the water she was able to take a really deep breath without gagging.

The Beach and The Quay were almost as busy as normal, despite the pall of sickness lying over the town. Men worked aboard those trawlers in harbour, repairing rigging, swabbing down the decks. Others had damaged nets spread over the cobbles, seeking the rents in order to repair them. The sound of hammering rang round the town from the shipyards, waking the gulls into squawking, protesting flight. A late fish cart

rumbled past, on its way to Brixham Road to catch a
train to London, its dripping burden adding one more
ingredient to the cocktail of odours already infesting
the air.

'I hope he catches his train,' remarked Francis,
guiding her around the assorted ship-chandler's wares
spilling from the shop into the road.

'If not he'll do as they do in the morning,' guessed
Charlotte. 'The train has a long wait at Newton, so if
the carter pushes his sweating horses hard through
Paignton and Torquay, and on up through St
Marychurch, he can catch it at Teignmouth.'

'Does that often happen?'

'If the fishing-smacks come in late.'

'Then for the animals' sakes it seems an excellent
idea for Brixham to have its own railway!'

'Most people seem to think so,' responded Charlotte
non-committally.

Francis looked out towards the broken Breakwater,
a brooding expression on his face.

'Will it be repaired?' he wondered, nodding in its
direction.

Charlotte shrugged. 'Something will be done, I
expect, but there are not the funds to extend it, which
is what it really needs. At least we shall have a lifeboat
soon, thanks to a collection made by the people of
Exeter.'

'Indeed. To be launched in October, I believe.'

'Yes. It will be an improvement on our previous
reliance on Insurance Society gigs and smugglers' vessels for rescue.'

'Smugglers' vessels?'

She smiled mischievously. 'Do not tell me you do not
know that smuggling has always been a local industry?
And those engaged in that activity have need of ships

which can sail in the worst of weather, for then the
Revenue Cutters are at a disadvantage!'

'And those law-breakers are prepared to go to the
rescue of ships in distress?'

'When they are free. Mostly, of course, they would
be engaged elsewhere, but if in port they are always
ready to assist. Such is the unwritten code of the sea,'
she informed him proudly.

Leaving The Beach behind, they quickly arrived
within a few yards of her home. Charlotte wanted
nothing so much as to escape the web of enchantment
he was weaving about her. If she did not, she would be
caught up in his spell, unable to free herself. Unable to
deny him whatever he wanted. She removed her hand
from his arm and this time he did not attempt to stop
her.

'I must bid you good day, Mr Langford,' she said,
her manner stiff to counteract the silly weakness which
was afflicting her knees. 'I have much to do indoors.'

'I am glad we met, Miss Falconer. I trust we shall do
so again, in less harrowing circumstances. Good day to
you.'

And he lifted her hand to his lips.

Charlotte almost snatched it back, curling her fingers
into a ball as she hurried indoors, wondering what the
neighbours must be thinking. People were bound to
have seen. And they so loved to gossip.

The back of her hand still burned where his lips had
touched. The weather being so hot, she had not been
wearing gloves. No lady would think of going out
without gloves. But he knew she was no lady — and had
still kissed her hand.

She had cause to be extremely wary.

* * *

The cholera lingered on in the town, postponing the launching of the lifeboat. On the newly appointed day in November the townspeople gathered on the harbour shore just inside the Breakwater to watch proceedings. His Worship the Mayor of Exeter performed the ceremony, naming the boat, appropriately enough, *City of Exeter*.

Standing so near to where Sammy had died brought back much of the old grief. Charlotte resolutely refused to allow the tears to fall, concentrating instead on the sight of the reddish-brown sails being hoisted up the twin masts, and on the steady rhythm of the oars as the crew of ten volunteer fishermen, in the absence of an adequate breeze, took the sturdy, self-righting boat on a lap round the harbour while the band of the Brixham Artillery Volunteers played rousing tunes.

Everyone was there. She dared not look to where Francis Langford stood with the younger Bradgates — Sir George and Lady Bradgate were seated in the temporary grandstand erected for the ceremony — though she was aware of his presence with every fibre of her being. Instead, she concentrated on studying the man she now knew to be her father. She had never been so close to him before, and might never be so again.

She could not help a feeling of interest and pride, despite her deep-seated resentment. He was a fine figure of a man, well-built yet not stout, dressed in a double-breasted frock greatcoat with a silk hat set upon dark hair greying slightly at the temples. His moustache and beard, still quite untouched by grey, added to a distinguished appearance. He must be in his mid-forties, she supposed, in fact about Pa's age, though Samuel Falconer's hard life had added lines which were missing from George Bradgate's face. His features had not coarsened with age, and Charlotte could still see in the older man the face of the youthful seducer who stared from her mother's treasured photograph.

Francis watched her with a certain amount of disappointed irritation. He had been looking forward to seeing her smile at him. What must he do to break down her reserve? And why did he wish to accomplish so profitless a victory? That was a question he was not prepared to pursue.

'Good-looking female, that,' observed Tristram, fidgeting at his side and following his companion's gaze out of sheer boredom. His brown eyes devoured Charlotte's face and figure, still clad in the black of her funeral finery. 'Fancy her, do you, brother?' he chuckled. 'Wouldn't mind a dalliance there myself.'

'She is not the kind to indulge in dalliance, Tris.'

Francis dragged his eyes from Charlotte's intent face, alarmed that he had allowed his interest to show. He clenched his jaw. He must curb this ridiculous longing to know the girl better. Angry with himself, he bent a hostile eye on his stepbrother. Tristram, good-looking, shorter than himself by several inches and inclined to plumpness, was noted for his conquests, his excessive indulgence in food and drink and his hard riding. He had little mercy on his horses — or his women, Francis suspected, and the idea of Tristram's pursuing Charlotte Falconer brought cold sweat to his palms.

He tolerated but did not particularly like his step-father's son, but felt it necessary to offer an explanation for his interest in the girl. 'It was her brother I got soaked attempting to rescue,' he told him with an offhand shrug.

'I would have thought she'd have been eager to show her gratitude,' drawled Tristram, giving him a meaningful nudge in the ribs. 'You are too noble, Frankie. Now had it been me——'

'You would not have exerted yourself on her brother's behalf,' snapped Francis, who hated being called Frankie. Tristram did it to annoy him. 'So she would have had no reason for gratitude.'

'Oh, I would have found *something* to make her owe me a favour. In fact,' mused Tristram, his narrowed eyes fixed on Charlotte, 'I think——'

'You will leave her alone,' grated Francis, peering down his nose at his annoying brother, 'or you will answer to me!'

'Really?' Tristram's smooth-shaven features, almost too pretty for a man, registered both mockery and pained surprise, but Francis's expression held no glimmer of humour so he held up a palm in a sign of peace. 'All right, all right, you can keep her, Frankie!' He made an expansive gesture. 'The world is full of succulent armfuls!'

'Who are you two talking about?' enquired Felicity archly, realising that Francis was behaving in a most odd manner and that Tris was baiting him. If Francis was interested in another woman, it behoved her to know.

'No one,' said Francis repressively.

'Just one of the Quay women,' grinned Tristram.

'Well, thank goodness this dreary ceremony is almost over,' said Felicity, hiding a yawn and putting her hand on Francis's arm. He, perforce, extended it politely for her to hold, so that she could reach it comfortably without moving too close and tipping her crinoline against his legs. By some quirk of breeding she was as fair as Tristram was dark. Her baby-blue eyes flirted up at Francis as she fluttered her thick, pale lashes. Yellow ringlets framed her face from under the brim of a pale blue feathered hat, whose wide ribbons were tied under her chin in an enormous bow.

Felicity had returned from a second Season in London without a prospective husband in view. She was a reasonable-looking female, small and dainty as fashion demanded, but Francis did not wonder at her lack of success. Her fortune was not large enough to tempt any but the most impecunious, and her nature did not appeal. In fact Francis liked her as little as he liked Tristram, but he could not be rude.

He glanced across to Charlotte again as he reluctantly escorted Felicity up the slope to their waiting carriage. After his stepsister's crimped hair and fussy clothes, her appearance reminded him of a deep, calm pool. But. . .

He frowned. She was still gazing at his stepfather with a look on her face he did not like: considering, assessing, definitely interested. Almost mesmerised.

Surely she could not be attracted to a man old enough to be her father! The very idea turned Francis cold. He had warned Tristram off, but he could hardly warn his stepfather to leave the girl alone! Especially as it was she who was displaying all the interest.

If he was to warn anyone off, it should be her. If she set her cap at Sir George his mother would be the one to suffer, and Vicky, too.

But, he mused dourly, she had no way of furthering the relationship. She would have to be brazen beyond belief to gain Sir George's attention. He had nothing to fear there.

But he did begin to wonder whether Charlotte Falconer was as innocent and honest as he had thought.

CHAPTER FIVE

FOR weeks before Christmas excitement reigned in the household. Charlotte adhered to all her mother's old traditions, determined to make the festival as cheerful as possible for the children.

Eyes and noses ran as onions were pickled. Making the plum pudding had always been a great event. Everyone had a stir, from Pa down to little Jackie, who was toddling by now, though in effect the child did little more than bang the side of the basin with the wooden spoon. The smell of boiled cloth, followed by the rather more appetising aroma of cooking fruit and spices, pervaded the kitchen for a whole day as the huge round pudding bubbled away on the hob.

Clandestine shopping expeditions resulted in a store of brightly packaged gifts passed to Charlotte secretly and tucked into a hiding-place known only to her. When she came across a square parcel hidden here and a long one secreted there as she swept and cleaned, she smiled to herself and pretended not to have seen them, knowing such gifts were intended for her.

Danny had contrived to secure a large branch of fir to plant in an old bucket. Prince Albert had introduced the Christmas tree and every family who could possibly manage it endeavoured to have one. Charlotte turned out the doll her mother had dressed as a fairy only the previous year, while heavy with the unborn child which had killed her. Ironing out its crumpled muslin skirts through a haze of tears, she impatiently dashed them away before fixing the smiling doll to the spike of fir at the top of the tree. The older children helped her to decorate the branches with ribbons and glass baubles and last of all she fixed the small holders in place and inserted the candles.

With those alight it looked pretty and cheerful standing in the corner of the parlour with all the gifts piled beneath. A blazing fire burnt in the hearth all through the holiday, fed by logs collected over a period by the boys and sawn into neat lengths by Danny. Charlotte was proud of him — proud of them all, and grateful to Pa for providing the extra housekeeping needed to enable them to celebrate in style.

Widowed Aunt Ada joined them for the festivities, hiding her own sadness at the recent death of husband and sons, all taken in a matter of hours by the cholera despite her devoted care.

After allowing the children to delve into their Christmas stockings Charlotte shepherded the entire family to church. On their return, spirits were high and laughter rang through the house as the presents accumulated under the tree were opened, admired, tried on or played with. Exciting aromas of exotic cooking wafted through the house with the laughter. The plump goose Charlotte and Aunt Ada cooked between them, followed by large helpings of the Christmas pudding, brought on an inclination in the older generation to snooze in the afternoon, and Pa remained in the kitchen after the dirty dishes had been cleared to enjoy a pipe in his chair by the range.

Time had softened the blow of loss, but even so the celebrations held an underlying note of sadness. The yawning gaps left by the absence of Ma and Sammy, not to mention Uncle Davy and their cousins, could not be entirely papered over at such a time, even by holly and mistletoe, trees, paper-chains, hilarious games,

exciting gifts and the fun of picking charred chestnuts
from beneath the roaring fire to sting their fingers and
burn their tongues.

The New Year of 1867 came in on a quiet, cold night,
to the ringing of church bells, the boom and rattle of
drums, the ululating notes of coach-horns and the blare
of fog-horns from ships in the harbour. That cacophony
of sound had not long died away before Charlotte heard
the raucous singing of men reluctantly leaving the
public houses to wend their unsteady way back to wives
patiently waiting indoors with the little ones tucked up
in bed.

Some wives, of course, had refused to miss the fun
and had either left the children to look after themselves
or dragged the youngsters along to wait on the pave-
ment while they celebrated with their men in the
taproom. That explained the thin wails of tired and
frozen children, abruptly cut off by a cuff and a roar or
a shrill stream of abuse from a reeling parent.

Charlotte shivered, thanking God that the young
Falconers had never been treated so. Like her mother
before her she had no inclination for any such
expedition and tonight, as every other night, she had
remained indoors while Pa made his way to the Blue
Anchor.

Danny had gone with him, now he was considered
old enough. Rose and Albert and even young Lizzie,
who had begged so hard that Charlotte hadn't the heart
to refuse her, had stayed up to see the New Year in.
Aunt Ada had come round so as not to be all alone in
her cottage, and they had all drunk each other's health
and happiness in ginger beer, hugging and kissing each
other. Bertie's whoops had threatened to keep the
whole street awake.

Charlotte had laughingly shooed them all to bed

immediately the noisy celebrations outside died down, and Aunt Ada had left soon after.

She should go upstairs herself before Pa returned. His temper had become uncertain of late, though it was not in his nature to be truly violent, even in the drink. Her mother had been right in calling him a good man. He had been grateful and generous over the last year, seemingly determined to woo her into remaining to look after the family. He'd had no need. Love had dictated that she stay. But. . .

Charlotte pulled her shawl more tightly around her. She disliked being alone with her foster-father since her mother's death. They had never broached the subject, yet knowing he was not her real father and knowing he knew it made a difference. The old ease in his presence had gone.

He was so familiar, so — no, not exactly loved. Yet she could not deny an affection for the man who had been a stern but in so many ways a caring father to his ever-growing family over the years. Her real quarrel with him had always been on her mother's behalf. He should have governed his appetites, should have spared his wife the regular annual travail which had eventually killed her.

Although — if a man's wife happened to be fertile, how was he to avoid getting her with child? He had his needs, and she was there to satisfy them. Would Ma have preferred him to seek the services of a prostitute? Charlotte doubted it.

There were ways to stop breeding — she couldn't help hearing the talk among the women of the town — though none was reliable, grumbled those who had fallen despite the application of herbs, early withdrawal, flour and lard plugs, douches, choosing their time and all the rest. There were even ways of ridding

oneself of an unwanted baby before it was born, but
they were positively dangerous. Women died. Her
mother had never considered any of these things,
welcoming each new member of the family God sent
with tenderness and love.

Charlotte felt almost ashamed of her thoughts. Her
mother had cast no blame on her husband, so why
should she castigate Sam Falconer for something so
entirely natural and right? She sighed wearily. Life
seemed so difficult sometimes.

She had not been sleeping well of late. Bed held no
attraction for her, so she sat on by the banked-down
grate wondering why a pair of accusing blue eyes should
so deprive her of sleep. At the launching of the lifeboat
she had emerged from her rapt contemplation of her
father to see Francis Langford about to escort Felicity
Bradgate to their waiting carriage. Before leaving he
had looked her way. She had been quite near enough
to see his grim expression, the accusation, the anger,
the disappointment in eyes whose smile could set her
heart thumping. Startled, she had stared back, her own
features blank with shock. And he had turned away
without so much as a nod.

The look in his eyes she could not understand. Of
what was he accusing her? Why was he angry? What
had she done to disappoint him? Not that it mattered,
since he was ashamed to acknowledge her in the
presence of members of his family.

She had known he would be. So why did she feel so
totally destroyed? Why did his eyes haunt her into
sleeplessness? 'Dear lord,' she prayed desperately,
'help me to forget him!'

Sam's return, when it came, took her by surprise.
She must have dozed, though thoughts and vague

pictures had still been whirling in her head, giving the illusion of wakefulness.

'Still up, are you? Waiting for me?'

His words slurred slightly and he held the door-frame for support. Charlotte's eyes searched the darkness of the scullery behind him, looking for Danny. Not seeing or hearing anything of her brother, she sharply enquired as to his whereabouts.

Sam chuckled as he lurched forward to prop himself up against the table. 'Gone off with Janie Prowse.'

'What do you mean, Pa? Gone off with Janie Prowse?'

'What I says, of course. He be gone off to get some experience in the petticoat line. 'Bout time, too, if you ask me.'

'He's — he's only just seventeen,' protested Charlotte faintly, her stomach lurching. 'How could you let him, Pa? Supposing — supposing he gets her breeding?'

Sam's drunken snicker chilled her through. She had never seen him in this state before. 'She'd never be able to pin it on our Danny, never you fear!' he claimed. 'Whole town knows she be free wi' her favours, though she's no doxy to want paying an' all. She'll teach the lad what he needs to know. He's been throwing his weight about lately, demanding a steam engine to drive the crank; 'tis time he became a grown man.'

'Oh, Pa!'

Charlotte's distress was genuine. Of course, it was different for men, but she could not help but feel that Danny should have reserved his first passion for someone more worthy of it, not a young woman notorious in the town for her loose ways. Better, almost, to have paid Moll Fryday, the prostitute who lived a few doors up the road; she was a kindly soul, a widow driven to her profession by sheer necessity but condemned by all and sundry just the same. Danny's need would have been widely understood, and he could have experimented without fear of unpleasant consequences — except perhaps the pox. She shivered.

'What's the matter with you, girl? Jealous? Or are you too much of a prude to indulge in a bit of carnal pleasure?'

The growling tone of Sam's harsh challenge pierced her misery. She looked up quickly to see his hot, bloodshot eyes fixed on her jutting bosom.

Her breath caught in her throat. Blood rushed in a confusing flood up her neck and into her cheeks. Clutching her shawl about her, she jumped to her feet and took a step towards the stairs.

'Come here!'

The gruffly uttered command stopped Charlotte in her tracks. Obedience to Pa was too ingrained for her to ignore such an order. Her heart hammered as panic rose to close her throat.

'I must go to bed,' she managed desperately.

'No hurry, girl.' He staggered across, bringing the stench of the alehouse with him, and took her by the shoulders, first tearing the shawl from her trembling fingers and casting it aside. 'Come to your old pa.'

His sweaty face was too near. 'Pa!' she pleaded.

'I'll not hurt you, lass. Just a kiss, eh?' he wheedled. 'Then, maybe, you'll be ready to share my bed. You'd enjoy that, I can promise you.'

'No!'

The word wrenched itself from Charlotte's throat just before Sam's mouth fastened on hers. She clamped her lips together, battling his attempts to force them apart, standing rigid in his embrace, resisting his assault with all the determination in her young body. But she could not help the shudders of fear which racked her as she felt his hard form pressed against hers. He had never kissed and cuddled her as a child; she was not used to his touch. This was different, anyway. By no stretch of the imagination was this a fatherly embrace. His hands were everywhere, squeezing and hurting.

Pa was drunk, his senses over-stimulated by beer and Danny's escapade. Damn Danny! Why hadn't he come home with Pa? And, she remembered with a sinking stomach, it was almost a year since Ma had died. She didn't know whether Pa had been with other women since then. But he was a lusty man, and if he hadn't. . .

At last his lips lifted from hers, though his arms kept her tightly bound. Wafts of heavy, beer-laden breath fanned her face and she could feel the urgent vibrations which shook his body. She almost retched.

'Lottie! I need you. You're so like your ma was. I miss her, girl. Let me love you instead.'

The thick voice, the hot, pleading look in his eyes touched some inner well of compassion and strength. She was calm now. She knew she must handle him carefully if she was to escape without causing grievous harm. She could scream, wake the children and cause a scandal, but that would be little better than doing what he demanded. It might save her, but the family would suffer.

'It would not be right, Pa,' she argued quietly, though her voice shook uncontrollably.

'Why not?' His voice had descended to an obstinate growl. 'You're no kin of mine. There's no blood tie between us. You know that, don't you?'

'Yes. But no one else does. If we did. . .did. . .' She gave up trying to articulate the action. 'It would be bound to come out. Supposing I——' She swallowed hard, forced the words from her parched throat. 'Supposing I fell for a baby?'

'I'd marry you, Lottie. That's it! We'll be wed!'

It was the drink speaking. Sober he would never have contemplated such a preposterous proposal. Or would he? Had all the consideration, the presents, been leading up to this? Sickness almost overwhelmed her again.

'We cannot.' She drew an essential, sobbing breath. 'It would mean admitting I was. . .' Words failed her again.

'A bastard,' supplied Sam ruthlessly.

'A love-child,' whispered Charlotte shakily.

Pain seemed to rack her whole being as she clung to the assurance her mother had given her. She was no casual by-blow, but the child of a great love. Her eyes were enormous, filled with anguish, and Sam recognised it through his alcoholic haze. He sucked in a harsh breath.

Suddenly, he flung away and threw himself into his chair by the fire.

'Go on, then, go to bed,' he growled.

Charlotte needed no second bidding.

Danny was up late next morning, tired, but hungry and smug. He could not quite wipe the smile from his face.

Pa kept his head down while he drank his ale, supped his porridge and bit on a slice of bread and marmalade. But whenever she turned her back Charlotte's spine crawled. She was certain he was eyeing her with the same lust she had seen last night. She had heard him go out again, probably driven to visit Moll Fryday, she thought miserably.

As soon as she knew it would be convenient, Charlotte wheeled Jackie round to Mill Tye to visit Aunt Ada.

Aunt Ada was a few years older than her brother-in-

law, for her husband had been some ten years Sam's
senior. Charlotte supposed she was almost fifty. She
was sprightly enough, having been spared the eternal
pregnancies suffered by so many women, though
whether by luck or guile Charlotte had never discovered. Ada had lost a lot of weight since the summer's tragedy. She visited the King Street cottage
regularly, in search of company. She never minded
looking after Jackie once she had finished her work in
the fish market in the mornings. Thanks to her,
Charlotte had planned to begin teaching again after the
holidays, two afternoons a week.

Ada had not long returned from work. She kissed
Charlotte warmly, wrapping her in motherly arms. A
smell of fish still clung to her flesh and clothes, but
Charlotte was used to an aroma which seemed all-
pervasive anywhere near the harbour. Besides, Rosie
brought it home with her, too, and so had Sammy.

'A happy New Year again, my love. Are you all quite
recovered from the celebrations?'

'Yes, thanks, Aunt Ada.'

'And how's my favourite boy, then?' demanded Ada,
picking Jackie from the three-wheeled push-cart Sam
had made for his young children to ride in many years
before.

She held him on her arm, her rather plain, now thin
face beaming. Jackie stopped whimpering, grabbed the
grey-streaked hair, an act which threatened to dislodge
her bun though she did not seem to mind, and began to
laugh instead.

'Come in, come in.'

Once indoors, Ada scrutinised her niece shrewdly.
The hollows under Charlotte's eyes told of sleepless
nights. Red rims to her lids indicated recent tears.

'What ails you, Lottie?' she asked gently.

'I have to leave home.'

The bald statement raised Ada's eyebrows. She set Jackie down to play on the floor and busied herself reaching for the cocoa before she asked, 'Why?'

'I—I just need to get away, to make my own life. Rose is fourteen now, old enough to take over really, but I wouldn't like to leave her the responsibility—Aunt Ada, would you look after them? The children all love you, and you work wonders with Jackie. I wish he'd be like this at home!'

Jackie was occupied with an old saucepan and a wooden spoon, making as much din as he could and crowing delightedly.

Ada smiled briefly as she handed Charlotte a steaming cup, drew up a chair and sat down knee to knee with her niece.

'You mean move in?' she asked with a doubtful frown. 'Sam Falconer might not like that.'

'Once I was gone I don't think he would mind, so long as the children were off his hands and he got his meals regularly.'

'You should not be expected to cope with them all on your own; he shouldn't ask it,' muttered Ada. 'It bain't fair on you, my love. But you're not leaving because you can't manage, for you know very well I'd help out, nor yet because you want to throw off the responsibility, so don't try that one on me! Out with it! Or I won't even consider your suggestion.'

Charlotte took a nervous gulp of the cocoa and burnt her mouth. She gasped in annoyance and put her cup and saucer down on the hearth. 'Too hot,' she explained, gathering her wits to concoct some story which would satisfy her aunt.

'Is it your pa?'

The question took her by surprise. She blushed

furiously and avoided her aunt's sharp eyes. 'W-what do you mean?' she stammered.

'You know what I mean. I'm not blind. I've seen the way he's been looking at you of late, and it bain't right; it bain't right at all. 'Twould be a mortal sin if he violated his own daughter. To think he is my own dear Davy's brother, too!' Ada finished indignantly.

'You. . .you mustn't blame Pa——'

'Then who should I blame? You?'

'No! You are wrong! Really you are!'

The flush had gone, leaving Charlotte bone-white. She was breathing as though she'd been running up a hill. Ada's eyes narrowed and she pursed her lips doubtfully before she spoke.

'Then if I be wrong, tell me what *is* up with you, Lottie. I want the truth, mind. I won't lift a finger otherwise.'

There was no help for it. Aunt Ada was no gossip, neither was she easily shocked. Charlotte considered her other options and decided she had none. The whole story came pouring out.

'So you see,' she ended in a whisper, her head bent in shame, 'Pa wasn't committing a mortal sin. I am not his daughter.'

Ada's expression had changed from shock to disapproval as the story progressed. 'Well, well!' she exclaimed now. 'I would never have believed it of Lizzie! But then, you never can tell, can you?' She did not expect an answer, and Charlotte offered none. 'So you are a love-child, eh?' went on Ada after a moment's consideration. 'And Samuel Falconer knows it! It were still sin enough on his part, him having brought you up from a babe as though you was his own!'

'He knew she was breeding when he married her. He. . .he's been so good all these years. . .but now. . .'

Ada sniffed, but she had taken Charlotte's hands in a warm, comforting hold. 'It were no sin of yours to be born so, though many's the parson who would condemn you. I don't, my love.'

The tears gathered in Charlotte's eyes as she lifted her head. 'Oh, Aunty!'

'No need to be grateful, child! Though it wouldn't do for the story to come out, now would it? So perhaps it is best for you to get right away. And I cannot deny that I would welcome a move from here. Without my man and the boys it be lonely, and that hard to find the rent. But to think of Samuel — why, it fair makes me shiver. . .'

'Pa had drunk too much.' Charlotte was still making excuses for him. 'Promise you'll never let him know I told you?'

Ada squeezed her hands. 'I'll not mention it; you have my word.'

'Thank you, Aunt Ada. But I cannot be certain it will not happen again, so I must leave. You do see that, don't you?'

'Aye, child, I do, I do. But — where will you go?'

This question had been exercising Charlotte's mind since she'd flown up the stairs the previous night.

'London,' she pronounced firmly.

'Have you money? You'll need plenty of it if you're to manage there.'

'I still have a couple of guineas Ma left. But I'll get some more. Ma said to ask my real father. He'll give me money, if only to keep me quiet.'

'Lottie! You wouldn't . . .?'

'Not unless he forces me,' responded Charlotte grimly.

* * *

The climb up to Higher Brixham seemed particularly exhausting that afternoon — perhaps because her mission was distasteful. For whatever reason, Charlotte's feet were dragging by the time she turned into the lane leading to Bradgate Hall. She had scarcely plodded a hundred yards when she heard sounds of a horseman approaching round a bend.

Charlotte's nerves tightened. She shrank against the high bank supporting the bare hedgerow, staring in dismay at the unwelcome sight of Francis Langford. She had hoped to avoid meeting him.

There was nowhere to hide.

She stood rigid as he drew near, saw the sudden stiffening of his body as he recognised the sombre figure pressed against the side of the track. A forbidding frown drew creases between his eyes. The gait of his horse did not falter. He acknowledged her nervous nod distantly as he passed her by. Unsure of his mood, she gave him a half-smile, which he did not return.

Charlotte drew a deep breath as she stepped back on the track. So he was still unaccountably annoyed with her. What could possibly have happened between their leave-taking during the cholera in August and the launch of the lifeboat in November? Not that it mattered.

He would probably guess where she was headed. There were scarcely any cottages near by. She had confessed to not coming up here often. What would he think?

She tossed her head. Like his strange withdrawal of offered friendship, it did not matter! Once she had her money and went to London she would never see Francis Langford again. So what he thought could be of no possible consequence at all. Neither could his opinion of her, she told herself defiantly. Life here was becom-

ing altogether too difficult. She would be glad to be
gone.

Her heart told her otherwise. All the people she
loved were here, and loneliness lay ahead. She would
not think about it.

She quickened her steps and hurried towards the
gates of Bradgate Hall. Best to get her unpleasant task
over. But having arrived she almost lost her nerve again
and had to force her hand up to pull the chain to ring
the bell.

A man came in answer to her summons. Jess's
husband, she guessed, and smiled as confidently as she
knew how.

'Yes?'

Sawyer was not inclined to friendliness, though his
expression did relax slightly at sight of her smile.

Charlotte schooled her voice. 'I wish to see Sir
George Bradgate,' she informed him calmly.

'Do you now! And what makes you think he'll want
to see you, my girl?'

'This.'

Charlotte held the locket out on the palm of her
gloved hand. Sawyer made to take it through the bars,
but Charlotte curled her fingers over the precious
object.

'No,' she said, 'you may look, but I am not allowing
this out of my possession.' The slender chain was about
her wrist, but would break if he snatched at the locket,
and she did not intend to take the risk. 'Understood?'

He shrugged. 'Let's see it, then.'

Charlotte uncurled her fingers and Sawyer studied
the familiar coat of arms enchased on the gold.

'Where did you get that?' he demanded suspiciously.

'No business of yours. Take me to see Sir George.'

Sawyer hesitated, then opened the small wicket gate forming part of the heavy main ones.

'I can take you up to the house, but I'm not saying the master will see you.'

'Thank you.'

Charlotte still sounded calm enough, but inside she was churning with nerves. Relief at getting this far made her legs weak for a moment but she quickly recovered to follow Sawyer up the gravelled drive. He called to his wife as he passed the lodge, telling her to see to any further callers.

Just beyond the lodge her guide diverted their steps to a narrower track, which for a while followed the general direction of the elms marking the line of the main drive, though it was on the far side of screening azaleas and rhododendrons. Charlotte realised he was taking her along the path used by tradesman's carts.

The house had looked large from the gates, but as they came closer Charlotte saw that it was enormous, with chimneyed wings, not visible from a distance, running back from the main block and then spreading sideways.

It must have been built a long time ago. The rather austere lines of the façade had been softened by virginia creeper, a few brilliant leaves of which still clung to its otherwise denuded tendrils. Elsewhere, deep swaths of ivy clung to the stonework. Both creepers encroached on a number of the windows lined up like soldiers in the walls.

Their path had diverged from the main carriageway by this time. A smooth swath of grass, being cleared of fallen leaves by a gardener and his lad wielding birch brooms, together with its twin on the far side of the drive, opened up an impressive approach to the pedimented porch protecting the massive front door. The path they were following led to the service quarters. Charlotte stopped by a carriageway linking the stables and coach house with the great sweep of gravel fronting the Hall, debating whether to insist on using the main door. If she wanted to gain access to her father, she must surely do so. He would be less likely to consent to an interview with someone who sought entry by way of the service door.

'I will go to the main entrance,' she told her guide with far more assurance than she felt.

'I can't take you there!' protested Sawyer in alarm. 'I would lose my place!'

'Then do not. I will go alone and take all responsibility.'

Charlotte swept off, her stride long and determined, though her knees felt weak. Sawyer's anxious cries grew fainter as she approached the entrance, and died away altogether as she stepped inside the porch.

There was a bell. She rang it.

It seemed an eternity before sounds of movement came from inside, though it could only have been a minute. The huge oak door swung open and she was confronted by a young man in footman's livery, who took one look at her and began to close the door again.

'You want the tradesman's entrance,' he told her loftily.

She stepped forward quickly and put her hand against the wood.

'I wish to speak with Sir George Bradgate. Please inform him that I am here.' Her tone brooked no argument. The footman was not to know that her voice sounded high and strained in her own ears.

He raised sceptical eyebrows, his glance sweeping up and down, assessing her dress. 'You have an appointment — miss?' The final word passed his lips on a disdainful sniff.

'No.' The door began to close again. In desperation, Charlotte thrust the locket through the narrowing gap. 'Tell him I have this!'

'Who is it, Blackler?'

'Some young female, Mr Parsons.'

The footman stepped aside. Charlotte discovered that the sonorous tones belonged to a severe-looking personage in butler's garb, who took his place.

The man's eyes assessed her briefly, then flicked down to fix on the object in her hand. Finally they lifted to scrutinise her face with vast suspicion.

He repeated Sawyer's exact words. 'Where did you get that?'

Charlotte returned the same answer, but in a more imperious tone. 'How I came by the locket is no business of yours. Please inform your master that Miss Charlotte Falconer wishes to speak with him — on a family matter.'

'Wait here.'

The door shut firmly in her face. She did nothing to stop it this time, but sank down on the stone bench lining one side of the porch. Her knees had given out at last.

The butler was not away long. The door opened wide, and he stood to one side in reluctant invitation.

'The master will see you in the library.' His whole attitude implied severe displeasure at Sir George's decision to admit this unlikely visitor. 'This way.'

Charlotte drew a thankful breath and, iron heel-tips ringing, followed him across a large, flagged hall furnished with a couple of settles and several polished-wood rout chairs. He led her past the foot of an impressive, carved-oak staircase, which led up to a wide half-landing, where it divided to sweep off in opposite directions to the floor above. They passed under one of these narrower flights to reach a room at the back of the house. Everywhere she looked, cheerful yuletide decorations abounded.

The butler knocked. A strong, pleasant voice bade them enter.

'This is the young person, Sir George.'

Charlotte stepped past the disdainful servant and halted, scrutinising his master, who stood near an armchair by a blazing fire. He wore country clothes, top-boots and breeches with a tweed riding coat. He looked no less impressive than in his formal overcoat and tall silk hat.

A desk littered with papers stood by a window which commanded a distant view of Tor Bay and overlooked a formal garden beyond a wide terrace. Charlotte imagined he had been working there before her arrival.

He eyed her steadily, stroking his carefully trimmed beard, then waved a dismissive hand.

'That will be all, Parsons.'

'Very well, sir.'

The butler made a dignified retreat and Charlotte was alone with her father for the first time in her life.

CHAPTER SIX

'PARSONS tells me you have a locket with you. May I see it?' Sir George enquired quietly.

Charlotte moved across the polished boards towards him, her heels embarrassingly loud and hollow, though shelves of books and linen-fold panelling absorbed much of the sound, which was hushed altogether when she reached the Turkey rug before the fire. In here, the Christmas decorations were minimal, a mere swath of greenery lavishly scattered with red berries fixed above a portrait over the mantel.

She glanced down at the glittering object in her hand. Then, with an unconsciously defiant gesture, she held it out to Sir George.

'My mother gave me this when she was dying,' she informed him in a dismayingly husky voice. She cleared her throat.

'Thank you.'

His even tones steadied her. She watched as he studied the crest, fondling the locket as though it meant more to him than the worth of the gold. After a glance which sought permission, he put a thumbnail under the clasp to spring it open. For a long time he studied the face staring up at him from the inside.

'You know who this is?'

The question took her by surprise with its abruptness.

'You,' she said, and swallowed, hesitating before adding firmly, 'My father.'

He sighed, and snapped the thing shut.

'You will wish to keep this.'

With a muttered word of thanks, Charlotte took back the precious keepsake, clenching it in her hand. He had not denied her claim. She waited.

'I knew she had died,' said Sir George at last. 'I followed her progress as well as I could — yours too, though it became increasingly difficult as the years passed by and I took on — other commitments. Please believe you have my deepest sympathy. Your loss must be grievous.'

She stood with her head bent, silent. How could he know how she felt? Why should he care?

'I expected you before this.'

Her eyes flew back to his face. 'You did?'

He smiled slightly. 'I guessed she had not told you. But I also guessed she would, before the end. I expected you to come to claim your birthright.'

'What birthright?' asked Charlotte bitterly. 'You abused my mother's love and left her to. . .to marry a man she did not love — then. But she did afterwards,' she added, wanting to hurt this man who had so hurt her mother. 'She joyfully bore him all the children he wanted. He is a good father. We all love him,' she insisted, perhaps a trifle too defiantly.

She watched him wince with secret relish. But he made no other response to her gibe.

'Was she happy?' he asked instead, and there was something in his voice which made Charlotte ashamed of her deliberate cruelty.

'She was not unhappy,' she told him truthfully.

'I was,' he asserted on a sigh. 'Until I married the present Lady Bradgate. She has brought me the happiness my first marriage did not.' He straightened, throwing back his head. 'But why *are* you here,' he demanded abruptly, 'if it is not to claim kinship?'

'I need help, that is all. Enough money to take me to

London and keep me for a year until I am settled. I have experience of teaching in school. I will either find a position, or take in pupils myself.'

His eyes narrowed. 'Have you any idea of what London is like? And why choose to leave now? Why not a year ago when your mother died?'

He was asking too many questions. Charlotte compressed her lips in annoyance, but knew she had no choice but to satisfy his curiosity.

'I shall manage. A year ago my eldest sister was too young to leave in charge — she still is, but an aunt is a widow since the cholera and she is willing to see to the family. So I am free to make my own way.'

Put like that her ambition sounded somewhat selfish, but Charlotte could not help it. Sir George frowned, but in thought rather than disapproval.

'I cannot allow you to go to London alone, my dear; you would never survive. Besides, I would like to become acquainted with my daughter.' He paused. Charlotte waited in silence for him to elaborate. Before he spoke again his brown eyes met hers steadily. 'I loved her, you know. The locket you have was my token of the deepest affection in which a man may hold a woman.'

'Then why did you let her——?'

He cut her off with an impatient wave of his hand. 'I was called away on business. I had no idea she bore my child in her womb. If I had——' He broke off with a helpless shrug of his shoulders. When he resumed he had his voice under control. 'I returned to find that she had already entered into matrimony with Samuel Falconer. She refused to see me, or to accept my help.' His face contorted momentarily, then he half turned away, making a defeated gesture which touched

Charlotte's sensitive heart. 'I was deeply hurt. I never saw her — to speak to — again.'

'What could you have done? You had a wife!' accused Charlotte.

He turned slowly to face her again. His eyes remained steady on hers as he spoke.

'The marriage was arranged by our families when we were both very young, too young to rebel successfully. We were not suited, and were both deeply unhappy. When I met your mother I could scarcely believe such paradise existed.'

He shut his eyes, as though reliving those distant memories, his features mirroring a private anguish Charlotte did not wish to see.

'Believe me, Charlotte,' he went on gruffly, 'she brought real joy and contentment to my life. I would have seen she wanted for nothing; she must have known that, yet she chose. . .' He tailed off, then gazed steadfastly at his boots as he began again. 'I feared she had stopped loving me.'

A vision of her mother's dying face and some element in the man's voice made Charlotte whisper, 'She loved you to the end.'

He reached out a hand and touched her hair. Charlotte stood without flinching, though the effort cost her dear. 'Thank you.' His features relaxed into a smile. 'Even now, that knowledge gives me happiness.' Studying her face intently, he shook his head in wonder. 'You are so like her. You are the child of our love, the issue of my loins. You belong here, with me. You must come here to live.'

Charlotte stepped back a pace. 'Live here? How can I? Think of the scandal —— '

Her heart knocked inside her breast and she emitted

a small gasp. She would be forced to see Francis
Langford every day!

Her father indicated the chair.

'Sit down, Charlotte, my dear.'

She did so, never taking her eyes from his face as he
stood with his back to the fire, his hands clasped behind
him. He rocked backwards and forwards from heel to
toe several times. Charlotte realised he was probably as
nervous as she, though he had regained control of his
other emotions.

'I should be proud to claim you as my daughter were
it possible,' he began thoughtfully. 'You are beautiful,
well educated and well mannered. I should have
expected no less of Elizabeth's child. She was a rare
woman, your mother.'

Charlotte blushed at his words of praise, yet resented
them. He had no right to assess her so. She nodded
stiffly. 'I have always known that.'

Deep in his own thoughts, Sir George ignored her
interruption. 'Quite out of place as a housemaid here,
of course, but circumstances had driven her to take the
position. She deserved so much more than —— ' He
stopped abruptly, and for a moment a bitter expression
touched his mouth. He sighed and shook his head, as
though to banish unwelcome memories. 'But no matter.
Much as I regret it, acknowledging you will not be
possible.'

Charlotte stared at him. She had not expected him to
so much as consider the possibility. 'No?' she murmured uncertainly.

'No. For your sake, mainly, for as far as the world is
concerned you are Samuel Falconer's legitimate daughter, and the records bear this out. I doubt whether my
protection would outweigh the disapproval of church
and society — you would be made to feel shame, and

that would be unfair. The fault was mine and your mother's — if fault it was. We could not feel it a sin to love as we did.'

He paused, flapping the short skirts of his cut-away coat, again lost in memories of the past. He brought his mind back with an obvious effort.

'But also for my wife's sake,' he went on quietly. 'The present Lady Bradgate has brought me unexpected happiness over the last few years, and I cannot allow her to face the scandal such a course would raise.'

'So your suggestion that I live here is impossible, isn't it?' rejoined Charlotte cuttingly, adding tartly, 'Even if I wanted to, which I do not!'

'Not impossible, no.' He cleared his throat again. A coal dropped into the red centre of the fire with a soft shuffle which sounded loud in the silence of the room. Charlotte waited, sitting bolt upright in the chair. Her father brought his warm brown gaze up from the carpet to meet hers again.

'Victoria, my youngest daughter, has a nanny, but at going on seven she needs a governess, too; I have been thinking so for some time. You teach, you have the qualifications; it is really quite fortuitous. I can arrange to make you a generous allowance without arousing comment. Nanny Bridges will continue to look after Vicky in general terms — get her up, put her to bed, see to her clothes and food and so on. You will give lessons most mornings and afternoons, join the family for meals and spend the evenings with us when we are at home — visit with us when invited.'

'Impossible!'

'Not at all.'

George Bradgate met her indignant rebuttal gravely. At length he smiled.

'We will tell the truth — in part, at least. The servants know of your locket and will gossip.'

'I am sorry if I have caused you embarrassment,' put in Charlotte quickly, not quite sure why she was apologising. 'I felt I had no alternative but to show it.'

'Of course not. I fully understand. So we will say your mother gave it to you, as indeed she did, and that she obtained it from her parson father, who was a distant connection of another branch of my family. We need not go into detail, and no one will see the photograph it contains — or recognise its subject if they do,' he observed wryly, 'but the explanation will give reason for my readiness to appoint you and to draw you into the family circle. It will also give you status in the household.'

'As a poor relation!'

'Would that be so terrible, my dear? You would be treated well; my wife has a tender heart. A young girl, destitute and seeking roots, will win her sympathy, you may be sure.'

'I am not destitute. Pa has not turned me out. I have chosen to leave home.'

'Then we will merely say that you seek to relieve the pressure on the family budget now that you are no longer needed at home for practical reasons.'

'If I agree, any money I receive will be a remuneration not an allowance!' she protested, feeling the need to keep some semblance of independence.

'We will not quarrel over terminology, my dear! Will Samuel Falconer object to your coming here?'

'I do not know.' Would Pa be angry when she told him she was leaving? Would he threaten to disown her as his daughter? She could counter with the threat to tell everyone of his shocking behaviour. . .

But maybe, since she would not co-operate in satisfying his carnal desires, he would be glad to see her gone. She had to hope so. 'I do not think he will,' she said at last.

'Then what further objection can you have to accepting my proposition?' demanded her father quietly.

Charlotte remained silent for a moment, thinking. She needed the money. Experience of living in a wealthy household might prove useful in the future. Her father was offering both. And much more, were she prepared to accept his love.

The prospect subtly enticed. She would willingly weather any awkwardness the move might cause were it not for Francis Langford. She could foresee his presence creating difficulties, for she doubted whether his heart was as tender as his mother's was reputed to be. Her father remained unaware of that complication. If she decided to accept his offer she would be forced to avoid his stepson as much as possible.

A new thought gave her additional pause.

'If I claim relationship through my grandfather, people will think all my brothers and sisters connected too. They will expect you to help us all! Had you thought of that?'

Sir George stopped rocking on the balls of his feet and stood still. He brought his hands round from under the skirts of his jacket and stuck them into his trouser pockets. He frowned, pursing his lips.

'No. I had not.' The frown quickly disappeared to be replaced by a wry smile. 'But if that is your only problem I am vastly relieved. It makes no difference. They are Elizabeth's children, therefore I am more than willing to do what I can for them. As far as they are concerned you have taken a position here, and any help comes from you. Explain nothing to them unless you are forced. My family will not question deeply, and will not necessarily expect me to entertain your brothers and sisters, or to treat you all alike.'

'I hope you are right!'

He smiled, reached out and pulled her to her feet. 'You will see!' He looked down into her candid eyes and a slightly grim smile touched his lips. 'I had feared your dislike of me would prevent your accepting my suggestion. I am delighted that it is not so, and hope that one day I shall win your regard.'

'I have not yet agreed, but if you will help me in no other way I have little choice, since I wish to leave home but not to starve!'

'Now I have met you, my daughter, I am not prepared to let you go again without a struggle! This arrangement will be for the best; of that I am certain. And who knows what opportunities will present themselves to you in the future? You are of an age with Felicity. You could perhaps act as her companion from time to time. In any case, as a member of the family you will move in society. So do you agree?'

Charlotte nodded, the ramifications of her decision only just beginning to penetrate her rather numbed mind. Still holding her hands, Sir George pulled her towards him.

'Welcome home, Charlotte,' he murmured, and kissed her cheek.

He smelt of bay rum and tobacco. His whiskers tickled her cheek. Charlotte evaded his embrace as soon as she was able, uncomfortable with his nearness. Events had moved too swiftly. She was not yet ready to accept his fatherly affection, though she was finding it difficult to maintain the dislike she had built up in her mind for a man who could betray a serving-girl as he had betrayed her mother. Maybe she should not judge too harshly.

'I will take you up to the nursery now,' he told her.
'If you dislike your half-sister — or she does not take to
you — I shall not force you to keep to our agreement.'

From what little she had seen of the child such an
eventuality was the least of Charlotte's worries. 'I am
sure we shall deal well enough together,' she assured
her father.

'I believe so, too. This is Tuesday, the first day of a
new year. Provided my wife approves, you can move in
here as soon as you are able to make the necessary
arrangements. Perhaps Saturday?' She nodded and he
smiled. 'A new year, a new beginning, daughter. May
all your dearest wishes be realised.'

Francis entered the house through the gun-room, its
outside door being the entrance nearest the stables. He
had rushed his errand in town, distracted and unable to
rid his mind of thoughts of Charlotte Falconer. Had she
come to the Hall? He had not liked to question the
lodge-keeper.

But if so, for what purpose? She had an interest in
his stepfather, that had been plain enough to see in
November, but surely she was not pursuing it further?
If she had visited the Hall, had she already left? He had
seen no sign of her on his way back.

About to step into the main hall, he came to an
abrupt halt. Victoria's childish treble floated down from
above, saying a shy goodbye in response to Nanny
Bridges's gruff yet kindly tones enjoining her so to do.
She was answered by the light, clear voice with the
fascinating burr which had haunted his mind for a year
now. Then came his stepfather's deep tones, growing
louder as he escorted Charlotte down the stairs to the
hall. What was going on?

Francis stepped back, unwilling to confront the girl

inside the house without first discovering her purpose for being there. Sir George was seeing her out himself, an unusual circumstance, since he would normally ring for a footman. Francis watched from the shadows as his stepfather led Charlotte across the echoing hall. At the door they paused, speaking quietly, so that he could not hear what passed between them. Then he stiffened as Sir George took her hand and drew her near. For an angry moment he thought his stepfather would kiss the girl! But if any such impulse had seized him he resisted it, merely murmuring something more before letting her out.

Sir George stood for several moments watching Charlotte retreat before closing the door behind her. He stood absently stroking his beard, deep in thought, before the entrance of a housemaid on an errand brought him out of his abstraction and he returned to the library.

Francis swiftly crossed the hall and followed Charlotte from the house. He could see her trim figure stepping briskly down the main carriageway between the avenue of trees. She greeted the gardener and his lad as she passed. Perhaps she knew them — they were both local men.

He lengthened his stride, determined to catch her before she reached the lodge. He wanted no witnesses to the interview he intended conducting with Charlotte Falconer.

She heard his fast approaching steps and turned. Seeing who it was, her face flooded with colour. Facing him made her uncomfortable, he saw. So be it. Innocence did not stain cheeks with guilty red!

He chose to ignore the times young girls had blushed on greeting him in saloons and ballrooms, in gardens and drawing-rooms. They were silly young misses with-

out a thought in their heads but of how to catch a
husband, and he dismissed them out of hand. Charlotte
Falconer was a continent away in attitude and experience, and no such vapourings were likely to assail her!
His mood was such that he refused to remember
previous occasions when she had blushed and he had
thought it charming.

'Miss Falconer!' His tone was sharp. 'A word with
you, if I may.'

It was not a request. Charlotte detected the simmer-
ing anger beneath his outward calm and waited apprehensively for him to catch her up. She was upset enough
after her interview with her father. She did not relish
another trying encounter, but could scarcely ignore
him, or run away. Besides, it was time she discovered
the cause of such an abrupt change in his attitude
towards her.

When he reached her he took her arm in a bruising
grip and urged her off the drive, halting behind the
screen of a rhododendron bush.

'Good morning, Mr Langford.' Charlotte kept her
voice steady with an effort as she obeyed the insistent
pressure of the fingers on her arm. Francis Langford
was most definitely still annoyed with her. 'You wished
to speak with me?' she asked politely.

'What are you doing here?' he demanded.

Charlotte lifted her chin, hiding a sudden unease at
his question. 'I came to see Sir George.'

'Why?'

She stiffened. 'I do not think that any business of
yours, sir!'

'I believe otherwise,' he told her harshly. 'What
concerns my mother concerns me. What is your
relationship with my stepfather?'

Charlotte gasped. The colour drained from her face and flooded back. 'R-relationship?' she quavered.

'Relationship!' He forced the word through his teeth, seeing her guilt written clearly on her face. 'What are you up to, Charlotte Falconer? I've seen the calculating way you regard him! If you entertain designs on him and his purse, if you think you are going to seduce him behind his wife's back, you are mistaken! I will not allow it!'

'And how would you stop it?' Charlotte snapped back, relief that he had not in some way guessed the true state of affairs renewing her courage. She shook his hand off her arm, where it still gripped, detaining her. 'Let me go, sir! I do not like your insinuations! My relationship with Sir George is perfectly above board, and none of your business! But for your information I have just met your mother, who approved my appointment as Victoria's governess!' Let him digest that! she thought indignantly.

'Vicky's governess? I do not believe you!'

She smiled mirthlessly at the look of blank astonishment on his face. 'Why not, sir? She needs a governess. I am fully qualified to teach her.'

'It is a cover!' he exploded. 'He has not spoken of seeking a governess for my sister! And why should he choose you, a stranger from Brixham Quay? How were you apprised of the position?'

He was too near the mark, asking far too many questions she could not answer. Charlotte took refuge in anger. 'You are insulting, sir! I have no more to say to you!'

She turned to stalk away, but Francis reacted with a speed which took her by surprise. Before she had time to realise what was happening his arms were around her, steel bands turning her about and clamping her to his taut frame while his mouth swooped on hers.

Charlotte began to struggle. Every nerve in her body had leapt into life, responding to his nearness in a way that dismayed and frightened her. Pa she had resisted with rigid determination, but she could not stand still in Francis Langford's embrace. Her every instinct impelled her to throw her arms around his neck, to clasp him close, to revel in his nearness, even in the brutality of his kiss. So she had to fight to escape his hold or subside into boneless acquiescence.

He seemed determined to vent his anger on her, to punish her for whatever it was he thought her guilty of. Her struggles were only inflaming him further. He was bruising her lips, had split one in fact, and perhaps it was the taste of blood which brought him back to rationality.

He lifted his head eventually to glare down on her flushed, angry face, his chest heaving, his breath coming harshly through flaring nostrils as he fought for control. Gold-flecked eyes locked accusingly with blue as Charlotte deliberately licked the blood from her bottom lip.

He had been suppressing a desire to kiss her for as long as he had known her and had allowed anger and frustration to dictate his actions. He had not meant to hurt her so, but the feel of her in his arms had roused a fierce tide of desire, which he had sought to stem with anger. He had felt her first instinctive response and her subsequent struggles had fuelled both his libido and his fury.

'That is how I will prevent your designs on my stepfather!' he declared harshly as he pushed her away, severing contact and further temptation.

She was as attracted to him as he was to her; of that

he was certain. The trembling and quick breathing she could not conceal might be partly due to anger but experience suggested it to be mostly the result of arousal. The knowledge gave him power.

His own hands were far from steady, and he thrust them into his pockets. 'You will leave him alone!' he ordered grimly. 'If you are looking for a gentleman to seduce, I am available.' He smiled, but the expression on his face sent a shiver down Charlotte's spine. 'I am able give you anything you desire — in fact rather more than Sir George can, since I have the advantage of youth in addition to fortune. You would, I fancy, find my attentions more acceptable than those of a man old enough to be your father——'

He stopped on Charlotte's outraged gasp. 'Sir,' she cried, 'I have misjudged you! I thought you a gentleman, courageous, courteous and kind. I find I was gravely mistaken!' Tears of anger and disappointment streamed unheeded down her cheeks as she sought to control her emotions. 'I want nothing from either of you except my due as a governess! Good day to you, sir!'

This time he let her go, feeling unaccountably abashed at actions so at variance with his normal behaviour. Rarely did he allow his forceful, passionate nature such free rein, but then, seldom had another person so attracted, annoyed, disappointed and challenged him as had Charlotte Falconer. And he was still uncertain of her true motives and intentions.

Her move to Bradgate Hall went more smoothly than Charlotte had expected.

When told of her decision, to the astonishment of the assembled family Sam Falconer muttered, 'Good riddance to bad rubbish,' and from then on ignored her.

Rose was frankly envious.

'What did Pa mean, Lottie?' she demanded, but Charlotte refused to answer with more than a shrug. 'Well, I wouldn't mind Pa's displeasure if only I could live up there!' she told her grimly silent sister.

Danny appeared sceptical of Charlotte's motives, telling her she was backing a loser if she hoped to net Francis Langford. Charlotte was astonished at his having noticed the brief partiality Francis had shown towards her.

'Don't be silly, Danny,' she scolded; 'you imagined it. There was never anything between Mr Langford and me!'

'You know your own business best, Lottie,' he admitted with a shrug. 'But if you ask me he fancied you. You'd better look out, or you'll be in trouble.'

'He is a gentleman!' she defended tartly, memories of his recent ungentlemanly behaviour bringing heat to her cheeks.

'So are most of them, until they get a girl in the family way.'

Danny was growing up fast, and Charlotte did not know whether to be glad or sorry. She was grateful for his concern, but could have done without his uncomfortable remarks.

'Do not concern yourself over me!' she retorted, with so much more asperity than his warnings warranted that Danny pulled a face.

The younger children swung between tears at the prospect of her imminent departure and excitement at the promise of future largesse.

Sir George sent a groom with a gig to transport her and her meagre belongings, causing a stir among the neighbours. The carved wooden box containing her mother's small treasures had fitted in on top of her few clothes and spare pair of boots, in a grip which had also belonged to her mother. Her grandfather's books, wrapped in sacking and tied into three neat bundles, went on the floor at her feet, with the grip strapped on behind.

The final farewells were tearful, though Sam ignored her going by the simple expedient of not being there. Ada, who had already moved in, kissed her goodbye.

'Everything will work out, you'll see,' she prophesied.

As they approached the Hall Charlotte could barely disguise her nervousness. She had had no choice but to come here, she reminded herself miserably, having been caught between the devil and the deep blue sea — she could not remain under the same roof as Sam Falconer, and yet had no wish to share one with Francis Langford. She rubbed her arm, where the bruises made by his fingers still showed a yellowing blue. His harsh judgement and rough handling had wounded her deeply, and she dreaded the moment when they would meet again.

The confrontation was not to be immediate, however. On arrival she was taken straight to her room by a servant — a housemaid she recognised as Jennifer Hoddy, a youngster of barely fourteen from the Quay, who had occasionally attended the school where Charlotte had taught.

'I'm right glad to be looking after you, miss!' she exclaimed. 'If there be anything you wants, just you let me know.'

'Thank you, Jenny. You cannot imagine how glad I am to see a familiar face! You are looking very smart in that nice uniform! The cap suits you. Are you happy in service here?'

'Oh, yes, miss.' Jenny's round, youthful face shone.

She self-consciously straightened the frilled white cap perched on top of her mop of brown hair. 'The mistress is kind enough despite her being a foreign lady, like, and although old Parsons is a bit toffy-nosed he's not so bad really. Cook's a terror in the kitchen, but I knows how to get round her, so she don't bother me. If you wants a bit of left-overs, she's the one to make a friend of. I'm quite happy here, and treated better than some I knows of in other places. But up here I'm called Hoddy, miss.'

'I can see no reason why I should not continue to call you Jenny, as I have always done,' smiled Charlotte. 'You say Lady Bradgate is kind, but what of the rest of the family?'

Charlotte knew she should not encourage gossip, but the opinion of a girl like Jenny could provide valuable guidance for her own behaviour in the future. She was glad enough to have her assessment of Cecily Bradgate confirmed, so why not discover what she could of the other members of the family?

Jenny chuckled and blushed, managing to look both pert and shy at the same time. 'Master Tristram, he be a one! Can't keep his hands to hisself, he can't! You want to watch out, miss! Snatches a kiss, or two even, if us'll let him!'

Charlotte frowned. 'Don't let him go too far, Jenny!' she warned. 'You could find yourself in trouble.'

'Oh, I know all about that, miss; me mother warned me afore I come up here. He'll not have his wicked way with me, never you fear! Nor the master nor Mr Francis, neither, though there's not much risk of it with them — they're not like Mr Tristram. Keeps their hands to theirselves, they do, and never a look out of place, neither.'

'I'm glad to hear it, Jenny.' The sudden lifting of

Charlotte's spirits could only be because her reluctant admiration of her father was proving justified. 'What about Miss Felicity? And Miss Victoria?'

'Miss Felicity!' Jenny sniffed expressively. 'She don't notice the likes of me, miss, and I don't have no call to deal with her, thanks be; she has her own lady's-maid, she do. Thinks too much of herself, that one, and she be that desperate for a husband.'

'You shouldn't speak of your employer's daughter like that!' admonished Charlotte rather belatedly, and with little censure in her voice.

Jenny grinned impishly. 'You asked me, miss! As for Miss Vicky, she be a little darling. Mr Francis dotes on her, he do. It's my belief she's what keeps him here. That and that blessed railway.'

'Well, thank you, Jenny. I had better unpack, I suppose.' She looked around her new domain with wondering eyes. 'This is a lovely room, isn't it?'

'Beautiful, miss. It's known as the Blue Room — you can see why. Mr Francis's is the Gold Room, though there isn't much gold if you asks me, only yellow; his dressing-room backs on to yours, through here, see?'

Jenny trotted across the bedroom to open a door leading to a small room dimly lit by high windows borrowing light from the corridor. 'That's his bed-room——' she pointed straight ahead '—and this is his dressing-room.' She walked across and rattled the handle of a door set in the wall opposite the borrowed lights. 'It's locked right enough,' she observed reassuringly. '*His* dressing-room windows be in the outside wall. It's a lovely bright room. You could do with the light in here.'

'I'm sure it must be.' Dear lord! Francis just the other side of a locked door? She pulled her thoughts

back from threatened incoherence. 'But this will do me
well enough. Where is the key to that door?'

'The housekeeper do keep that, miss, unless someone
asks for it special, like. Sometimes, when there be
guests, these rooms are used by married couples, you
see. But not since Mr Francis has been staying here, of
course.'

'I see.' She did not wish Jenny to guess at the nervous
apprehension sending perspiration trickling down her
spine. She quickly changed the subject. 'My! I shall
never fill this wardrobe! But my books will sit well on
the writing-desk in the bedroom.'

'There's a closet stool over there, miss, and a pot
cupboard by the bed, but the master had one of them
new contraptions what empties away down a pipe, with
water and all, if you prefer to use that. It's at the end
of the corridor near Miss Felicity's room, and it's all
right so long as they remembers to pump the water up
into the tank. There's water for washing in the jug on
the wash-stand, miss, but if you'd like some hot I'll go
and fetch it. And any time you'd like a bath just pull
the bell and let me know. Any time you wants anything,
just give the bell a pull.'

'I will. A pitcher of hot water would be lovely for
now, thank you.'

Jenny disappeared, threatening to help her unpack
when she returned. Charlotte wondered whether the
maid realised how nervous she was at having to deal
with a servant. How different life here would be! So
used to doing everything for herself and all the others
at home, she was not keen on someone else interfering
with her things. The true implications attached to being
transported from cottage to gracious manor house had
only now begun to emerge.

Would the strangeness of being able to order someone else to do things for her ever wear off? Would the awe she felt, on looking about the huge bedroom she would have all to herself, die away in time?

Silken damask hangings on the old tester bed matched the sumptuous counterpane spread over it. Blue velvet curtains hung in slightly faded folds on either side of a wide window which framed a view over hedged, sloping fields, some ploughed, some left for grazing, dotted with clumps of leafless woodland.

She felt the bed and found soft feathers rather than the lumpy flock of the mattresses at home. The inlaid wood of the desk felt like satin under her wondering fingers. She eyed the plush fabric of the upholstered chair ruefully, knowing she would have to overcome her reluctance to sit on it for fear of making it dirty.

She quickly unwrapped her precious books and stood them on top of the row of little drawers set at the back, behind the writing surface of the desk. She fondled them lovingly as she stood them there. There was a Bible, of course, showing signs of much use, bound in calf with lettering and a cross on the front, embossed in gold. Next came a collection of sermons, followed by an atlas of the world, a copy of Dr Samuel Johnson's dictionary and, most treasured of all, for it had given her endless hours of vicarious excitement, a book called *Adventures in the Rifle Brigade* by a soldier called John Kincaid. The remaining books covered a miscellany of subjects. Her grandfather's interests had been wide, a constant cause for her gratitude.

She found more drawers underneath the writing surface of the secretaire — and a chest of them for her clothes. So many drawers! So much cupboard space! Far more than she would ever use. She had no need of Jenny's help to unpack her scanty belongings!

It was all strange, but by the time she had made use

of the hot water Jenny brought, combed her hair and smoothed down the black skirts of her one decent dress, she felt able to face whatever Bradgate Hall held in store for her.

This *was* where she belonged. She knew it with growing inner certainty. Here she could expand, become her true self. She would not allow bitterness towards her father or the uncertain feelings she held for Francis Langford to spoil this opportunity to enter into the heritage her mother had assured her was hers. Somehow, she would learn to be the lady she had been born. Granddaughter of a parson, daughter of a baronet, she had at last been offered the opportunity to discover her true identity.

CHAPTER SEVEN

HALF an hour before dinner Sir George sent a footman to escort Charlotte to the library. They passed Francis's room and the nursery suite on the way down, but she saw no one except a housemaid — not Jenny — and a couple of other footmen hurrying between the green baize door separating the kitchen and servants' quarters from the family's part of the house, and the dining-room. None of the servants took the slightest notice of her. Her escort did not speak other than to deliver his message, and she felt rather as though she had ceased to exist. No one from the family had greeted her on arrival. Her previously buoyant mood deserted her, turning to mild resentment tinged with apprehension. Perhaps no one truly wanted her here.

However, her father's welcome was warm enough to bring her some belated comfort. Once the footman had retired he moved forward to take both her hands in his.

'How are you, my dear? I do so regret not being here to welcome you, but must plead unexpected but necessary business which took me from the house. Have you settled in? Is the room to your liking?'

'I am quite well, sir, I thank you, and my room is most comfortable,' she returned, stiffly uncomfortable in his presence.

'Good, good. And how did the journey go? I trust Jeffries saw that your removal was accomplished smoothly?'

'Indeed, sir.'

Charlotte remembered the young ones' tears as she

had quitted the cottage and resolutely suppressed her own. There was no point at all in allowing homesickness to overcome her.

At Sir George's invitation she perched on the edge of the armchair she had used before, her back rigid, her hands clasped tightly in her lap. Her father's attempts to put her at her ease were proving unsuccessful, since she was not only battling incipient homesickness but bracing herself to meet the remainder of his family. And dreading the renewed confrontation with Francis Langford. After what had passed between them — above all that disturbing kiss — she would have the gravest difficulty in looking him in the face.

'You will be out of mourning soon,' Sir George remarked genially into the silence which had fallen. 'Lady Bradgate must send for the dressmaker to fit you out with new gowns.'

'I shall be in half-mourning for another six months yet,' objected Charlotte, finding unacceptable the thought of allowing the outward signs of her grief to disappear so soon. Added to which the prospect of having clothes sewn by an expert especially for her was a strange and rather daunting one, for she had always made her own dresses, except for the black gown she was wearing, of course. Delay seemed overwhelmingly attractive on both counts.

'Dove-grey should suit you admirably, my dear, and with a touch of white at the throat will look quite delightful, I am certain, though my wife is the authority. You may rely on her taste. I will mention your needs to her after dinner.'

'Please do not trouble yourself——'

'My dear, you must allow me to provide the gowns which will befit your new position as my daughter's governess. I provide all household staff with uniforms, so there is nothing to cause you or anyone else to remark. But you will not be considered merely an employee but one of the family, and therefore you will need a completely new wardrobe.'

Charlotte looked down at the black dress Pa had bought her almost a year ago, and flushed.

'There is nothing wrong with my dress!' she protested.

'Nothing at all!' he assured her soothingly. 'And you shall wear it as much as you like. But you will need others. Do try to quell your pride, my love,' he added softly. 'It is a sin.'

'Do not preach to me of sin!' hissed Charlotte fiercely. 'And be circumspect in your manner of address, sir! If you are not, then I cannot remain here!'

He bowed in acquiescence. Behind the wry amusement, sadness lurked in his eyes. 'From this instant on I shall be as circumspect as you could possibly ask, my dear Miss Falconer. I wished only to make certain you knew you were welcome in my house.'

'Thank you.' Charlotte acknowledged his good intentions with a brief nod, rather ashamed of her behaviour in the face of his genuine kindness. She could detect no trace of condescension in his manner and some of her apprehension began to dissolve. But her response was still stiff and wary. 'I will do my best to be a good governess and to conform to your other wishes.'

'You should achieve both ends without difficulty. My wishes will be neither onerous nor distasteful — I have the reputation of being somewhat easy in my application of discipline, I believe!' He smiled ruefully, and Charlotte found herself smiling back.

His expression suddenly sobered. 'It would please me greatly if you would call me Father — just once?'

The expression in his eyes stirred something in

Charlotte's heart. 'Just this once then—Father,' she obliged him in a soft voice which shook slightly. 'But how shall you explain the fact that you are meeting my dressmaker's bills? Everyone will be aware that I do not have the means to purchase new gowns.'

'True.' He waved a hand airily, though his eyes were suspiciously bright and he cleared his throat of a betraying thickness before he went on. 'But as a newly discovered, though distant member of the family some latitude will be expected. They can be told that much of the cost will be met from an advance on your salary.'

'I shall be obliged if you will indeed deduct the cost from the money due to me.'

'We will see.' He held up a hand to stop her as he saw her mouth open to protest. 'No, do not argue! And you will need a small sum for your immediate use. I will see that you receive it tomorrow.'

'Thank you.' She tried to sound grateful, and in a way she was, with the part of her that did not still blame him for seducing her mother. Since he would brook no denial she would use the money to buy each of the children some small gift.

'Good!' he exclaimed, delighted with her ready acceptance. 'And now shall we go through to the saloon, where I believe the remainder of the family will be assembled awaiting the dinner gong? Take my arm.'

Charlotte placed her hand on the lustrous black superfine of his sleeve and drew a breath to sustain her through the moment she had been dreading.

Everyone turned as they entered the large room. Charlotte was too confused to properly take in the stuffed sofas and chairs draped with antimacassars, the ornate gilt-framed mirrors festooned with greenery, the drawn wine-coloured velvet curtains with gold-tasselled fringes and pelmets, or the unlocked tantalus containing cut-glass decanters from which Tristram was dispensing pre-prandial drinks, though her eyes were drawn to the enormous, sparkling Christmas tree alight with myriad candles, which dominated the room.

'Here we are!' Sir George's voice sounded a little over-hearty to Charlotte's sensitive ears. 'I would like you all to welcome Miss Charlotte Falconer, who is to be little Vicky's governess.'

He led her forward. Charlotte curtsied to Lady Bradgate as her mother had once taught her, unconscious grace disguising the awkwardness of an unaccustomed gesture.

'My lady!'

'Welcome, my dear Miss Falconer. I am glad you could come so soon. Vicky has been eagerly awaiting your arrival!'

Cecily Bradgate had the same inflexion in her speech as her son. Her voice seemed a little strident to Charlotte's ears after her own mother's soft tones, but warmth and kindness shone from eyes which had from the first left Charlotte in no doubt from whom Francis inherited his. She was dressed elegantly in blue, with ruffles and pale lace edging her neckline and decorating the skirt of her billowing crinoline. The brilliant light from the glittering chandelier overhead brought highlights from the fading golden hair escaping a delicate lace cap to frame her rather long but still attractive face.

Sir George continued the introductions. 'You have not met Felicity, my daughter, I believe, nor Tristram, my son. And this is my stepson, Francis Langford, who is here on a visit to his mother.'

Charlotte acknowledged each introduction with a small dip and bow of her head.

A stiff smile failed to hide the calculating expression

or the hostility in Felicity's pale blue eyes. She was wearing a crinoline in a shade of yellow which managed to clash with her hair. Charlotte imagined she had flouted any advice her stepmother might have offered in favour of her own poor taste, and thought it unlikely that she would often be called upon to act as the girl's companion. Some would call her pretty in an orthodox way, but the inner quality required to bring her regular features to attractive life was lacking.

Tristram on the other hand gave her a most welcoming, charming smile, carried her hand to his lips and held her fingers for a moment too long. He was quite like his father in looks and Charlotte began to understand the fascination the young George must have exerted over her mother. But Tristram's reputation had gone before him, and Charlotte found herself amused rather than flattered by his over-zealous attention.

Francis Langford bowed politely, barely touched her hand at all, and dropped it as though it were contaminated. He did not claim a previous acquaintance.

All the men wore informal dress clothes. Black trousers and white shirts with high collars finished by various designs of necktie were common to all. Sir George sported a grey waistcoat under his black superfine, Tristram wore a white one under a dark blue coat with very wide revers in some kind of satiny material, and Francis a silver-grey, under a simple wine-coloured velvet.

Charlotte found it difficult to tear her gaze away from the last's tall, elegant figure, although she had not yet dared to meet his eyes. The deep ruby-red suited his clean-cut, fair looks to perfection.

Cecily Bradgate smiled encouragingly and patted the sofa beside her.

'Come and sit by me, child. Sir George tells me that you are related to him in some way?'

A stifled gasp from Felicity and a sudden movement from Francis told her that her father had not warned his children of any family connection. This was confirmed when Tristram brought her a stemmed glass of sparkling crystal, filled with sherry.

'My, my,' he said, his eyebrows raised in calculating amusement as he handed it to her with a flourish, 'so we have gained a delightful new relative, eh? But I believe you already know brother Frankie, don't you?'

Charlotte looked puzzled. 'Frankie?'

Francis spoke up. 'He is referring to me, Miss Falconer.'

'Oh! Yes,' she admitted, 'we met on the night of the great gale, a year ago now. Mr Langford bravely attempted to rescue my brother, who drowned in the harbour. I was—and am—most grateful to him.'

She pointed a brief smile in his direction and turned back to Cecily Bradgate, to find the older woman eyeing her son with fond admiration.

'I did not discover the connection until my mother's death, which occurred at about the same time as the gale,' Charlotte went on to explain. 'She was distantly related to Sir George through her father, a parson who unfortunately died penniless. The revelation came as something of a shock to me.'

'I am sure it must have done!' exclaimed Cecily Bradgate. 'But a pleasant one, I trust?'

'Oh, yes.' Charlotte extracted the locket from under the collar of her dress and held it so that her father's wife could examine the crest. 'She left me this keepsake.'

'How very pretty! But how sad that you should lose both your mother and your brother, and so close together, my dear. You are most welcome to look upon this as your home.'

'Thank you, ma'am. You are very kind.'

Charlotte raised her eyes to find Francis Langford's gaze fixed on her face. She lifted her chin and spoke quite deliberately. Although she was, on the surface, addressing Lady Bradgate, she was speaking to him.

'I had no intention of presuming upon the relationship, any more than my mother had done, but circumstances at home forced me into seeking Sir George's financial help.'

Francis uncrossed his long legs impatiently and emptied his glass. Charlotte sipped her sherry with lowered gaze, exceedingly conscious of the worn barathea of her skirt. For the first time, an ambition to be dressed elegantly, like his mother, rose in her. She would not stint when the dressmaker called, and she would certainly be guided in her choice by Lady Bradgate, who in her opinion showed excellent taste.

'And I suggested that, rather than my advancing her the money to set off alone for London to seek a position there, as she requested, she should come here to us, where she can be usefully employed in teaching Vicky,' Sir George concluded.

Charlotte lifted her eyes to Francis's face again, to see it wiped clear of expression apart from the slightly puzzled line etched between his straight, absurdly blond brows.

At that moment a gong resounded through the house and Parsons opened the door which connected with the dining-room to announce dinner. All finished their drinks and rose to their feet.

'Tris,' said Sir George, 'will you bring Miss Falconer in?'

'With the greatest of pleasure! Come, coz!'

Tristram offered his arm. Charlotte hesitantly put her hand in its crook as Felicity, smiling complacently, placed hers on Francis's arm.

'How convenient!' she simpered. 'Now everyone has a partner!'

Charlotte found her mouth so dry that swallowing her food became extremely difficult. She was petrified of making a fool of herself, of branding herself socially unacceptable by oafish table manners. She eyed the array of cutlery laid by her place with acute trepidation, unable to concentrate on Sir George's sonorous recital of Grace.

However, by watching the others she managed to push the cook's succulent offerings around her plate with the correct implements, and raised an apologetic smile as the footman removed her leavings. How the family at home would have enjoyed the delicacies she was sending back to the kitchen! The plump, succulent chicken such as she had previously tasted only on special occasions. Vegetables she had never seen before — asparagus was one, cooked to perfection and served in a white sauce. But her throat had closed up with nervousness and the food she did chew around in her dry mouth tasted of nothing. She took another mouthful of watered wine but it did little to relieve her problem.

She was afraid to look up, because if she did she would see Francis studying her across the white damask, his brooding, puzzled eyes searching for answers over the crystal glasses and the silver serving-dishes. He was eating in silence. Felicity, sitting on his left, had given up trying to make conversation with him, just as Tristram had ceased attempting to draw her out.

Sir George sat at the head of the table between

Francis and Charlotte. After an initial attempt at conversation about horses and farming, the state of the country and the Reform Bill Disraeli was attempting to push through Parliament, he, too, had lapsed into silence, wishing he knew how to set his daughter at her ease but afraid of saying the wrong thing and precipitating an awkwardness. He eyed first the unusually silent man on his left and then the girl, sensing some undercurrent flowing between the young people but unable to imagine what could be its cause.

Lady Bradgate, oblivious of the tension gripping the other end of the table, chatted to her children, addressing only occasional remarks down its length to her husband.

The interminable meal ended at last. Lady Bradgate led the two younger women to the drawing-room, where the tea-tray waited.

The room was smaller, more intimate than the saloon where they had met earlier, with French doors which could be opened on to the terrace, though rose-coloured velvet curtains were drawn across them. In here the decorations were more lavish, and Christmas cards had been set out on every conceivable surface. Soft light from a number of lamps and candle-sconces threw interesting shadows across the solid, comfortable furniture and upwards to play tricks with the superb plasterwork with which this ceiling, like those of all the other main rooms, was decorated.

'You had no appetite,' observed Felicity rather accusingly from the small armless chair she had chosen. 'But no doubt you were nervous. Our way of life must be strange to you — so very different from that to which you have been accustomed.'

Charlotte had scarcely eaten at all, but in her nervousness had drunk a full measure of the watered wine, to which she was completely unaccustomed. On top of the sherry it had given her a rather pleasant, muzzy feeling, loosened her tongue and bolstered her courage. The tea moistened her mouth in a way the wine had not and she found that once she had cleared her throat she could speak quite normally.

'Very different,' she agreed pleasantly, carefully replacing her cup in its saucer and leaning from her armchair to put it on a nearby table. 'At home I would not have had strangers watching my every move, seeking to find fault.' She ignored Felicity's suddenly heightened colour and went on smoothly, 'Do you not find the constant presence of servants distracting? You have so little privacy.'

'The servants do not count!' observed Felicity sharply, setting her cup and saucer down with a rattle.

'I noticed you spoke as though they were not there. However, they have eyes and ears, and surely they have feelings, too? Do you imagine they never laugh privately at the things the gentry do and say? Never gossip? Or resent the way some people treat them?'

'It would be more than their position was worth! They know their place! You are, of course, speaking as one of them,' finished Felicity with a snap.

'Children, children!' admonished Cecily mildly. 'Do not begin your association by quarrelling over servants! I agree they are human beings, Charlotte, my dear, as are indeed Negroes — why, my son Francis fought to free the slaves in the Southern States, the poor things! But servants are trained to be discreet and, as Flissy says, they know that to abuse their position of trust would lose them their place.'

'I am sorry, ma'am,' Charlotte assured Lady Bradgate in genuine contrition. She had not intended to precipitate a quarrel, but Felicity's needling had

brought out her fighting instincts. Her relief that Francis
had fought for the Yankees and not the Confederates
brought a new light to her eyes and a smile to curve the
tender line of her lips.

'You would do well to consider the servants more
than you do, Flissy. And you will remember that
Lottie — we may call you Lottie, my dear? — is not a
servant, but more like a sister to you and Tris, certainly
a cousin, though she will take on the duties of governess. I hope you two girls will become fast friends. There
are so many things you could do together. . .'

She trailed off at the look on Felicity's face. Charlotte
was confirmed in her opinion that the girl automatically
opposed any suggestion made by her stepmother.

The men joined them soon after, saving the need for
further embarrassing exchanges. To his father's obvious
displeasure, Tristram made his excuses and took horse
to a local hostelry, where he could consort with more
lively company. Francis and Sir George engaged in a
game of chess.

Lady Bradgate and Felicity brought out embroidery
and sat stitching elaborate designs on squares of linen
intended as cushion covers. Felicity did not work fast.
Most of her attention was given to the men. Charlotte
watched her watching Francis and could not deny the
knot of jealousy forming in her stomach.

Felicity was seeking a husband. Jenny had told her
gleefully of Miss Felicity's failure to secure the promise
of a match during her Season in London. 'What man
would want a sourpuss like her, miss?' she'd wanted to
know.

Sourpuss or not, there was no barrier of breeding
between those two. And although Francis showed no
especial interest in his stepsister, neither did he hold
her in contempt.

The full weight of her own disadvantaged position struck Charlotte so forcefully that she was obliged to square her shoulders to prevent their slumping. Francis had barely glanced in her direction since he had joined them in the drawing-room. Did he believe the truth now? Or did he still brand her an adventuress?

Had it been only hours earlier that she had congratulated herself on belonging here, on finding her true identity? How wrong she had been! However hard her father and his wife tried, she would never be accepted as one of the family. Tristram would flirt with her, Felicity ignore her and the servants — with the exception perhaps of Jenny — treat her with the disdain they reserved for all upstarts. And Francis — Francis, if he believed in her innocence, might offer friendship, as he had before. But to hope for any deeper relationship must lead to heartbreak.

Lady Bradgate chattered on, content with the occasional, 'Yes, ma'am,' or, 'Really, ma'am?' Charlotte interjected while pursuing her own dispiriting thoughts.

'We must find some work to occupy your hands, my dear,' Cecily said at last. 'Is there anything you fancy to do?'

Charlotte brought her mind to bear with an effort. 'I have always wished I could tat, ma'am,' she confessed after some hesitation.

'Then I shall teach you! I will search out my shuttle and some thread tomorrow, and you can make a start after dinner! Tatting makes such excellent trimmings!'

'Thank you, ma'am. You are very kind.'

Felicity's lips had set in a petulant jut. She ceased pretending to work. Rising impatiently to her feet, she thrust aside her embroidery frame and rustled over to lean against the high back of Francis's chair.

'Who is winning?' she enquired, fluttering her stubby eyelashes at Francis in a way that made Charlotte's stomach curdle.

Her father greeted her with an exasperated frown. 'Do not interrupt, Flissy! We need to concentrate!'

'It is only a game!' She pouted prettily. 'Are you not bored, Francis?'

'No,' he replied gravely. Then he smiled, and although it was only to himself it transformed his face. Charlotte caught an involuntary breath. The smile became a chuckle. 'Perhaps because I am winning!' He leaned forward to move a rook. 'Check!' he announced.

'Oh, Francis! How clever of you! Can you escape, Papa?'

'Be quiet, child! How did you do that, my boy? I did not see it coming. . .'

Sir George frowned over the board. Francis sat back. Felicity put her hand on his shoulder. Charlotte wished to look away, but her eyes seemed glued to the couple. She bit the inside of her lower lip to stop the tears but despite this they blurred her vision, forcing her to blink in case she was wrong. But she had not imagined the grim set of Francis's lips or the way he moved his body so that Felicity was forced to remove her hand.

He glanced her way. She could not be absolutely certain, for her vision was still impaired, but his eyes seemed to hold an expression remarkably reminiscent of wry resignation. It was the most intimate look he had given her since. . .since the launch of the lifeboat. That was when things had gone wrong between them, when Francis had mistaken her interest in Sir George for something else. . . Warmth crept into her cheeks, a reflection of that which had touched her heart.

Shortly afterwards Sir George, deciding the position of his king was irretrievable, resigned. Francis took the

opportunity to make his apologies and retire for the
night. Lady Bradgate and Felicity soon indicated their
intention to follow suit, and Charlotte joined the
exodus with immense relief.

The evening had proved as tedious as it had nerve-
stretching. How she had longed to be back in her
mother's kitchen with her brothers and sisters for
company and plenty of household tasks to keep her
busy!

Francis Langford would not have been there, though.
She remembered the night when he had been, when
there had been no misunderstanding between them,
and wished his opinion of her had not been so unfairly
debased since then.

But he knew the truth now — or almost the truth, she
amended her thoughts hastily. Dared she hope he
would withdraw his groundless censure? He owed her
an apology, though she doubted whether she would
receive one.

After the evening just spent in his company she could
no longer deny to herself that his opinion of her did
matter. She desired his approval above everything.

So she had something to prove, to him as well as to
herself: that she was worthy to take her rightful place
in her father's household.

Charlotte woke early. Dawn's grey fingers had barely
touched the winter sky when she let herself out of the
front door.

No one saw her leave. The under servants were
about, in the kitchen and the main rooms, clearing
grates and laying new fires. The upper servants were
receiving cups of tea and hot water in their rooms and
preparing to rise.

Her own tea and hot water would be delivered about

eight, so Jenny had promised. Breakfast would be
served at half-past, after which the family would pre-
pare to attend church, it being Sunday.

She felt she needed a brisk walk. Needed exercise to
clear her head before facing any member of the family
again. Needed, too, to escape the proximity of Francis
Langford, which had kept her awake for hours last
night, conscious as she had been of his sleeping no
more than a few yards away. She would get used to the
idea. She must, or become a nervous wreck.

The gravel crunched underfoot as she made her way
around the house, taking a direction away from the
kitchen block and stables, where activity would be the
greatest. At the far side of the house she paused to look
up, knowing this must be the wing in which her bedroom was situated. It was impossible, in the near-
darkness, to work out which was her window, for she
could detect no colour in the curtains to guide her. She
was not yet familiar enough with the internal layout of
the house to make a guess without that aid.

A path of flat paving-stones led off across a lawn
towards a clump of trees and the fields beyond. She
took it. The trees screened a coppice. A thick layer of
fallen leaves clothed the path ahead. Her boots raised
the earthy, pungent aroma of leaf mould as she walked.

She came to a gate, swung it open and passed
through, closing it carefully behind her. Sheep dotted
about the field lifted their whey faces nervously at her
intrusion. A few scattered bleats accompanied her
progress through their midst. So far that winter there
had been no need to take the flocks into shelter.

Charlotte strode on, her heavy cloak clutched about
her, the hems of her garments soaking up the moisture
from the wet grass, while small tendrils of her hastily
brushed hair curled about her face, responding to the

misty dampness of the atmosphere. Under the hood it
hung loose about her shoulders.

The sky had lightened considerably by the time she
was brought face to face with a herd of cows gathered
around a gate, patiently waiting to be milked. She
leaned on the top bar, reluctant to challenge the bunch
of curious cattle for a passage through their midst. A
distant clock had already chimed the half-hour. If she
returned now she would be back in good time to receive
Jenny's offerings of tea and hot water.

She accordingly retraced her steps and was almost
through the coppice, with the screening trees and lawn
a few yards ahead, when she saw a shape unexpectedly
detach itself from one of the trunks. Although it was
quite light by now, the trees created their own dimness
and shadows. Charlotte let out a stifled cry of alarm
before she recognised the man who had stepped out to
intercept her.

'Mr Langford?' she gasped incredulously.

'Good morning, Miss Falconer.' He lifted one of the
round-crowned hats Mr Bowler had made fashionable,
and bowed. 'I hope I did not alarm you, but I saw you
walking in this direction, and hoped to catch you on
your return.'

'I — No. You surprised me. But — how did you see
me? It was still dark when I set out!'

'Nevertheless, I recognised you as you walked
beneath my window. I think perhaps I would recognise
you anywhere, Miss Falconer.' His voice had held a
curious tinge of self-mockery, which left it as he added,
'I had to speak with you in private. Is it true?'

'Is what true?' demanded Charlotte, stiffly defensive.
Her heart was thumping so loudly that he could probably hear it, and it was not with fear. Why did his
proximity affect her so?

'You know very well what I mean; do not demean yourself by pretending otherwise,' he insisted with quiet intensity. 'I have misjudged you, I believe, and behaved extremely badly, which I regret.'

Charlotte made a dismissive gesture, but he allowed her no time to speak.

'I seek to clarify the situation. Are you indeed related to Sir George? And if so, why did you not say so before this?'

'It is true. As for why I did not——' She broke off, uncertain of what to say. When she resumed, she chose her words with some care. 'The relationship is. . .distant. It seemed to have as little bearing on my life as it had had on my mother's.'

She found his sudden smile as blinding as the fiery rim of sun which had just appeared over the horizon to dispel the mist with its brilliance.

'I confess that I do not understand her reticence, or yours. However,' he went on, reaching for her hand, 'I am certain your reasoning was sound in your own eyes at least, and I have no intention of allowing such a minor consideration to further disrupt the friendship I had believed to be forming between us. Charlotte — I shall call you Charlotte, for are we not distant cousins by marriage? — will you forgive my past folly and allow me to escort you back to the house?'

Her heart had begun to unfurl like the petals of a rose in the sun. 'Willingly, sir,' she told him breathlessly.

'Francis!' he instructed firmly, placing the hand he held in the crook of his arm. 'You must address me as Francis if we are to be friends and cousins! Tristram and Felicity will expect it.'

Charlotte's hand lay nervously on the tweed sleeve of his jacket. She could feel his muscles flex beneath her fingers and the old familiar tremor of excitement raced to her heart. She smiled, and was quite unaware of the sweet radiance he saw on her face. 'Very well — Francis. But everyone calls me Lottie ——'

'I shall not,' he told her firmly, leading her through the formal garden towards the terrace at the back of the house. 'Charlotte is a pretty name; it is a pity to shorten it. And I know how much I dislike being addressed as Frankie!'

'Well, I do not exactly dislike Lottie, but I do confess to a preference for Charlotte. And Frankie certainly does not suit you!'

'My own opinion exactly!' He laughed suddenly, his face boyish in the brilliance of the sunrise. 'Shall we go in this way? I am certain the terrace doors will be unlocked by this time.'

They parted by her door. Her hood had fallen back and her gorgeous hair rioted about her face like molten copper. Her eyes shone luminous and almost green. Francis sternly controlled the impulse to kiss her. He had abused his privileged position once, to his deep regret. He could not do so again without losing his self-respect — and probably earning her renewed scorn.

But his hand had lifted before he could control it, seeking to touch the shining abundance of her hair. He let it drop back to his side.

Charlotte saw the cut-off gesture and laughed self-consciously as she lifted her own hands to smooth the tangled tresses back into some kind or order.

'I am sorry, but I did not trouble to arrange my hair before I went out,' she apologised breathlessly. 'I did not expect to meet anyone before breakfast. It must be terribly untidy. I must go and make my toilet.'

'Do not apologise, Charlotte. You have beautiful

hair; it is a pity to keep it so tightly confined. I will see you at breakfast.'

He turned abruptly and sought his own room before his resolution dissolved and he gave way to the temptation to gather her into his arms.

CHAPTER EIGHT

CHARLOTTE closed the door behind her and stood perfectly still for a moment, attempting to control her trembling. Her cheeks glowed with a colour not entirely attributable to a brisk walk in the cold air.

'Why, miss,' cried Jenny, who was tidying the room, having brought the tea and hot water a little earlier, 'I was wondering where you was! Your tea is getting cold, and you'll be washing in tepid water afore you knows it!'

'I am sorry, Jenny!' Charlotte's colour rose even higher. 'I decided to take a walk, and went a little too far, I'm afraid.'

'And met Mr Francis — I saw you walking back with him. Be putting Miss Felicity's nose out of joint if you're not careful.'

'Oh, I do not think so. Mr Langford was just being courteous.'

'He usually goes riding in the morning, not walking.'

'Perhaps he felt like a change of exercise! Really, Jenny, you must not attribute any deeper meaning to a casual meeting! Besides, it is not your business, and gossiping could lose you your place. So be careful of that tongue of yours!'

'Yes, miss.'

Jenny grinned, not at all abashed, her urchin face alight with speculation. Charlotte began to remove the old black skirt and greying-white blouse she had donned for her walk, glad that the cloak had covered them so completely — then decided she was becoming far too self-conscious about the quality of her clothes and how she looked. On the other hand she did not wish to shame her father or his household. Nor, she had to admit, did she wish to appear ill clad and unattractive in Francis Langford's eyes.

But until she obtained the new wardrobe her father had promised she would have to continue to wear the only respectable clothes she possessed. Francis must already have recognised the black dress and would know the coat she proposed wearing to church as the one she had worn to the funeral.

Why should she feel ashamed? He knew her family was not rich, though better off than most in the town and certainly not destitute and threatened with the workhouse, like some poor folk who lived in daily fear of being turned out of their homes.

Francis had said he liked her hair loose. She brushed out the tangles and studied the effect before she pulled the thick, springy waves back and twisted it into a loose chignon instead of a tight bun and allowed a little more fullness in the hair which framed her face. Pleased with the softened, flattering effect even such a slight adjustment to her coiffure made, she wondered if, one day, she would find the courage to change it more drastically. Felicity kept her hair in tight, artificial ringlets, a couple of which hung down her cheeks, with the remainder gathered together at the back of her head. Charlotte grinned with sudden, slightly malicious pleasure. She would have no need of curlers if and when she decided on a more dramatic change to her own style.

She did not meet Victoria until the family assembled to depart for church. The little girl was dressed in a short pink crinoline with white frilled pantaloons poking down to cover her legs and ankles. A small bonnet tied under her chin hid most of her fair hair, while a thick white mantelet and tiny fur muff protected her from the cold.

The ladies were to travel in a closed carriage, while the men went on horseback, the under servants walked and the upper servants rode in an old chaise. The child greeted her shyly, but seemed quite content to sit next to her with her back to the four matched horses while her mother and stepsister squeezed their skirts into the more comfortable seats facing forward.

Francis helped the ladies to step up into the carriage. His hand was warm on Charlotte's, and did she imagine it, or did his smile hold extra warmth as he saw her settled into her place? He met Victoria's trusting, friendly gesture as she tucked her hand into that of her new governess with a small nod of approval.

Lady Bradgate and Felicity provided any conversation during the short journey. Victoria kept silence in obedience to endless injunctions to be seen and not heard, while Charlotte was overcome with nervous anticipation as she realised that some of the congregation were bound to recognise her and wonder at her taking her place in the Bradgate pews. Although she normally worshipped at All Saints, she knew plenty of people who attended St Mary's, at least by sight. Her presence was bound to become the subject of gossip and speculation.

Sir George and Lady Bradgate led the way down the central aisle, followed by Tristram and Felicity. Francis had hung back to attend his little sister.

As she walked with them Charlotte's awareness of the whispers and curious glances from some members of the congregation brought an uncomfortable flush to her cheeks, but she kept her chin up, reminding herself that this was but a minor hurdle compared to some others she would be called upon to clear.

The squire ushered his wife and older children into the front pew and would have stood aside for his stepson except that Francis had already guided Charlotte and Victoria into the pew behind, and followed them in. Although Victoria's small crinoline kept them well apart, Charlotte was aware of Francis's presence with every fibre of her being.

An angry colour had stained Felicity's cheeks. The two ladies' crinolines filled so much of the front pew that there would not in any case have been room for all of them to sit in it together. Had she expected Francis to abandon his small sister and her governess and leave them to sit alone in the row behind?

Charlotte always enjoyed church. That day, despite her self-consciousness, her voice rose, sweet yet rich in tone. Francis's strong tenor rang out tunefully, and from time to time he smiled at her over Victoria's childish treble. Charlotte smiled back, the shared intimacy of looking after the little girl a source of new delight.

After the service, while pleasantries were being exchanged in the yard between the regular members of the congregation, Charlotte became aware of a few hostile glances among the curious ones being thrown her way. Her elevation from tradesman's daughter and part-time teacher down Quay to governess in one of the leading households up Town appeared to be a cause of resentment to some. But then, the rivalry between the two communities had always been keen, often resulting in brawls. Up in Higher Brixham she would be considered an interloper.

Felicity annexed Francis, while Tristram appeared at Charlotte's side. Heavy drinking the night before had dulled his eyes and the smell of stale spirits still hung upon his breath. But his smile was full of confidence and conscious charm.

'You must allow me to escort you to the carriage, coz,' he told her with a bow. 'I cannot allow that dog Frankie to monopolise your company. I,' he pointed out, 'am the heir. Frankie will be sailing back across the ditch quite soon, but I shall still be here and at your service.' He accompanied his last words with an elaborate, mocking bow.

'Sir,' returned Charlotte tightly, 'I do not seek the favours of either of you. I am here to educate Victoria.' The child was still clinging to her hand, and Charlotte pulled her between herself and Tristram, placing her hands on Vicky's shoulders. It was scarcely right to use the little girl as a defence against the man, but she could think of no other way to fend him off. At that moment she envied Felicity her crinoline, for the wide skirt would have kept him at a safe distance.

'I can provide you with all the things a young woman desires —' he began persuasively.

'I desire nothing from you, sir!' broke in Charlotte angrily.

'Do call me Tris,' he grinned, quite unabashed by her sharp repudiation. 'You will not be able to maintain your distant manner for long, coz, that I'll wager! I guarantee we shall soon become more intimate than brother and sister.'

Charlotte could not hide her agitation. 'We shall not, sir!' she declared. 'Please desist from these improper suggestions!'

'My dear Lottie, I am not trying to seduce you — yet!'

Charlotte forced herself to relax and managed to raise a smile to answer his mocking grin. She did not wish to make an enemy of him. He was, after all, her half-brother, incredible as it seemed. Any intimate relationship of the kind Tristram undoubtedly had in mind was an impossibility even had she been willing. His overtures must not be taken too seriously, she reminded herself. Was he not a rake who adopted a seductive manner with every woman he met? Jenny had warned her. But, unversed in the precepts of upper-class flirtation, she found herself at a loss to know how to deal with the situation. But surely if she let him know she regarded the episode as light philandering on his part he could not take offence?

'I am delighted to hear you say so—Tris,' she responded lightly. 'And I must warn you, you would be attempting the impossible! And I do not believe you can be serious, for your father would not approve.'

'Father,' said Tris with a rueful grimace, the bitterness almost but not quite hidden, 'dislikes almost everything I do. So that would be no strange thing. But,' he added softly, 'I take up your gauntlet, sweet coz. Nothing is impossible.'

Charlotte was suddenly very warm indeed. She had not intended her warning to be taken as a challenge! She was seeking for appropriate words with which to put him down when Victoria made a welcome interruption.

'I am cold!' Her plaintive voice rose between them. 'May we get into the coach? Please?'

'I am sorry, Vicky!' cried Charlotte, immediately concerned that she was neglecting her duty. 'Tris, you offered——'

'Allow me.' Francis's incisive voice cut in.

Charlotte turned to him with a radiant smile of relief. 'Francis! How kind!'

He stepped between her and Tristram, but directed

his words to Victoria. 'Come, poppet. Would you like
a lift?'

'Yes, please!' squeaked Vicky, clinging to his neck as
she was lifted in his strong arms. 'Tris was trying to
make Miss Charlotte do something she didn't want to.'

'Shut up, Vicky,' muttered Tris. 'You're telling tales
again. I've warned you before ——'

'Do not threaten the child!' burst out Charlotte, her
resolution to be friendly quite forgotten. 'If you choose
to speak in front of her you must expect her to repeat
what she hears!'

'And what exactly did she hear?' asked Francis, in a
voice which spelled danger for someone.

'Nothing that matters,' Charlotte quickly assured
him. 'Come, let us go to the coach.'

Francis gave her a measured look, then a brief nod.
Tristram stood grinning after them. But Charlotte did
not like the resentful gleam in his dark eyes or, when
she glanced back, the scowl which had quickly replaced
the smile on his face. Francis was only a few years his
senior, yet Tristram seemed an irresponsible, truculent
boy compared to his stepbrother.

Thereafter Tristram reverted to his original, lightly
flirtatious, cousinly manner, particularly in front of his
father, though Charlotte was often conscious of his
calculating gaze turned her way. His presence made her
uncomfortable and she was inclined to fear him.

Francis made no further attempt to seek her out.
Charlotte told herself she was glad, for there could be
no future in any deepening of their relationship. But a
feeling of disappointment persisted.

She and Felicity avoided each other by mutual
consent.

Her entry into her father's household had become
fraught with undercurrents she had not anticipated.

Only the genuine friendship of Cecily Bradgate and the instant rapport which had sprung up between herself and her pupil prevented her from going to her father and pleading for release during those first difficult days.

Charlotte spent most of her time in the schoolroom with Vicky, whom she quickly came to love. Nanny Bridges proved no problem, willingly sharing the responsibility for her nursling, who in truth had become rather more of a handful than the elderly woman could manage alone.

The child learned quickly, and showed an interest in things Charlotte might have thought to be beyond her years. Teaching her became a delight and were it not for having to face the silent hostility of Felicity, the over-zealous courtesy and sidelong glances of Tristram, and the equally disturbing measured friendliness of Francis, Charlotte would have thought herself extremely fortunate.

The dressmaker, a diminutive woman whom everyone called Miss Matty, came to the Hall despite the advent of frost and threatened snow, exclaimed over Charlotte's lack of stays and insisted that her gowns would not look well without their aid. Reluctantly Charlotte agreed to be laced into whalebone to reduce the size of her waist for formal occasions. For everyday wear she adamantly refused to be so confined and restricted. She could scarcely breathe or move in the corset and knew the wearing of it would be torture.

'You will get used to it, my dear,' consoled Cecily Bradgate with a wry smile. 'We all do. Fashion demands many sacrifices to comfort. But you will find the cage of the crinoline leaves your legs wonderfully free of petticoats, so that particular fashion has at least one redeeming feature! But it is inclined to tip up and show the ankles, so you will need pantaloons for

modesty's sake. What do you think of this for every
day? The material will be warm for the winter and
spring.'

Charlotte fingered the soft cloth. Fine white stripes
had been woven in to relieve the duller, dove-grey
wool.

'It is beautiful, ma'am.'

'Then we will have two gowns made from it for you
to wear in the schoolroom. With white collar and cuffs
and black buttons and other trimmings, I think.'

'A most sensible choice, my lady,' enthused the tiny
seamstress. 'The stripes can run down the bodice at the
back, form a chevron in front and run horizontally
around the skirt. How wide a crinoline do you wish?'

'I would rather wear ordinary petticoats,' put in
Charlotte. 'I am not used——'

'But must become used to moving in a crinoline,'
pointed out Cecily shrewdly. 'If you have a cage petticoat made to go under these you can practise managing
it in the schoolroom, and will then find no difficulty on
social occasions.'

Charlotte could not deny the sense in this, and
accepted her mentor's advice with good grace.

'A small crinoline, then,' she agreed.

For dining at home Cecily thought it necessary for
Charlotte to have two dinner gowns in the latest style,
the skirt falling fairly straight at the front but belling
out at the back over the new egg-shape now being given
to the watch-spring hoops. One of these was to be in
black silk, the low neckline emphasising the flawless
creaminess of Charlotte's skin—although she privately
envisaged wearing it with a shawl—the other in a silvery
green damask the colour of downy chestnut leaves as
they unfurled in the spring. It was almost grey, and
Charlotte could not resist its instant appeal, especially

when both Cecily and the dressmaker exclaimed over
the way the hue suited her colouring. This one had a
higher neckline and would be trimmed in sober black,
but so arranged that the contrasting colour could be
changed to something brighter when Charlotte finally
came out of mourning.

For more formal occasions — the prospect of which
Charlotte viewed with some anxiety — a white gown in
expensive silk taffeta shot with gold thread was proposed, so *décolleté* that Charlotte wondered whether
she would ever summon up the courage to wear it. But,
when the gown was delivered it took her breath away.
Even the fittings had not prepared her for the finished
effect. She had never expected to own anything so
beautiful.

'Lottie, my dear, I do declare you look quite lovely!'

The expression of disbelief on Charlotte's face as she
eyed herself in Cecily Bradgate's cheval-glass made the
older woman laugh.

'Did you not know how well you could look, my
dear?' she enquired softly. 'With your hair expertly
dressed, and dainty slippers on your feet, you will draw
the admiration of every male at the dinner party we are
to give next week! But beware the jealousy of the
women!'

'Oh, ma'am!' Charlotte turned to Lady Bradgate
impulsively, and the belled skirt of the dress billowed
and swayed about her, displaying a quite indecorous
amount of ankle, happily soon to be covered by lace-
frilled pantaloons. She ran across the boudoir and
would have dropped to her knees except that her tightly
laced stays prevented easy movement and she remembered the pristine white skirt just in time. 'How can I
thank you?' she asked breathlessly. 'Why are you being
so good to me?'

'It is Sir George's wish,' responded Cecily simply, 'and my pleasure. Is it not a pleasure to dress such a lovely young woman, Miss Matty?'

'Indeed it is, my lady.'

Charlotte turned again as the seamstress spoke, to find the creator of her wonderful gown beaming with pride.

'And my most sincere thanks and admiration to you, too, Miss Matty! Lady Bradgate assured me you were a treasure, and now I can appreciate why! The other gowns you have made for me were beautiful, but this is magnificent!'

'Thank you, Miss Falconer!' Miss Matty flushed at the praise and dipped a respectful curtsy. 'I am honoured to have served you. I think you will agree that the stays do enhance the smallness of your waist.'

'Oh, I do! I just wish I could breathe more easily!' lamented Charlotte, who had submitted unwillingly to the ministrations of Cecily's lady's-maid. Hanging on to the solid chaise-longue with the woman's foot in her back while the laces were tightened had been an experience she was not anxious to repeat too often.

Yet perhaps the result was worth the physical discomfort, she thought, eyeing herself in the mirror once again. Would Francis admire her in this dress? Would he be able to span her waist with his hands? She doubted it, for not all the lacing in the world would bring it down to a fashionable eighteen inches.

She would know if he liked her in it, when the time came. He had approved of the previous additions to her wardrobe — a day gown and the black dinner gown; she had seen it in his eyes.

The second day dress and the grey-green dinner dress had also been delivered that day, but the 'special occasion' garment had overshadowed her delight in them. The grey-green did suit her well, as her advisers had predicted. She resolved to wear it that very evening. Although he not infrequently dined out, Francis had not indicated his intention of so doing that day.

Miss Matty inspected the fit of the special gown with sharp, expert eyes. 'Further adjustment will be unnecessary,' she decided.

'Excellent! And now shall we try *my* new gown?'

Both Lady Bradgate and Felicity had ordered several new garments, but Felicity, as usual, had insisted upon having her fittings before Charlotte's, leaving the room immediately the dressmaker had finished with her.

Now, unusually, she returned, to halt in the doorway, completely taken aback.

'Flissy, my dear!' Cecily broke lightly into the dense silence which had fallen. 'Have you not seen Lottie's evening gown? Miss Matty has quite excelled herself.'

'Fine feathers,' spat Felicity, having speedily recovered herself, 'do not make a fine lady!'

With which acid cliché she stormed from the boudoir.

'Oh, dear!' grimaced Cecily comically. 'We seem to have ruffled hers! What an excessively rude thing for her to say! Take no notice, Lottie, dear. Flissy has never been the easiest of young women to get along with. I believe she resents me, and therefore everything and everyone I favour.'

'How could anyone resent you?' cried Charlotte in distress. 'You show nothing but kindness, and have brought her father happiness. . .'

'Perhaps that is the trouble,' murmured Cecily quietly with a glance towards Miss Matty, who was busy at the far end of the room unpacking another gown from layers of rustling tissue paper. 'Sir George has put me in her mother's place, and she cannot forget.'

'But she cannot possibly remember her real mother!'

'True, but that does not alter the fact. And for years she and Tris were disciplined only by Nanny Bridges, and she is the softest of creatures. Whatever the cause, Flissy has never forgiven me for marrying her father.'

'And yet she wishes to have you for a mother-in-law!'

The words burst out before Charlotte had considered the wisdom of putting her own fears into words. Cecily eyed her shrewdly before answering.

'As my son's wife she would spend most of her time in the United States. She would be rid of my presence almost entirely.' She paused. 'But Francis will not marry her, Lottie.'

'You do not think so?' asked Charlotte doubtfully. Felicity's assualt on his affections was most determined.

Cecily shook her head. 'No. He is not greatly attracted to either her or Tris. They have so little in common. Such a marriage would be a disaster for him, and he knows it.' Her breast heaved as she sighed deeply. 'I believe both Bradgate's children by his first marriage must take after their mother, for I can see nothing of my dear husband in either of them!'

'I am glad you and m——' she caught herself up quickly '—Sir George have found happiness,' cried Charlotte impulsively, and quite sincerely. 'You have both made me so welcome here, and shown me how felicitous a marriage can be!'

'We pray that you find such happiness yourself one day, my dear. You will undoubtedly make a good match in due course——'

'No.' Charlotte shook her head and smiled to soften the harshness of her interruption. 'I do not think so. No one of consequence will ignore my lowly origins. Even should a man be so tempted, his family would forbid the match.'

'There are those who will consider your connection

with Sir George's family to far outweigh the more
immediate circumstances of your birth,' pressed Cecily
gently.

Charlotte did not argue further. Lady Bradgate was
unaware of the truth. And she could never marry
without revealing it, for to keep such a secret would be
a breach of trust which would eventually destroy all
happiness.

Francis entered the saloon early that evening, to find
her seated alone under the brilliance of the myriad
candles illuminating the chandelier. His eyes lit up with
more than friendship. Admiration flared at sight of the
soft, downy green damask billowing about her, the
sheath-like bodice emphasising the jut of her full
breasts, the draped neckline allowing a glimpse of
creamy skin, the slender neck bearing its load of
chestnut curls.

Charlotte had at last found the courage to sweep her
hair back and to brush the ends round her finger into
ringlets, which fell in a cascade of colour to touch her
shoulders. Her eyes glowed with new assurance in the
knowledge that her appearance equalled that of the
lady she aimed to become.

'Charlotte!' He bent his gleaming head courteously
over her hand. They had not met previously that day,
since he had breakfasted early and not returned for
lunch. 'May I congratulate you on your gown?'

His voice had deepened. He held her hand for much
too long. Charlotte's fingers trembled in his and rich
colour flooded her face.

'You should congratulate your mother, sir,' she
returned, 'for it was chosen upon her advice.'

'Her taste is beyond reproach, as usual.' His eyes
met hers. She saw a flame in their depths which both

excited and frightened her. 'But Mama did not create the beauty and grace with which you endow it.'

'Francis!' protested Charlotte, laughing to cover her embarrassment. 'You will turn my head with your flattery! I expect such nonsense from Tris, but not from you!'

'Then perhaps it is time you began to.' He released her hand at last and added quietly, 'I have never been insensible to your charms.'

'Please stop your teasing, sir!' Charlotte feared that by showing the intense pleasure she felt at his words she might give away the tender feelings which had needed little encouragement to burgeon in her own breast over the last weeks.

'I am not teasing.' His smile, and the fact that he dropped down to sit on the sofa beside her, brought more confusion to stain her cheeks. 'I would like your permission to take Vicky on an outing tomorrow. The weather promises to be reasonable. May I take her? Will you accompany us?'

'An outing? Where to?' Charlotte was suddenly breathless.

'My sister has shown great interest in the new railway line. I promised her she should follow its progress, but the severe weather since the New Year has prevented our visits.'

'She shares your enthusiasm for the venture?' Charlotte wondered, and shrugged her elegant shoulders, attempting a nonchalance she was far from feeling. 'I can see no reason why she should not accompany you, Francis, for I am certain you will keep her safe. The outing should be most educational.'

'And for you too, Charlotte. I do not think you will have seen such extensive excavations and engineering works before.'

'No, I have not. I have seen something of the wheel and pumps being placed in the leat at Parkham Wood, and of the pipes being laid to take the water up to the station on Furzeham Common, but that is all.' She pretended to consider, though nothing would have prevented her from accepting his invitation. 'Very well, Francis. I will accompany Vicky, with pleasure. At what time should we be ready?'

'After breakfast. Shall we say half-past nine?'

She smiled somewhat uncertainly, still thrown off balance by the sudden change in his attitude. 'I shall look forward to it,' she assured him.

Sir George and Lady Bradgate entered at that moment to see the two bright heads, so close together, bathed from above in soft candle-light. They exchanged an involuntary glance which the pair on the sofa did not see.

Felicity soon followed them in. In Tristram's absence, Francis had already risen to dispense the sherry.

The few moments of intimacy were over, leaving Charlotte barely aware of anything but Francis, her thoughts entirely centred on the morrow's expedition. After weeks of apparent indecision, he had sought her company. Did she dare allow herself to enjoy his?

Why not? she reasoned. She was strong-minded enough to resist any temptation to follow in her mother's footsteps and enter into a disastrous liaison, should he seek to form one. But she simply could not live under the same roof and behave with cool aloofness when her entire being clamoured to engage in the closer friendship he appeared to be offering.

CHAPTER NINE

CHARLOTTE had difficulty in hiding her amusement when she collected the child for the outing next morning. Vicky had not known until she was woken that the treat lay in store, and all lessons in decorum had been cast aside.

'I hope Nanny has wrapped you up well, for it will be chilly!' she warned, with a smile for Meg Bridges, who had managed to dress the little girl in warm clothes despite all her jumping about with excitement. 'Your brother is taking us in an open pony trap. Do not forget your muff!'

'I have it here! Ooh, Miss Charlotte, I am so glad you are coming too!'

Charlotte squeezed the small shoulders as she knelt to re-tie the strings of Vicky's bonnet, which had somehow come adrift. 'So am I!'

'Behave yourself now,' warned Nanny as they departed. 'Otherwise Mr Langford will refuse to take you anywhere again.'

She grinned wryly at Charlotte. They both knew that Francis Langford found it difficult to deny his small sister anything, but for discipline's sake it was best the child did not realise this — though privately Charlotte suspected Victoria was well aware of the power she exercised over her big brother. Francis needed children of his own, she thought suddenly, and wondered why he had never married.

Charlotte hustled the child down to the stable yard, shivering slightly as they emerged into the raw air. Not

only did she now possess a wardrobe of new gowns, but
a long, thick, sleeved mantle, several shawls and
becoming bonnets, a pair of warmly lined kid gloves, a
fur muff and two pairs of dainty calf button boots. She
should not be cold, swathed in the new mantle and with
her hands, now almost free of chap and chilblains,
cosseted in gloves and muff.

When she had first walked down to visit the family
dressed in her new finery, Rose and the others had
scarcely known her at first. But once the exclamations
had died down and she had removed her bonnet and
coat and tied the strings of a borrowed apron about her
the old Lottie had emerged, to everyone's relief.

They were all still so dear. Even Victoria's present
excitement could not equal that of Lizzie, Willie,
Georgie and Annie when her gifts, bought on a recent
shopping expedition, were received. An illustrated
story book, scarlet-coated lead soldiers, a box of
brightly painted bricks, a rag doll — anyone would think
them made of pure gold! Danny and Bertie had been
less demonstrative over their neckties, but no less
appreciative. Jackie had squalled because he did not
like having his new bonnet put on his head. Aunt Ada
had laughed and assured her that he would wear it
happily enough when next she took him out. But he
had not whined or grizzled the entire afternoon and
looked more robust than Charlotte remembered. Perhaps their fears for his survival had been groundless
after all, thanks in no small part to Aunt Ada.

Charlotte had bought tobacco for Pa, as she still
thought of him, presenting it diffidently in case he
resented her bringing him gifts. But he thanked her
civilly enough.

'You didn't have to leave, you know, Lottie,' he
growled, so that only she could hear above the din

made by the excited children. 'I didn't rightly know what I was about, that night; I'd drunk more'n a few over the eight — you know that. But I be glad you're so well settled, girl.'

'Perhaps it was for the best, Pa.'

'Maybe so.'

'Aunt Ada seems to be managing well.'

'Aye. We couldn't do without her.'

He said no more, but stuffed his pipe with part of her gift and sat puffing by the range while high spirits were let off all about him.

Both Rose and Aunt Ada accepted the warm gloves, intended to comfort their chilblains, with unfeigned gratitude. And everyone exclaimed over the end of a joint of beef, the raised pork pie, the generous chunk of fruit cake and the bag of small buns and tarts Charlotte had begged from Cook. Meat had been expensive for the last couple of years and had it not been for the abundance of fish even the Falconers might well have felt the pinch, so the beef and pie were especially welcome.

'Mrs Lane — Cook — is generous with the left-overs if she likes you,' Charlotte explained when the cries of astonishment had died down. 'Jenny — you remember Jenny Hoddy? — advised me to cultivate her friendship, and I have. I love the kitchen, with its wonderful aromas, and I think she appreciates my taking an interest.'

'You were always one for the cooking,' grimaced Rose, who hated it.

'Yes. It is the thing I miss most up there — apart from you all, of course!'

It had been a good afternoon, saddened only by the leave-taking. But she had been astonished to discover the eagerness with which she hurried back to Bradgate

Hall. Any lingering remnants of homesickness and guilt had been finally banished with that visit.

Not only was the weather raw this morning, but murky as well, the sky laden with lowering grey clouds. However, it had remained dry. February had not yet taken its leave, though it seemed to have spent most of its rain. January's blanket of snow and unusually hard frosts had long given way before the recent spell of wet weather, and the March winds were yet to come.

Francis lifted Victoria aboard their conveyance, sitting her on one of the side-benches. Her bonnet bobbed expectantly over the high side-rail of the vehicle as he helped Charlotte to negotiate the step at the back and take her place beside the excited child. Finally, he leapt up himself to sit on the opposite seat. A groom closed the back gate.

Charlotte spread a tartan rug over Victoria's and her own knees, and arranged the hot stones ordered for their feet. Francis took up the reins, nodded to a second groom to let the pony have its head, clicked his tongue and flicked his whip. The pony pricked its ears and walked forward, changing its gait to a brisk trot in obedience to a further command.

Francis glanced sidelong at Charlotte. A grin touched his lips to match the teasing gleam in his eyes. Charlotte's nerves quivered in response.

'Do you know what kind of a conveyance this is?'

'No.' She ignored her wayward senses while considering the vehicle doubtfully, realising that Francis's expression signalled some secret amusement. 'Is it special?'

'I had it brought out and spruced up. It is quite an age, you see, for it was used last when Tristram and Felicity were young. It is a governess cart,' he told her with a chuckle.

'Really?' Charlotte eyed the smart little trap with some interest. Such fancy forms of transport were outside her previous experience.

'Really.' His grin widened. 'Hence the back entry and high sides, for safety. I gather it is known locally as a jingle. Can you drive?'

'Of course not.'

Charlotte felt peeved that he should ask, so making her admit her lack of expertise in that field. He knew quite well that Samuel Falconer owned no horses.

Mock astonishment replaced the grin. 'Not even a donkey cart? Most children can wheedle round someone to let them take the reins once in a while!'

'Oh, well, if that is what you mean!' She laughed back at him, her temporary pique forgotten. 'I even drove the carter's dray along Fore Street once!'

'And the horse did not bolt?' he teased.

'It did not! Neither did the baker's donkey,' she admitted, by now grinning as widely as he.

'Excellent! Then we do not have to fear that you will frighten the animals!'

He waited while Sawyer opened the main gates for them to pass through before he resumed the conversation.

'Both you and Vicky should learn to drive,' he told his passengers as he turned the sturdy pony's head towards the turnpike road. 'I shall appoint myself your instructor. You must be able to travel around independently if you wish.'

'I can drive a donkey cart already!' claimed Vicky importantly. 'And I can ride my pony, too. May Miss Charlotte learn? Then we could ride together.'

'I can see no reason why not, poppet. If she wants to?' The last addressed to Charlotte with a questioning lift of his brows.

Astonishment overtook her that he should even consider the suggestion. 'I should enjoy riding on horseback, I believe,' she answered honestly, 'but I have no suitable dress, and I have already spent far too much on my clothes. It will take me years to repay Sir George all I owe him.'

A strange expression settled on Francis's face. 'He has merely loaned you the money?'

'Oh, yes! I insisted. He has been more than good to offer me a home and a position which brings with it a generous income.'

'I see.' The expression disappeared as he eyed her thoughtfully. Charlotte wondered whether he believed her, but his voice was warm enough when he spoke again, so he probably did. 'In that case, perhaps my mother has one she no longer wears. It would need lengthening, I believe, but may not require much alteration otherwise. Ask her.'

'Should I?' Charlotte was hesitant. 'She has already shown me so much kindness. Will she not think me presumptuous?'

'I doubt it, but I will dispose of the possibility by making the request myself.'

'And she would do anything for you,' observed Charlotte with a soft smile curving her lips.

He grunted. 'She probably would, nowadays. I am to be indulged while I am on this visit! A sense of guilt combined with a case of absence making the heart grow fonder, I imagine.'

'I am certain you never lacked your mother's affection!' protested Charlotte.

'Then why,' demanded Francis, suddenly grim, 'did she not return to me ten years ago?'

His sudden show of resentment shocked Charlotte. She had never suspected him of harbouring such feelings against his mother. She had thought them on the best of terms.

'Because she met Sir George, and fell in love. Can you not understand that, Francis?' she begged.

He shook his head, sighing. 'Now, yes. I am exceedingly glad to see her so happy. But at the time I found it difficult.'

'Surely you could have joined her over here?'

'Oh, yes.' He flicked the pony's flank with the whip, encouraging him to a faster gait. Charlotte thought he did it to gain time, perhaps to swallow back bitter words that had sprung to his lips. 'But she had no need of me in her new life,' he explained evenly. 'I understood that well enough. Besides, I am American-born. The fortune my father left is in the United States and I needed to be there to administer it. She would not have been pleased to lose her income.'

'You are half-English, are you not?' questioned Charlotte diffidently. 'Your grandfather——'

'Cut my father off without a penny as a result of some youthful adventure with a married woman. It happens all the time, but he could not forgive. Yet my father was the best and most faithful of men, as I remember him, and an excellent businessman, as his success in building a fortune in railways demonstrated.'

'I should like to have met him,' said Charlotte sincerely. 'But what of your father's family here?'

'The present Earl shows no inclination to heal the breach; he has no need, with a castle full of heirs. Not that I have the slightest ambition in that direction!' he added, with a laugh signalling a return to good humour. 'I am content with life in the United States. But ten years ago, when I was scarce seventeen, I confess to feeling abandoned.'

'I am sure you were not,' persisted Charlotte earn-

estly. It seemed important that she should defend
Cecily Bradgate, should attempt to heal any lingering
breach between mother and son. 'But your mother
could not be in two places at once! She had to choose
between her own future happiness and your temporary
need of her. You were almost a man. Possibly you
seemed more independent to her than in fact you were.'

'Possibly. In any case, I survived.' Why was he
talking to this girl of things he had kept close to his
heart for so many years? And with Vicky's long ears
pricked close by! Though the child was singing noisily
to herself, thoroughly absorbed in the passing scene.

The unburdening of his secret, almost unrecognised
resentment had brought release, which manifested itself
in a buoyant mood. 'But enough of such introspection!'
he cried. 'Once we have passed through the toll-gate
you may take the reins!'

The pony was particularly well behaved, and
Charlotte found little difficulty in controlling him, with
Francis to instruct her and reassuringly close by to
retrieve the reins when a coach approached from the
opposite direction. From time to time he vaulted from
the jingle to assist the pony up an incline, protesting
that the weight of two adults and a child in such hilly
country was really too much for the beast. By the time
they reached the works at Churston Ferrars Charlotte
was confidently envisaging herself venturing out alone
with Vicky on many a future occasion.

For she could hardly expect Francis to accompany
her whenever she wanted to make an excursion. The
whole purpose in teaching her to drive was to ensure
her independence.

This thought took the edge off her excitement and
pleasure in her accomplishment, but Francis's words of
praise kept a glow on her cheeks as he disembarked to

coax the pony to breast a final muddy rise so they could reach a vantage-point.

At first the scene before them appeared chaotic in Charlotte's eyes. Soil had been thrown in great random mounds. Men, apparently caked in mud from boots to shoulder, their caps pulled down tightly on their heads and wielding long-handled shovels in heavily gloved hands, swarmed everywhere. Charlotte eyed their stalwart figures with considerable interest, for the navvy gangs had become notorious throughout the land. Brixham considered itself lucky that their camp was well away from town, for the men had a rumbustious reputation. They appeared harmless enough as they heaved and dug, and so far had given no cause for alarm in the district.

But her attraction was diverted from speculation by Francis's voice as he leant against the side of the cart to unfold the pattern of the works to her.

A cutting was being hewn from earth and solid rock. At the Brixham end navvies squelched in the wet ground, shifting vast quantities of mud to expose the limestone beneath. Near by, men were working on a road-approach to a half-finished bridge which would span the line. Towards Brixham Road in Churston, where the junction with the existing line would be made, the cutting petered out and soon became an embankment. Piles of bottom ballast — the limestone already blasted out and removed from other places — had been dumped ready for breaking up as a foundation to the track.

'This is only one cutting,' Francis told his audience. 'The entire length of the line will be just over two miles, and because the countryside it crosses is fairly flat the deepest they will have to dig is about eighteen feet, with embankments elsewhere of a similar height.'

'Will there be many bridges like this one?' asked Charlotte, eyeing the solid masonry from which the arches supporting the road would be sprung. Carpenters were already erecting the centring the masons would use to turn them.

'Eight in all — three like this, with the road crossing above the track, the others spanning the carriageways to form viaducts for the line to run above.'

'Like that planned up on Furzeham Common, where the station is being built?'

'Exactly. You have seen the works there?'

She shook her head. 'Only from a distance. They had barely been started when I moved.'

'I believe they are further forward now.'

'No doubt. Will the railway be a good thing, Francis? Opinions are divided. Mr Wolston has immense enthusiasm, but most people are uncertain. The fish carriers will be out of work, and so will the coach drivers who ferry passengers from Brixham Road.'

'The catch will still have to be carted up the hill to the station and people driven down. And there will be porters needed there. The railway brings prosperity to any town, Charlotte. Shoals of passengers have already been brought here by the existing line, so I am told. Mr Wolston is doing Brixham a great service by bringing them right to the town. You can expect even greater numbers, and will need additional hotels, more shops and houses. . .'

'You believe the town will grow? I wonder if that will prove a blessing or a curse?'

'Look forward, Charlotte! You must move with the times! I had not thought you unadventurous.'

'I am not!' protested Charlotte indignantly. 'It is not for my own livelihood I fear, but for those of my friends down in Brixham Quay.'

'Then do not! With delivery to London in seven hours, the fishing industry will thrive, as will all those who depend upon it — including rope-makers,' he added with a significant grin.

'And perhaps, with more visitors coming, the Local Board will do something about the drainage and water supply!'

Francis chuckled. 'You have seen the bright side at last! And look, the sun is breaking through! We need sun to dry out this wet ground if the line is to open on time.'

'Francis! Someone is coming!'

Victoria's cry turned their attention to a gig trotting in their direction. 'Stewart!' exclaimed Francis. 'Excuse me.'

He left them to descend the slope and greet the newcomer, a ruddy-faced, stocky man in high silk hat and black top-frock.

'Can I get down?' demanded Victoria, shaking the cart as she jumped eagerly to her feet.

'No,' decided Charlotte, eyeing the muddy ground. 'You'll get your boots and clothes dirty, and what will Nanny Bridges have to say to that?'

'She wouldn't mind,' argued Vicky, but sat down again obediently, her eyes fixed on her brother.

The two men having spoken together for some moments, Francis led his companion up to where Charlotte and Victoria sat waiting, while the pony grazed the few sparse tufts of grass within its reach.

'Charlotte, may I present Mr Stewart, Mr Wolston's engineer? Stewart, meet Miss Falconer, Miss Victoria's governess, and a distant relation of the family. You have met my young sister in the past.'

'Ladies.' Stewart bowed, lifting his hat. 'You are interested in the line?'

'It is quite fascinating, sir,' replied Charlotte politely. 'I cannot imagine how you will manage to lay all the tracks in time!'

'The Danlzic timber for the sleepers, and the metal rails and bolts, are all on order, ma'am, and indeed we expect deliveries of both daily. The recent severe weather has delayed our progress, but we still hope to have the line completed by midsummer.'

'I quite look forward to riding on it, sir,' said Charlotte, who had just conceived the idea.

'And so you shall,' promised Francis quickly, before the engineer could reply. 'I personally shall escort you!'

'You will still be here?' wondered Stewart. 'I had not thought this little line would have been of such great interest to you. Two miles only, when you span the American continent with your railways!'

'Ah, but this line is of superior ingenuity, and affords me the opportunity to study its engineering closely. In America my interest is financial rather than practical! Besides, as you know, I am on a prolonged visit to my mother and sister.'

'Doubtless there are many attractions in the vicinity,' rejoined Stewart, with such a pointed look in Charlotte's direction that an embarrassed flush stained her cheeks. 'Well, ma'am, I am pleased to have met you. If you will excuse me, I must be about my business.'

'Of course.' Charlotte managed to cover her confusion, aided by the necessity to rein in the pony, which had been tempted by a lush growth just beyond its reach. 'Good day to you, sir,' she responded civilly. 'Vicky, say goodbye to the gentleman.'

If Francis noticed the engineer's innuendo or Charlotte's reaction, he chose to ignore both, taking his own leave of the man before grasping the pony's bridle and leading the reluctant, slithering animal down the muddy slope.

On the way back they stopped off a couple of times to inspect progress, and Francis directed Charlotte, who still held the reins, to drive up to Furzeham Common to view the station. The work was beginning to take some shape; she could see where the line and the platform would be and a number of retaining walls had been started. Even the outline of the station building was visible now, for the foundations had been laid. The new cart road Mr Wolston was building to bring the fish up from the quay was progressing slowly, but Charlotte could not wonder at this, for of necessity it had to be cut out of the face of the hill.

'The view from up here is wonderful in decent weather,' she remarked, sniffing the salty breeze with deep appreciation. Although Bradgate Hall was not far inland, the sea air had lost some of its distinctive flavour by the time it reached the estate.

'Yes, it is a shame about the mist; I thought the sun would dispel it. And the town, as ever, is shrouded in a pall of smoke from the chimneys!'

'It gets trapped in the valley, but not much rises this high. The air here comes straight off the sea! Not even Mr Wolston's iron-oxide factory and paintworks can spoil it!' she observed, eyeing the said enterprises, set on the edge of the cliffs where the products could be loaded by hoist into ships berthed beneath. His determination to bring the railway to Brixham was not all far-sighted, public-spirited philanthropy, she thought wryly. He stood to gain by a cheap and speedy method of distribution for his goods.

'No,' Francis agreed, 'the air here is healthily fresh. However, I fear we do not have long to enjoy it, for we should be heading for home. Otherwise we shall miss luncheon.'

'I am hungry,' announced Vicky loudly, and the two adults laughed until she followed that announcement with another. 'I want to drive home.'

'Not on a public road, poppet,' Francis decreed. 'You must practise in the grounds of the Hall first.'

'Miss Charlotte didn't!'

'Miss Charlotte happens to be rather older than you are, Vicky, and stronger. Now no sulks, if you please, or I will not give you a lesson tomorrow.'

Victoria immediately became all smiles and a merry party arrived back at the Hall. Charlotte had time only to remove her mantle and tidy the escaping wisps of hair before the luncheon gong sounded.

Since learning to drive was considered a necessary part of her education, Victoria's lessons took place during the mornings. Charlotte accompanied her, and learned with her. Francis was delighted with the progress of both his pupils. He was not just good with boys, Charlotte reflected, but also had an enviable way with little girls!

His mother responded to her son's appeal for a riding habit for Charlotte with a promptitude which almost embarrassed the recipient. But of course Lady Bradgate was still attempting to please her son in every way possible, not to mention her husband.

So a habit was produced, rather out-of-date, for Cecily no longer rode on horseback. But its dark, forest-green hue, though dull enough for her half-mourning, was colourful enough to enhance her complexion and to bring out all the lights in her chestnut hair. In short, it suited her to perfection, as did the small black top hat which went with it. A wide veil swathed the crown, the ends trailing down behind in a most becoming manner. Charlotte's only doubt was as to whether it would stay put on her head, until Cecily produced the skewer-like hat-pin designed to anchor it in place.

Aided by Cecily's lady's-maid, Hodgson, Charlotte let down the skirt of the habit, which had a good hem. The sleeves of the jacket were more difficult, but Hodgson unearthed a length of wide braid to sew to the cuffs. The outfit included a pair of gauntlets which would cover any deficiencies admirably. With a white blouse beneath the coat, the ensemble could hardly have been bettered. And there was not a single wire hoop to manage!

The alterations took only a couple of days, so it was not long before, with morning threading fingers of pale grey through the darkness, Charlotte received her first riding lesson.

Francis assisted her from the mounting-block into the saddle, his hands warm and firm as he lifted her. Charlotte desperately tried to control her accelerated breathing, hoping he would think it due to excitement. He made quite sure she was sitting correctly, with her right knee hooked firmly about the pommel, showed her exactly how to hold the reins, then took hold of the lunge-rein attached to the mare's bridle.

'First I'll walk you round in a circle,' he said, 'just to familiarise you with the motion.'

The ground looked so far down! The horse moved forward. The sensation aroused by undulating, quaking muscle beneath her bottom was nothing short of alarming. Quite certain she was going to slip off, she grabbed the horse's mane.

'Let go!' ordered Francis, quite unable to suppress an amused grin. 'You are quite safe!'

'I do not feel it,' gasped Charlotte, reluctantly releasing her grasp on her only source of security.

'Sit up! No! Do not drag on the reins like that; you will damage poor Minty's mouth!'

Charlotte did not wish to do that. She forced herself to relax and once over her initial panic was surprised at how quickly she became used to the motion. She did not fall off, and soon began to accommodate to the movement of the horse. Confidence blossomed. Francis taught her how to make her mount stop, start, turn to the left, then to the right — even how to make the animal back up.

'Now we will try a trot,' he told her, and instructed her on the signal required to make the docile mare change her stride.

Francis laughed as Charlotte bobbed and bumped, and grabbed the mane again. 'Find the rhythm,' he urged. 'You were doing so well, Charlotte. Don't spoil it now!'

After a time Charlotte found she could stop bouncing about like a rag doll on a bumpy see-saw and control her ups and downs to coincide with the motion of the horse. Francis removed the lunge-rein. She circled the yard unaided. Then exhilaration set in.

'Oh, Francis! Can we go for a real ride?' she pleaded.

He grinned up at her flushed, eager face, his hand on the horse's neck almost touching her knee. 'Not today, Charlotte.' His voice held a note of tenderness which sent her pulse leaping and bouncing in imitation of her previous antics on the back of the horse. 'It is almost time for breakfast, and I believe you have done quite enough for one day. You will undoubtedly be quite stiff and sore enough as it is! Let me help you down.'

She reluctantly unhooked her knee and slid down,

the feel of his hands on her waist doing nothing to moderate the urgent, erratic beat of her heart.

His touch was brief. Yet as Charlotte lifted her eyes to thank him she realised that it had affected him, too. His breathing had become quite irregular and, since he had clamped his lips tightly closed to disguise the fact, his nostrils flared. The eyes meeting hers held an expression she found it difficult — impossible — to interpret. He released her at once and turned away.

'We will ride out tomorrow,' he told her briskly.

'I will go and change,' she responded quickly, and hurried off before she gave herself away entirely. The urge to nestle in his arms had been almost overpowering and, given his response and her own situation, quite dismaying.

He kept his promise, and next day found them riding sedately in single file along narrow tracks beside ploughed fields or trotting side by side where wider bridle-paths permitted. Charlotte had managed to quieten yesterday's fears meanwhile, and her pleasure was so obvious that Francis was moved to remark, 'You are a natural horsewoman, Charlotte. You already have a good seat. It should not be long before we can enjoy a gallop together.'

She flushed at his praise. 'Thank you, sir! I believe much of my success must be due to the quality of the instruction!'

She drew rein and waited while he leant down to open the gate to a wide field which, in a few hours when the promise of the pinkish glow lightening the eastern sky had been realised, would afford an excellent view over the waters of Tor Bay.

He looked up as he stood his horse aside to allow hers through. 'Nonsense!' he laughed.

Charlotte's sparkling eyes had only an instant to meet

challenging, dancing blue ones before her mare took off at speed.

Shot forward in the saddle, Charlotte gasped and grabbed its mane. 'Whoa, Minty!' she cried desperately, but Minty, enjoying herself thoroughly, took not the slightest notice. Bumping inelegantly up and down, moving ever-nearer and nearer to the horse's ears, Charlotte made a last desperate attempt to clutch at reins and mane and stay aboard, but in vain. Soon she was hanging by her knee, but only for an instant, for the next she was on the ground, landing with a jolt which momentarily took her breath.

She had been dimly aware of a shout and flying hoofs behind, but it had all happened so quickly. She hadn't retained her seat much above a dozen strides before she had begun her descent, and there had been no time for Francis to catch her reins.

Francis flung himself from his own saddle and bent anxiously over her recumbent form.

'Charlotte! Are you all right?'

She felt his hand upon her arm and shot up into a sitting position, automatically trying to straighten the hat, which had been knocked awry. Her indignant gaze focused instantly upon her mount, cropping the grass a few yards away. In her agitation she did not register the concern in Francis's tone or see the anxiety in his eyes.

'I thought she was supposed to be placid! Why did she bolt?' she demanded heatedly.

'She didn't,' replied Francis, visibly relaxing, and smiled. She looked quite irresistible with her hat askew and her face flushed with exertion, vexation and embarrassment. 'She decided she wanted a canter over the open field,' he explained.

'Well, she shouldn't have!' cried Charlotte crossly. 'I did not tell her to!'

'But neither did you stop her,' he pointed out mildly.

Charlotte turned her attention to him for the first time, certain she had detected a hint of laughter hidden under that mild tone.

'I did not know how,' she accused acidly.

'You could have pulled on the reins ——'

'No, I could not! I was being tossed forward; I had no time! She should not have done it!' she repeated with renewed asperity.

'Horses may have small minds, but they are all their own,' he retorted mildly.

'They shouldn't use them when they have a rider on their back,' snapped Charlotte unreasonably. She felt utterly ridiculous, thoroughly deflated, and although he was now looking suitably contrite his eyes were still brimming with laughter.

'I suppose it was partly my fault,' he admitted. The quiver in his voice could have been due to earnest regret, but she doubted it. He held out his hand. 'Allow me to help you to your feet.'

The moment she had placed her hand in his she regretted it, for his touch precipitated a peculiar reaction that even her deep indignation could not overcome. She snatched her hand away as soon as she could, and registered his reaction. The amusement disappeared from his eyes.

When he resumed his explanation all trace of humour had left his manner, though it was warm and earnest, as though he sought to make amends for laughing at her. And so he should, she thought crossly, despite feeling slightly ashamed of her petulance. Although if he thought her snatching her hand away was due to pique he was wrong. But perhaps it was just as well.

'This is where the grooms bring the horses for exercise,' Francis explained. 'Minty expected to stretch her

legs and lungs and was so eager that she did not wait
for your instruction. How was the poor horse to know
that you could not canter, let alone gallop?' he
enquired, the smile returning, but he was laughing with
her, not at her.

He was quite irresistible, and Minty was staring at
her with soft brown eyes. Charlotte's lips twitched into
a reluctant answering smile.

'So teach me!' she challenged, walked briskly over to
Minty, and allowed him to lift her back into the saddle.

CHAPTER TEN

IN THE weeks that followed Charlotte found herself spending more time with Francis. This proved a source of both delight and distress, for she knew that by spring at the latest she must lose her love.

For how could she help but love him? She hugged the secret knowledge to herself, almost afraid to take out her emotions and examine them for fear of where her thoughts would lead. She forced herself to simply enjoy his company, to bask in his friendship, without thought or expectation for the future.

Their riding together became a daily routine, whenever the weather permitted. Once recovered from her initial stiffness she enjoyed the exercise, revelled in the speed of a gallop, but above all treasured the early mornings spent almost exclusively in Francis's company.

Once she had mastered the control of Minty they ranged far and wide over the surrounding countryside, alone apart from a groom, who now, for convention's sake, followed discreetly in their wake. Cecily Bradgate had decreed the precaution, fearing for Charlotte's reputation.

Curbing his speed to hers, Francis rode the huge stallion which had been his mount on that day, seemingly so long ago now, when they had first met.

To Charlotte's immense relief Felicity did not ride on horseback, except in the direst of dire straits, and was not prepared to rise at dawn even for the pleasure of Francis's company. Tristram rode only for convenience, or occasionally to hunt. Like his sister, early rising was not normally one of his virtues.

Besides, Felicity had a new beau and therefore no longer set her cap at Francis quite so keenly. Since the dinner party, held less than a week after Charlotte's fall, when Charlotte had still found it extremely difficult to sit without fidgeting, having landed on an unmentionable part of her anatomy, Felicity had almost stopped her pursuit.

Charlotte had been nervous enough on her first venture into society without having to cope with the problems of a sore behind and muscles that protested every time she moved. However, Cecily had loaned her the services of Hodgson to arrange her hair, Jenny had shown unexpected dexterity in helping her to dress, and she had entered the saloon knowing she had never been in better looks.

The white gown, with its golden sheen and the deep, lace-edged flounces threaded with gold ribbon which encircled the skirt and low neckline, looked even better on her with her hair expertly dressed and with all the indispensable accessories added—a filmy chiffon shawl, a tiny purse to hang on her arm, evening gloves to cover hands which still bore the traces of past hard work, dainty satin slippers, a fan, and, best of all, her mother's locket and chain gleaming richly around her throat.

Hodgson had not been free to begin dressing her hair until her mistress's had been arranged with all due care. Once started she had refused to be rushed, with the result that Charlotte was a little late.

The guests were already gathered when she made her belated appearance. A stir of interest rustled among the silken skirts and brocaded waistcoats. Tristram sprang forward, but Francis was before him, his eyes warmly appreciative, offering his arm. However, it was her father who, graciously but with a firm hand, led her forward to introduce her to his guests. Pride shone from his eyes, there for all to see, and Charlotte hoped no one would suspect its true cause.

It seemed they did not, attributing it no doubt to a natural pleasure in discovering so presentable a relative. Since that first day of her arrival he had treated her much as he did Felicity, showing no favour but denying her little of the kind of attention he afforded his other children. Only Felicity outwardly showed resentment. If Tristram felt any he hid it under his normal flirtatious, dashing manner. Francis had completely overcome his initial suspicions, accepting Sir George's interest as purely avuncular.

Some half-dozen guests had been invited that evening, including Mr Richard Wolston and his wife. Charlotte eyed the solicitor, frankly curious, as she was introduced.

In late middle-age he had lost none of the driving energy which had made him perhaps the most prominent businessman in the town. Because of his profession he had been appointed clerk to the Market and Harbour Commissioners. In addition to mining iron oxide and processing it on the cliffs at Furzeham and taking a proprietorial interest in his Iron Paint Company, as a final, strange flourish he held the position of Portuguese Vice-Consul—a result of the vast trade in port wine carried on between Oporto and the harbours constituting the Port of Dartmouth, of which Brixham was one. Yet in addition to all these diverse interests he still found time to finance, organise and oversee the building of a railway!

Somewhat overawed by his reputation, Charlotte accepted his greeting with a nervous curtsy.

The squire of a neighbouring estate, a bluff country-man ill at ease in drawing-room finery, had been persuaded to escort his plump and eager wife, and the pair had brought a visiting nephew. After introducing her to Mr Coleton and his spouse, whose blunt manners were more in keeping with Charlotte's previous experience and gave her little cause for awe, Sir George turned to the nephew.

'Mr Fitzroy Mannering, my dear,' he murmured gravely. 'Mr Mannering resides in London and is soon to be called to the bar.'

Charlotte curtsied, her eyes gleaming with an amusement which banished the last traces of her shyness. Mr Fitzroy Mannering's shirt-front was quite hidden behind a snowy white starched and stiffened scarf. The satin waistcoat with its prominent revers swelled and shimmered under a black tail-coat of exquisite cut, which topped black French Bottoms — an ensemble designed to impress both his modishness and his dignity.

He eyed her with approving and rather calculating interest before bowing solemnly over her hand. 'Miss Falconer! Servant, ma'am.'

'My congratulations on your advancement, sir.'

'Miss Falconer is a distant connection of my family and has been kind enough to take on the duties of governess to my young daughter, Victoria.'

As Sir George's dry voice spelled out her exact position in the household Charlotte saw the gleam of interest die from Mannering's eyes.

'Indeed, ma'am,' he responded stiffly. 'Most commendable, I'm sure.'

They passed on, and Charlotte was left wondering at the reason for her father's pointed declaration, torn between gratitude at being relieved of Mannering's unwelcome interest and, since he gravitated immediately to Felicity's side, a suspicion that Sir George was uncharacteristically putting her down in order to protect his daughter's interests.

At that moment she caught Francis's eye. His lips twitched. He winked. She blushed, entranced by his singling her out for such an intimate exchange. Mr Wolston appeared to dominate the room, at least his voice did, but in her view Francis did so by his mere presence.

She chanced a sidelong glance at Sir George and caught a quickly suppressed expression of mirthful satisfaction on his face. Surveying the room through lowered lashes, she saw only approval or complete disinterest reflected on the faces of the other guests, and breathed a careful sigh of relief. Her father had chosen to show Mannering up for the snob he was.

A younger couple, the Dugdales, and a single lady of indeterminate years, a Miss Emily Green, a badly dressed friend of Lady Bradgate's whom Charlotte had not previously met, due to schoolroom duties which occupied visiting hours and afternoon teatime, completed the party. The latter greeted Charlotte effusively.

'My dear, I have heard so many good reports of you from dearest Cecily! I am delighted to make your acquaintance at last!'

To which Charlotte could only respond in like vein.

Parsons flung open the doors and announced dinner. Sir George escorted Mrs Wolston. Lady Bradgate, elegant as ever in pale mauve satin, placed her hand on the arm of Mr Wolston, while Tristram escorted the squire's plump and beribboned wife. The squire offered his arm to Cecily's friend, while Felicity appeared more than content to enter the dining-room with Mr Mannering.

Charlotte found herself accepting Mr Dugdale's arm as the company filed through, with Francis escorting Mrs Dugdale. How truly distinguished Francis looked in his impeccably tailored black dress suit! She followed him in, her eyes irresistibly attracted to his broad shoulders and narrow hips. In view of the appreciation her own gown had won it seemed only fitting that it should billow out behind her to brush the floor with a triumphant slither of silk.

She barely suppressed a gasp on entering the dining-room. If the daily dinner setting had seemed sumptuous to her, the magnificence of the table that evening surpassed her wildest imaginings. The entire contents of the hothouse must have been imported for the occasion! How would one see the person sitting opposite, let alone speak with them, with that forest of greenery twining and wreathing between?

The tendrils sprang from tall urns set in a line along the middle of the table, two at either side of the central point. The swags of greenery had been caught up together like paper-chains and attached to the brilliant chandelier hanging above the centre of the table, giving a tent-like opening through which she could see Felicity and Mannering opposite if she peered around the enormous stand of fruit and did not allow the intervening candles in their silver candelabra to dazzle her eyes. Tristram was off to her left, with the squire's plump wife on his far side and with Mrs Dugdale and Francis as buffers between him and herself. He could not resist flirting, even with Mrs Coleton, Charlotte noted, and was somewhat reassured, for his manner towards herself was a source of constant misgiving. She could not rid herself of the feeling that he was awaiting his opportunity to pounce.

But for the moment she was safe, seated between

Francis and Mr Wolston. Francis bent towards her,
leaning close despite the width of skirt separating them.
'You look quite enchanting tonight,' he murmured. 'I
hope you do not intend to disappear at midnight!'

Charlotte, who, though tense, had been stimulated
into high spirits by the occasion and a full glass of
sherry, dimpled at him. 'I shall endeavour not to,' she
whispered back, 'though I fear Cinderella must return
to the schoolroom tomorrow!'

He chuckled. 'Enjoy the ball while you may!'

'But there is to be no dancing!' she retaliated mock
tragically.

'Then you must make do with eating, drinking and
making merry!'

'On watered wine?'

'Don't argue, woman!' he commanded, his warm
eyes filled with teasing laughter. 'Sir George is about to
say Grace!'

The exchange of banter succeeded in abating her
nervousness at dining in such elevated company. However, from the outset Mr Wolston dominated the conversation with a non-stop account of the problems and
successes he had met with in carrying out his pet
project. In particular, he lamented the lack of enthusiasm among other local businessmen to take up shares
in his company and bemoaned the escalating costs. But,
to offset this, he told them with satisfaction, the con-
tractors were now in possession of all the necessary
land and work was progressing at a good speed, a fact
Francis was enjoined to confirm.

The cream of chicken soup and poached halibut had
been succeeded by sirloin of beef before the conversation became general, so Charlotte was free to concentrate on remembering every nicety of etiquette she had
learned during the weeks spent at Bradgate Hall with-

out having to worry about making small talk. The dinner passed off without incident, and when the ladies rose to leave the men to their drinks and cigars she knew that she had not let herself or anyone else down by her behaviour.

That evening proved a turning-point in her new life. She lost her nervousness in company and even began to enjoy the dinners and suppers she attended and, as spring progressed into summer, the picnics organised by hospitable friends and neighbours, for Vicky could be included in those excursions and lessons were excused. As she passed out of her period of mourning the dressmaker was called in and new, brighter, more summery gowns ordered.

'You're quite the lady of fashion now, but not too grand as to forget your family, I'm glad to see,' remarked Aunt Ada, critically eyeing the blue spotted muslin Charlotte wore. 'Mr Langford not with you?'

'No, not today.'

She usually visited on a Sunday, after partaking of the cold luncheon usual on that day to allow the kitchen staff to attend morning service and to have the afternoon off. Francis had escorted her on several occasions, insisting that he enjoyed the walk and the company at its end. And he did seem to, fitting into the family circle and seemingly less aware of the poor surroundings than Charlotte, who was seeing the relative poverty of her old home through newly awakened eyes. Aunt Ada did not possess her mother's knack of keeping the place shining, though it was neat and tidy enough. But although she might begin to criticise their home Charlotte would have brooked no criticism from others, and would never cease to love the half-brothers and sisters who lived there.

'You love him, don't you?'

Startled, Charlotte gazed at her aunt in confusion. They were alone for the moment, in the parlour examining some gingham Ada had bought for summer dresses for the younger girls.

'I hold him in great regard,' she admitted, 'but I cannot love him.'

'Cannot? Whatever do you mean, Lottie? Cannot? Of course you can, and you do, and I can't say as how I blames you, either; he's a fine young gentleman, no uppish airs with him. And he's in love with you.'

'Oh, no! You are mistaken there, Aunt. He likes me, we get along well together, but he knows my origins are here. He could never love me.'

'I shouldn't be too sure,' observed Ada sagely. 'Coming here don't seem to worry him, and love takes a person all unawares. He's no more immune than any other man.'

'It would be quite impossible,' insisted Charlotte. 'I could not entertain his suit, even were you right. I would have to inform him of my true birth, and that I could never do, for my father's sake. And there could be no point, for if Mr Langford knew of it his feelings would change, he would surely cast me aside as not worthy of his regard.'

'Well,' Ada shrugged, 'it's up to you whether you tells or not, I suppose. But if you're considering your father's feelings you must be coming fond of him. He seems to treat you well.'

'Very well, and he is not the ogre or libertine I once thought him. I have found it impossible not to form an attachment to both him and Lady Bradgate.'

'And little Victoria?'

'Above all to Vicky!'

'Humbug! It's *him* you care for above all!' Ada could read her companion's true feeling more accurately than

Charlotte found comfortable. But as Charlotte opened
her mouth to voice indignant protest Ada waved her to
silence, her face, quite filled out again now, bearing a
half-shamed expression of remorse. 'Never mind me,
my love, 'tis your own business, and none of mine. But
what do you intend to do with your life? Live at
Bradgate Hall all your days?'

Charlotte herself no longer knew exactly what she
wanted for the future. Tempting visions of sharing her
life with Francis, however forbidden, often haunted her
dreams, combining with her unexpected and growing
affection for her father and his wife to obscure her
earlier determination on a path of independence.

'I do not know, Aunt,' she confessed. In truth, for
the moment she was more than content to enjoy the
good things so unexpectedly showered upon her as a
result of her mother's death and her foster-father's
unacceptable behaviour.

Charlotte believed in practical lessons, and drove
Victoria out on more than one occasion, among other
things showing her the remnants of the forts which had
been built on Berry Head to defend England's shores
against that monster Napoleon Bonaparte. Those
excursions provided the basis for several lessons on the
French wars.

'Some way had had to be found to combat the French
tirailleurs,' she informed her small pupil.

'In other words,' put in Francis, 'light infantrymen,
who went ahead of the regimented columns, firing from
every side and demoralising the rigid opposing lines
before the main body of Bonaparte's Grande Armée
reached them.'

'Exactly. I could not have put it better myself!'
responded Charlotte with sardonic sweetness, not

altogether pleased at having her carefully researched lesson interrupted. 'If Britain was to prevail against Bonaparte its generals realised they needed men trained in the same way — the army had to re-learn its almost forgotten art of combining fire — the shooting of guns,' she added quickly to forestall another interruption from the expert, 'fire,' she repeated, 'and movement, in a special system of drill. A famous and much loved soldier, Lieutenant-General Sir John Moore, was given the task of training a corps of officers and men in methods he had first used when he was fighting in the West Indies. You know where they are, don't you?'

'Yes, on the other side of the Atlantic, like America.'

'Excellent, Vicky. But to continue. Eventually the men of the Rifle Corps, as it was called, were issued with distinctive green uniforms with dark buttons and accoutrements, so that they would not be spotted by the enemy as they dodged from bush to bush.'

'I like red coats and shiny gold buttons,' Vicky informed her.

'Perhaps, but the green was more practical for them. Before long the Light Brigade was formed. It operated under carefully thought out rules, but they were really quite loose compared to the main army's. Each man thought for himself, instead of behaving like an automaton.'

'Automaton?'

'Yes, you know, one of those dolls you wind up and it moves.'

'Oh, yes! I saw one of those once! It was a monkey, and it saluted me!'

'There you are, then. But you couldn't make it do anything else, could you?'

'No,' admitted Vicky.

'So you see an automaton cannot be made to do

anything different. Anyway, the men of the Light Brigade gathered intelligence — information,' she interpreted hastily, 'and provided the Regiments of the Line — yes,' she grinned, as Vicky opened her mouth to ask, 'the automatons — with an invisible screen of marksmen watching the enemy from every boulder or bush. In skirmishing ahead or covering a retreat they became the wonder of the army.'

'They must have been very brave.'

'Very,' Charlotte confirmed. 'But despite all their bravery, and that of everyone else too, Bonaparte seemed invincible until Sir Arthur Wellesley — you've heard of him as the great Duke of Wellington, but he didn't become that until later — had been put in command of the British army.'

Francis knew more of millitary matters than Charlotte, who had gained most of her knowledge from Johnny Kincaid in his account of life in the Rifle Brigade. Once she had said her piece she encouraged him to contribute to the outdoor lessons. Vicky listened open-mouthed, especially when he wryly reminded them that America had declared war on Britain in 1812.

'That was precisely the kind of assistance we needed!' exclaimed Charlotte indignantly. 'We were practically alone in defying Napoleon Bonaparte, who everyone knew was out to conquer the world after he had subjugated Britain, and all America could do was to declare war on us!'

'But the Royal Navy was stopping our trade with the Continent!' protested Francis with a grin.

'Only because Bonaparte was blockading every Continental port against British trade!'

Francis held up his hands in mock submission. 'Pray do not lay the blame at my door! I was not born at the time!'

'It must have been a very long time ago,' observed Vicky in awe.

When the grown-ups chuckled, she faced them indignantly. 'Well, wasn't it?' she demanded.

'Over fifty years, poppet,' admitted Francis. 'Even your papa was not alive then.'

'And he is dreadfully old,' proclaimed Vicky, with such conviction that she was allowed the last word.

Even though Charlotte was now, as Francis conceded, an admirable whip, at least with the jingle, she found little chance to try out her new skill alone, for he somehow became part of the most prosaic outing she organised for Vicky and herself.

Berry Head offered other attractions besides the reminders of war. In early summer the three of them viewed the fulmars and kittiwakes nesting on the cliffs beneath the forts. Francis produced his field-glass, and it seemed as though they had only to reach out to touch the nestlings.

But reminders of war did rather dominate the peninsula and on occasions when they were there the Artillery Volunteers drilled on a parade ground cut from what had been No. 1 Fort.

'Did you do things like that in your war, Francis?' Vicky asked, eagerly watching the marching lines answering to hoarse, incomprehensible commands. She was already quite old enough to be fascinated by men in uniform.

'Too many times,' admitted Francis wryly, 'but on horseback, for I served in the cavalry. I fear I only did my duty, poppet. Soldiering was a necessity, but I could not make it my life, as some men do.'

He met Vicky's scowl with a straight look and silenced her protest with a wave of his hand. 'War is not at all like the parade ground, poppet. It is

uncomfortable, exhausting and extremely dangerous!
One is either hot, cold, dirty, wet, hungry or sick —
sometimes all those things together. One just endures.'
He paused a moment, a far-away look in his clear blue
eyes, and went on in a low voice, speaking more to
himself than his companions, 'Yet privation and adver-
sity bring out the best in most men, and the comradeship we shared was something I would not have missed.'
His eyes focused on his small sister again as he brought
himself back to the present with a self-deprecating
laugh. 'I was not cut out for army life!'

'You didn't like being a soldier?' accused Vicky,
outraged by the suggestion that he did not measure up
to her conception of a dashing military hero.

'I did not,' he told her truthfully. 'There was a job to
be done, and I could not dodge doing my share.'

He could have — of course he could; many men had
shirked their duty and made money while their fellow-
men died to free the Southern slaves. But not Francis,
thought Charlotte, her eyes resting on his virile form
with tender pride. He would do what he thought right,
whatever the personal cost or inconvenience. And what
he had just said explained the core of steel running
beneath his compassionate, easygoing nature. Like the
hoops in her crinoline, he would bend so far and no
further.

During the lengthening days of spring and early
summer they ventured abroad as far as Kingswear in
one direction, to see the naval training ships anchored
off Dartmouth on the far side of the river, and Paignton
in the other, seeking unusual shells on the expanse of
sand fronting that small community at low tide.

Charlotte had overcome her hesitation and come to
accept Francis's company with quiet pleasure. And he
never once threatened to overstep the bounds of friend-

ship. For which, she told herself rather too emphatically, she was heartily grateful. His reticence enabled her to drop the constant guard she had felt it necessary to maintain at first, and made it easier to hide those moments of confusion which took her unawares from time to time, always at the most difficult and sensitive of moments. Then, pleasure turned momentarily to the exquisite pain of denied love.

Felicity spent most of the Season in London with a sister of her long-dead mother, a woman who had married into considerable wealth. It had not been intended that Flissy should enter society that year, and when she first demanded to be allowed to travel both Sir George and Lady Bradgate vigorously declined the duty of accompanying her.

Tristram, for all his wild ways, appeared to hold London in some disfavour — perhaps, according to Jenny's gossip, because he had returned from previous excursions with empty pockets and serious debts, and his father refused to finance further periods of debauchery. For whatever reason, he kicked his heels at home all spring and early summer.

Francis declared himself most reluctant to undertake an unnecessary visit to a hot, dusty and malodorous town when Bradgate Hall offered exactly the kind of diversions he enjoyed.

No one suggested that Charlotte should make her début that year, or even accompany Felicity as companion, for the latter made her opinion on that point crystal-clear, without the need for actual words.

Permission having been granted for her excursion, 'I will travel after Easter when the weather will be better, and take my maid Newton,' she declared. 'She will be chaperon enough on the railway journey, and my aunt

Trestle will accompany me elsewhere. I shall not be a great expense to you, Papa; I shall only need a couple of new gowns and bonnets for I shall have no reason to attend many functions this year. Mr Fitzroy Mannering has promised to attend me every day at Hampstead and, as you must realise, it is for this reason that I desire to go.'

She blushed, batting her eyelashes, and gave Charlotte a smug sidelong glance before turning the guileless battery of her eyes on Francis. She had never completely given up her pursuit of him, though it had degenerated into a rather lame chase since Mr Fitzroy Mannering's advent in early March. Charlotte thought the girl would still prefer to ensnare her stepbrother, but recognising the extreme improbability of success had wisely settled for second best.

'He may ask to escort me back, so that he may request an interview with you, Papa,' she added with a smug little smile.

'He will be received with the utmost courtesy,' she was gravely assured.

Felicity returned in early July, Mr Mannering in attentive tow. Sir George granted the prospective barrister's eloquent plea for the gift of his daughter's hand in marriage and the household offered congratulations to the engaged couple. The wedding was fixed for the following June, almost a year ahead.

They were, thought Charlotte, well suited. Mr Fitzroy Mannering, at least fifteen years Felicity's senior, had income and prospects, but little capital and an insignificant social position. In marrying Felicity he would acquire a substantial dowry and become the son-in-law of a baronet. She would obtain a successful husband, and the independence of ordering her own house and servants in London, where she could be certain of meeting all the right people to further her social ambitions.

She was in a seventh heaven of content, and began to treat Francis with the cool disdain normally meted out to a suitor spurned. Francis smiled quietly to himself at the way she had turned her victory into a triumph over him, when he had been politely combating her advances for so long. But if it pleased her to treat him so he had no complaints. He was free of her pursuit at last.

He had a more pressing problem. He was not at all certain for how much longer he could continue so constantly in Charlotte's company without his control snapping. A dozen times a day he wanted to take her into his arms and make love to her, but convention and his own sense of honour prevented him. Yet he could not bring himself to avoid her.

He made no attempt to deceive himself. Much as he loved his small sister, his close attendance on Vicky was dictated by his obsession with her governess.

He faced a dilemma. He wanted the girl, yet he could not make her his mistress under Sir George's roof, even were she to consent — which he was by now quite certain she would not. Marriage he dismissed as out of the question. Charlotte would not do. There would be time enough on his return there to consider filling the lonely mansion awaiting him in the States. An American wife was what he needed, one who knew American ways, not an English tradesman's daughter, however superior and distantly connected to the family. Besides, she would never settle on the far side of the Atlantic, separated so completely from her brothers and sisters.

His best remedy would be to return to America forthwith, yet he suspected that even the width of the

Atlantic would not free him entirely from the toils in which he found himself. It would be a long time before he could forget her lovely face and elegant figure, her soft voice with its pleasant burr, her intelligence, her latent sensuality. The woman had got under his skin and he half resented, half relished the fact.

Although he had left his business in safe hands, and reports from his man of affairs gave no cause for immediate alarm, he was beginning to feel the need to resume personal responsibility for his interests on the other side of the Atlantic. Prolonged further neglect could land him in deep difficulty. But Wolston was expecting him to be at the celebrations planned for the opening of his line, and completion had been delayed until the end of the year.

Which gave him an admirable reason to ignore his conscience and remain in England until the spring.

CHAPTER ELEVEN

DURING the summer, the early morning exercise provided by their riding excursions kept Charlotte fit, and so ready to meet the demands of her busy schedule with energy and enthusiasm. She often wondered how she had survived the heat and squalor of the Quay in summer, and guilt sometimes took the edge off her enjoyment when she remembered her family still living there.

Her visits to her old home continued regularly, though still confined to a Sunday afternoon, for other days were spent in a constant round of duty and pleasure. She looked forward to August, when lessons would not be strictly enforced, when maybe she could find time to take the younger children out in the governess cart — Sir George had given her free use of the jingle once assured of her capability as a whip. The little ones would be thrilled by a trip into the countryside. She was absorbed in planning the treat as she entered the Hall via the gun-room one morning, having left Francis in the stables conferring with a groom.

She was halfway across the gun-room, absently removing her gloves and hat, when she heard the groan. It came from behind the heavy table used for cleaning, loading and priming the weapons.

Jerked from her thoughts, she peered in the direction of the sound, wondering who it could be — a sick servant perhaps? Moving round the end of the table to take a look, she came to an abrupt halt.

'Tris!' she exclaimed, scandalised.

He often returned late and staggering drunk, but normally managed to crawl up to his room. Why his man had not sought him before this she could not imagine. He must think his master had chosen to sleep elsewhere, as he sometimes did. No one dared to enquire as to where Tristram went on those occasions.

His presence here did at least explain the unbolted door Francis had remarked on earlier. As she had joined him in the stable yard he had greeted her with the smile that illuminated his face and made her heart flip and ache.

'Good morning, Charlotte, I was wondering where you were. I had thought you must be before me today, since the gun-room door was already open.'

'Perhaps Parsons omitted to lock and bolt it,' she had suggested.

'More likely it was left for Tristram, who forgot!'

She had responded to his slightly scathing remark with a laugh, and mounted Minty, thinking no more of the matter. Neither of them had noticed anything amiss earlier; there had been no reason why they should. Each had thought the other gone ahead. She would not have seen Tris now, lying behind the table, his body obscured by the bench-seat, had he not made a noise.

'Tris!' she repeated in exasperation, as another groan emanated from the recumbent figure.

Stepping briskly forward, she tossed her hat, gloves and riding crop on the table and bent over to grip his shoulder, trying to shake him into full consciousness.

He groaned again, rolled on to his back and gazed blearily up. His eyes gradually focused on her face. She saw recognition dawn.

'Lottie!' His voice sounded thick, but he seemed rational. 'Be so good as to remove that shen — censo-

rious expression from your face, coz!' he requested in a
pained tone.

Charlotte shook her head at him. 'Censure is no
more than you deserve, Tris, coming home in such a
state!'

'And who are you to criticise?' he demanded, his
face suddenly darkening into a scowl. 'Anyone would
think you quite scandalised, my virtuous coz, but you've
been out with Frankie again, haven't you? What do you
two do out there—apart from riding, of course? That's
what I'd like to know.'

Despite her first impression he could not be completely in control, yet he was not drunk. Hungover,
loose-tongued, bad-tempered, but not drunk. Charlotte
pressed her lips together to stop the rush of outraged
words on the tip of her tongue.

'I will ignore that innuendo, Tris,' she told him, her
voice quivering with anger, 'since you are hardly
responsible and it was not worthy of you. Now come
along, do; get up and I'll help you to your room.'

She bent over him again, her hand extended, braced
to help him to his feet. But Tris had no intention of
doing as he was told. With a gleeful chuckle he reached
up and dragged her down to the floor with him.

Taken by surprise, Charlotte could do nothing to
save herself. She fell forwards, landing across his body,
and ended up clamped in his arms.

'Give me a bit of what you give Frankie,' he
demanded. His arms held her in a vice-like grip, his
elbows digging in quite painfully while his hands
grasped handfuls of her loosened hair to clamp her
head still while his mouth searched for hers.

Charlotte squirmed, trying desperately to free herself
from his hold, until she realised she was just exciting
him the more. After that she endured the kiss, her rigid

body a silent protest. She tried to keep her teeth clenched shut against him, but he nipped her lip and as she gasped in pain his furred tongue invaded her mouth, almost throttling her for what seemed an eternity of torture, but at last lack of breath forced him to withdraw.

She took a shaking, indignant breath. 'Let me go!' she demanded furiously. 'You must still be drunk!'

'No, coz,' he denied, equally furiously, his hold on her head hardening painfully. 'Except drunk for you. You flaunt and tempt and you expect me to keep my distance. But I'll not endure such provocation a moment longer!'

'I do not!' she denied, hot tears of humiliation and indignation stinging her lids. How dared he accuse her of wanton behaviour?

But Tris was past arguing with. His hot, stale breath fanned her face, his full, wet lips sought hers again. She did not think she could stand another assault on her mouth. As she tried to twist her face away to avoid it, the first shiver of fear trickled down her spine. She was powerless in his grasp.

'No! Stop it, Tris!' she pleaded.

But he still held her head in that cruel grip and her last words were smothered to nothing as his mouth clamped itself to hers.

Though it had been hurtful, she thought despairingly, Francis's kiss had not been evil, or frightening, like this. In fact she was often haunted by the memory, reliving the incident with guilty pleasure, longing for him to kiss her again. Even Sam Falconer's assault had not repulsed her so. And to make matters worse this man was her half-brother! But Tris was not aware of that, so she could not accuse him of incestuous intent. Briefly, she toyed with the idea of telling him of their true relationship, but instantly decided she would merely exchange her own present distress for future grief to everyone concerned.

Somehow, she was beneath Tris now, where one of his hands was enough to hold her prisoner. He grabbed handfuls of her skirts with the other, scrabbling them up to explore beneath. Charlotte could feel his clammy hand greedily squeezing her thigh, hot through the cambric of her drawers. She could scarcely breathe; panic and sickness rose inside her as she realised the enormity of what could happen, and precisely how helpless she was to prevent it.

Her senses began to spin. With a last, despairing effort she wrenched her lips away from his. 'No, Tris!' she wailed, her voice wavering and reedy, little more than a thread, unable now to say the words which could save her even had she wanted to.

But Francis, entering at that moment, heard her cry, feeble though it was.

'What the devil is going on here?' he barked, his voice such as to make a trooper quail.

Hope leapt in a joyful surge as Charlotte realised Francis had arrived in time, had not chosen to linger unnecessarily in the stables or to enter the house by another door.

'Francis!' Her voice rose to a shriek as relief did strange things to her throat. She did not realise how desperate she sounded.

She did not see what happened next, only heard a string of expletives seldom voiced in polite female company, but suddenly she was free. She lay panting on the floor while Tris seemed to rise of his own accord to meet the anger of his stepbrother.

'You damned cur!' raged Francis, his voice deadly

quiet and the more awesome for it. 'You have deserved this for long enough!'

She heard the crack of bone on bone, twice. A heavy body went shooting across the stone-flagged floor.

'You poor damned fool,' gasped Tris's breathless, sneering voice. 'She was asking for it!'

'Get up!' commanded Francis, each word bitten out with grim deliberation.

By this time Charlotte had managed to drag herself up to sit on the bench. She leaned on the table for support, watching apprehensively, scarcely recognising Francis. This grim, militant avenger was so unlike the cheerful, courteous and gentle man she had left only minutes before!

Tristram continued to lie where he had fallen, nursing his chin and eyeing his adversary with wary hostility. Francis bent down, grasped him by his necktie and heaved him upright. Tristram swayed where he stood, at last made some pretence at defence, but failed to counter or evade the hard, lean fist aimed at his face.

Tris fell again, landing up sprawled against the wall. Francis stepped back, his whole attitude one of challenge.

'Come, brother! Stand up and fight like a man!' When Tristram continued to scowl at him from his position on the floor he made an explosive sound of disgust. 'So you will only attack women, is that it?' he accused. He relaxed his aggressive stance and waved a dismissive hand. 'If you will not defend yourself, take your unsavoury carcass off to your room and let your man clean it up.'

It looked as though Tris had a split lip and a loose tooth as well as a bleeding nose and a blackening eye. Charlotte almost felt sorry for him.

But his gentlemanly upbringing had instilled in Tris

little sense of honour, none when he was at a disadvantage. He pulled himself up from the floor with the aid of a wall rack above his head and as he did so he grabbed one of the pistols it contained.

Charlotte cried out in consternation. Francis dismissed the action with a short laugh.

'Not loaded,' he assured her laconically.

Tris knew this, of course, but it was a weapon once used by cavalry, and a heavy brass ball capped a butt designed to be used as a bludgeon once the pistol had been discharged. He grasped the barrel and swung the gun threateningly.

'Don't come any nearer,' he warned, as Francis advanced.

Francis ignored the threat. He caught a glancing blow on his shoulder before his superior fitness and old army training enabled him to wrench the pistol from Tristram's grasp and cast it side. Next moment Francis had his stepbrother by the scruff of his neck and the seat of his trousers and had turned him to the door.

'Get out!' he ordered brusquely. 'If you molest Charlotte again, I will kill you.'

'And hang for it?' sneered Tristram breathlessly over his shoulder. He was beaten and knew it, but could not resist a final verbal thrust. 'The jade is not worth it!'

Charlotte saw murder leap to Francis's eyes. He spun his victim round and grasped his neck.

'No!' she gasped. 'No, please, Francis! He cannot mean what he says!'

'He had better not,' growled Francis through his teeth. He relaxed his choking hold but moved swiftly to resume his previous grip on Tristram's collar and seat. He spoke harshly into his ear.

'I could be on a boat for America before the law caught up with me,' he assured his captive chillingly.

'So take no comfort from the thought that I should hang, my dear brother. Just believe me when I say that should you again molest your cousin, either by word or deed, you will pay for your folly with your life. Now — get out of my sight!'

He reinforced this injunction with a mighty shove which sent Tristram reeling from the room. Francis watched for a moment to make sure Tristram had truly departed, then closed the door and turned, leaning back against it, breathing hard.

He glanced across at Charlotte. Absently rubbing his bruised shoulder and sucking blood from a broken knuckle, he moved to pick up the pistol and replace it in the rack. His breathing was hard not so much from exertion, Charlotte thought, as emotion. It must have been exceedingly unpleasant for him to chastise Tristram so, in the other man's own home.

'I do not think he will trouble you again,' Francis remarked into the silence which had succeeded Tristram's departure.

Charlotte had already risen to her feet. At his words she gathered her skirts and flew across the room, reaching him before she had begun to think beyond the fact that she was safe and she had him to thank for it. He had been magnificent. As he had been on the beach when Sammy drowned.

Then, she had omitted to thank him at all. All her emotion had been spent on Sammy. Now her feelings spilled over into an overwhelming tide of love. Throwing herself at him, she wound her arms about his waist and buried her face in his waistcoat.

She felt him stiffen, which chilled her, but she could not blame him for holding her responsible for the unfortunate confrontation with his brother. She still clung to him, she seemed unable to let him go, though she expected him to put her aside. But instead he relaxed. His hands came up, slowly, to hold her lightly by her waist.

At his touch a sob racked her. 'Oh, Francis!' she gasped. 'I am so sorry! But it was not my fault, I swear! It was horrible!'

'What happened?' he asked quietly.

She told him, her voice choked, but trailed off as she came to the part where Tristram had begun his intimate fondling, unable to describe further the assault he had made on her. 'I was praying for you to come,' she finished on a choked whisper, and buried her face in his waistcoat again.

'Oh, my dearest!'

His hard-won detachment disappeared on the instant. His voice held near-desperation as his arms came round to hold her in a grip so fierce that she thought her ribs might crack, but gloried in the pain. These arms were hard, protective, passionate. And entirely, wonderfully, seductively acceptable.

She lifted her face on a surge of joy, realising that his stiffening, his lack of response, had been a matter of restraint, not anger. He smothered her features in quick, fierce kisses, tracking his lips across her forehead, his breath fanning tendrils of hair to tickle her skin. They lingered more gently on her eyes, picking up speed and passion again as they moved to her cheekbone, followed the line of her firm jaw, found the small cleft at its point and finally came to rest on her expectant mouth.

Now he was gentle, for he had seen the swollen bruising caused by Tristram's unwanted attentions. His kiss was tenderly deep and sweet. Charlotte responded without restraint, unable to subdue the tide of passion sweeping over her. As his arms moved hers crept up round his neck. She felt his crisp golden hair beneath her fingers, thrilling to the sensation it brought, aware that one of his hands had buried itself in the luxuriant waves of her own tumbling locks while the other gently traced the delicate line of her jaw. One kiss followed another, both participants lost in the exquisite joy of turning a long-held dream into reality.

The clatter of a housemaid's bucket from the hall brought Charlotte back from heaven to solid earth. She became aware of the urgency evident in Francis's body, of the singing, surging response in her own.

She had grown up in a house full of brothers and sisters. She knew the intimate details of the male anatomy, and had a reasonably factual idea of what union with a man entailed, unlike the gently nurtured young ladies of the middle and upper classes. Breathing rapidly, deeply, searching desperately for composure, she pulled away and put her hands against his shoulders, forcing a space between them.

Francis immediately dropped his arms. The high colour of his passion ebbed away as she watched. Bleakness filled his eyes, his jaw clenched in a struggle for control.

'I am no better than Tristram,' he declared bitterly. 'Please accept my abject apologies, Charlotte. Forgive me. I had not intended for that to happen, and I can promise you I shall not behave so despicably again.'

Dismayed, Charlotte could only stare at him. He thought her offended by his embrace — when she had simply sought to escape its inevitable conclusion! For it had become quite plain that he desired her. But with her past history she could never allow herself to succumb to temptation and abandon herself to the bliss of his arms. Ma's lined face and work-worn hands rose up in her mind to reinforce her determination never to indulge in the kind of illicit passion which had caused her mother's virtual ruin.

'No!' she gasped, feeling cold and weak without the comfort of his arms about her. 'No, Francis, it was my fault! I should not have behaved so shamelessly since I did not intend. . .' She drew a heaving breath. 'I was grateful,' she told him flatly, knowing she was killing the precious thing which had begun to blossom between them, 'and overwrought.'

'And I,' said Francis with a stiff little bow, 'am but a weak man, ever vulnerable to the charms of a grateful woman.'

'I am sorry,' Charlotte said again. 'I would not willingly destroy the friendship that has grown between us. Please say that my stupidity has not affected that?'

Francis closed his eyes against the anxious pleading on her beautiful face. She asked too much! How could he endure. . .?

He straightened his shoulders and met her golden-flecked gaze. 'You are safe, Charlotte,' he told her tightly. 'Tristram will not attempt to molest you again, even when drunk. Of that I am certain. He is not one of the bravest of men, and he knows I meant what I said.' He paused before adding stiffly, 'You have both my protection and my friendship for as long as you require them.'

Charlotte managed a wavering smile before lowering her gaze and moving to retrieve her things. Her heart demanded that she throw caution to the winds and follow its urgent prompting to give herself unreservedly to the man she loved. But self-restraint — bolstered by a strong sense of self-preservation — won, and she swiftly left the room.

* * *

As she had sadly anticipated, things were not the same after that interlude. The previously unacknowledged passion smouldering between them had momentarily burst into scorching flame. In order to keep the fire banked down and to avoid a new blaze, both, by mutual, unspoken consent, altered their behaviour, though not their habits, since they did not wish others to question the subtle change in their relationship. Besides, as far as Charlotte was concerned, Francis's company was too precious to be relinquished completely, however bitter-sweet each meeting had become.

Francis avoided close contact, though the stiff-lipped manner in which he had given his promise of continuing friendship had been replaced by an easy, comfortable style of behaviour Charlotte wished she could achieve with the same apparent ease. His passion had soon died, she observed sadly, which strengthened her still wavering resolution not to give way to her own wayward emotions. Susceptible to his merest touch, she was careful to use only the tips of her fingers when forced, for convention's sake, to take his arm.

When necessary a groom assisted her to mount and dismount. Francis further distanced himself by riding alongside the jingle on their excursions. With his long legs he had plenty of excuse for avoiding the cramped confines of the governess cart, yet he had seemed happy enough to share it in the past.

Charlotte felt the underlying emotional estrangement deeply, yet knew she must do nothing to court a return to the old, easy familiarity. By her loss of control after the incident with Tristram she had not only forfeited the right, but made any attempt to do so quite out of the question.

Damn Tristram! He had taken himself off to visit

friends in Dorset, or so he had announced before his abrupt departure. The Daltons had a daughter of marriageable age to whom Tristram had been asked to make himself agreeable. He would not be forced into a marriage, Sir George explained, but this match would be a suitable one, Miss Dalton being a young lady of character who would make an excellent mistress of Bradgate Hall when the time came. So no questions were asked, his departure being accepted with some pleasure by all, for differing reasons. The state of his face had been explained as being the result of a riding accident.

Immersed in preparations for her wedding, Felicity's attitude had changed from unspoken enmity to one of superior smugness. Charlotte wondered how that young lady would fare on her wedding night. Being delicately brought up, she probably had no idea what to expect, and would categorically reject any attempt Lady Bradgate might make to enlighten her beforehand. Mr Fitzroy Mannering did not impress Charlotte as a sensitive individual. But no doubt Felicity would manage as well as most young ladies launched all unprepared into the uncharted waters of the marriage bed.

It was September before Tristram returned, cheerfully behaving exactly as though nothing had happened. Both Charlotte and Francis, by this time once more enjoying an agreeable if rather less close association, accepted his reappearance without comment. Life went on at a pleasant, leisurely pace. Had it not been for her secret heartache, Charlotte would have considered herself both fortunate and happy.

One mellow morning, not long after Tristram's

return, the family were leaving the breakfast table when Parsons appeared.

'There is a young lad asking to speak with Miss Falconer,' he announced in his usual sonorous tones. 'He informs me that his message is urgent.'

'Who is it, Parsons?' asked Charlotte anxiously.

'I did not enquire his name, miss——'

'That was remiss of you,' interrupted Sir George impatiently. 'Bring the boy here.'

A few moments later the butler ushered a nervous Bertie into the room. The boy bore every sign of having thrown his coat on hurriedly and run all the way from Brixham Quay. Beneath his cap, his hair badly needed a comb. Sweat beaded his flushed brow and he was still dragging in his breath in painful gulps. His anxious gaze lit on Charlotte. He gave a cry of relief, darting forward to clutch at her hand.

'Lottie!' he gasped. 'Oh, Lottie, you've to come at once! Dr Stone has taken Rosie to his surgery; he says he's got to operate at once, before the poison reaches her heart——'

A gasp went up from all still present. Tristram had already left the room, but Felicity subsided into a chair demanding her vinaigrette, while Cecily Bradgate told her sharply to pull herself together.

'What poison?' demanded Charlotte, completely bewildered, her anxiety rising rapidly. 'Bertie, slow down; tell me what has happened!'

'Have the brougham brought round immediately,' ordered Sir George as he dismissed Parsons.

Charlotte barely noticed the by-play, all her attention being centred on her brother. He drew a deep breath and began again.

'It's Rosie. You know she cut herself the other day, at work, and it wouldn't heal?'

'I dressed the wound on Sunday.'

'Yes, well, first her finger, then her hand began to swell up, and now it's gone all up her arm, all red and angry, and she's running a fever this morning, so Aunt and Pa called in the doctor. And he says the infection has gone so far there's only one thing to be done.' Bertie hesitated and the tears began to roll down his cheeks. 'He's going to cut off her arm,' he blurted out, finishing up on a wail.

Charlotte swayed as a dreadful rushing sound filled her head and momentarily everything went dark. She felt a steadying hand on her waist and gratefully accepted the support.

'I'll escort you there at once,' said Francis, looking to Sir George for approval.

Parsons reappeared in answer to a pull of the bell.

'The brougham is ordered?' demanded Sir George.

'It will be ready in five minutes, sir.'

'Excellent. Instruct Hoddy to fetch Miss Falconer's bonnet, shawl and purse.'

On the butler's departure Sir George turned immediately to Charlotte, saying gravely, 'You must go at once, of course, and Francis has offered to escort you. Do not let the cost stand in the way of any treatment your sister needs; I will meet the bill.'

The room had come back into focus and Charlotte realised on whose strength she was leaning. Even after so many weeks of self-denial Francis's touch now brought with it no passionate response, only a healing sense of gratitude and release. Although her father was being practical and helpful it was upon Francis's support she instinctively relied.

'Thank you,' she whispered. 'Oh, poor Rosie! Such a small cut. . .she's had them so often before ——'

'But something got into this one,' gabbled Bertie

between suppressed sobs. 'The doctor says the knife must have been rusty or something; anyway it's poisoned and there's nought else he can do and we're afraid she'll die ——'

'No, she won't,' interrupted Francis stoutly as Jenny appeared with Charlotte's things. 'People survive worse injuries than an amputated arm. Stone has an excellent reputation; he treats this family, I believe.'

'He does,' confirmed Sir George, 'and be sure he puts his charges to my account. In addition to being a fine physician he is a clever surgeon who uses all the latest techniques, my boy, and I firmly believe your sister will recover splendidly.'

Such reassurances could do little to restore Charlotte's confidence as she threw the shawl about her shoulders and hurried to the waiting carriage.

In the close confines of the vehicle, Francis's presence seemed overwhelming. She made no objection when he placed a comforting arm about her shoulders, accepting the quiet strength he offered with a sense of inevitability. Bertie had elected to ride outside, beside the coachman, even at such a time enjoying a rare treat.

They made the journey in tense silence. The coachman drove straight to Dr Stone's substantial house in New Road, pulling up in the stable yard. Francis escorted his companions into the building, where they were immediately greeted by a strong smell of chloroform and carbolic.

The first person Charlotte saw, sitting disconsolately with his head in his hands, was Sam Falconer. He looked up as they entered the large reception hall where he was waiting.

The years rolled back as though by magic. Sam was once again the man who had stood solidly between his family and the world, harsh as he had seemed at times.

He stood up. Charlotte walked swiftly forward. Next moment they were silently clasped in each other's arms.

Charlotte stirred first, drawing back to look into Sam's face. The past year or so had etched new lines, deepened now by renewed suffering. Rose was his eldest true daughter, and in his own way he loved her deeply. She blinked back the tears which suddenly threatened. Since hearing the news she had remained remarkably dry-eyed, as though the tragedy was too great even for tears to express.

'How is she, Pa?'

'I don't know, girl.' Sam's voice was raw with emotion. 'Stone is operating now. He says there is hope, but even if she dies I cannot begrudge the cost of the operation. Doctor says I can pay bit by bit.'

'Don't worry about the cost, Pa,' Charlotte urged softly. 'Sir George is most concerned, and has promised to meet the doctor's bills.'

She watched Sam Falconer struggling with his pride. He wanted to refuse the help, but was in no position to do so.

'I'm grateful,' he muttered at last, tugging down the peak of his cap to shield his eyes, which held an expression somewhere between bafflement at the constant buffetings of fate, resentment at having to accept charity and the gratitude he expressed. 'It would have been a grave burden on me.'

'She will need nursing,' put in Francis, acknowledging Sam Falconer with a firm handshake, his expression unusually grave. 'Sir George told me to tell you she can be taken to Bradgate Hall to recover, where she can be near Charlotte.'

'He did?' murmured Charlotte.

'He did.' Francis essayed a smile, his lean cheeks stretching, his shapely lips taut, and took her hand.

'While you were putting on your shawl, my dear. He considers your sister entitled to the best treatment he can offer.'

Charlotte flushed, even in her distress recognising that Francis would consider such concern natural, while Sam would not. But neither man commented further on Sir George's generosity and the subject lapsed. Francis released her hand after seating her on the most comfortable chair available.

Bertie had remained outside with the coachman, which Charlotte considered for the best. All they could do was to sit stiffly awaiting news and making desultory conversation while their imaginations wandered to the small surgery where Rose was fighting for her life.

'The children must be home from school. Aunt Ada is with them?' ventured Charlotte unnecessarily.

'Of course.'

Sam relapsed into silence. Francis had removed his tall hat and placed it on the floor beside his chair. He sat with his long legs crossed, his hands still, a tower of quiet strength. A maid came in carrying a scuttle of coal with which she stoked the fire. Despite brilliant autumnal sunlight streaking through the window it was cold in the room, and Charlotte smiled her gratitude at the girl, who bobbed a curtsy and departed. Charlotte watched the motes dance in the shaft of light and noticed how it brought out the golden glints in Francis's fair hair.

He seemed to realise that her gaze was on him. He looked up. Their eyes met. Charlotte stretched out a hand and he immediately took it in one of his, giving it a comforting squeeze before dropping it again.

'How much longer must we wait?' she whispered.

Francis shook his head, but he produced his pocket

watch, snapped up the cover and consulted the time. 'It is almost eleven,' he told her quietly.

Midday came and went before the doctor appeared in the doorway, still drying his hands.

'The operation was successful. I have every hope that she will live,' he announced.

Charlotte shot to her feet. 'May we see her?' she demanded urgently. 'When may we take her to Brad-gate Hall?'

'You may see her when she wakes. No doubt she will be glad of someone to sit beside her bed. My nursing assistant will be on hand if needed. If all goes well, you may take her away in a day or so — to Bradgate Hall, you say?'

'Yes, Doctor. Sir George has been good enough to offer her sanctuary until she is recovered.'

'Can you recommend a reliable nurse?' asked Francis.

'I will nurse her!' exclaimed Charlotte quickly.

'Of course, but you will need help. And you have other duties,' Francis reminded her, with a small smile of reassurance to take any sting from his words. Left to her own devices, Charlotte would wear herself out nursing her sister day and night, and he had no intention of allowing her to do any such thing.

CHAPTER TWELVE

As soon as her condition allowed, Rose was removed to the comfort of Bradgate Hall. Charlotte insisted that her sister be laid in the big tester, herself using a small truckle-bed hastily set up in her dressing-room.

Francis, knowing there was nothing further he could do to help, had left Charlotte sitting beside her sister in the doctor's house while he walked back to Bradgate Hall to inform those there of the events in Brixham Quay. He left the brougham and coachman behind in case Charlotte should need them later.

But Charlotte dismissed Jeffries as darkness began to fall, for she intended to watch over Rose throughout the night and following days. She could walk to King Street for rest and meals, and promised to dispatch Bertie to ask for the coach to be sent when it was needed.

Francis arrived with the four-in-hand, mounted on his roan. He had visited the doctor's house several times in the intervening days, reassuring himself as to Charlotte's health and the patient's progress. Thus Bertie was saved the walk to Bradgate Hall, for Francis was able to convey her request. His care brought warmth to Charlotte's heart, though she knew it meant nothing beyond the friendship they shared. If he still desired her he hid it well, and in any case passion did not equate to love. No, he was merely behaving as any well-bred male would when a female of his acquaintance needed help.

He carried the sedated Rose to the coach, more

roomy and less draughty than the brougham, where he settled her safely in Charlotte's arms. Charlotte did her best to buffer her sister against the roughness of the journey, but neither careful driving by Jeffries nor her care could prevent the patient from being jolted.

Perhaps partly as a result of the difficult journey Rose developed a new and greater fever, but by then she was safely installed in Charlotte's bed. For several days she recognised no one, burning up one moment and shivering the next. Both Ada and Sam visited, Ada stepping diffidently into the Hall and speaking in whispers. Sam asked to see Sir George in order to thank him for his generosity.

Francis was in and out of the sickroom every day. As time passed his concern for Rose became submerged in exasperation with Charlotte.

'You must eat, Charlotte,' he told her firmly. 'If you do not, and will not rest, you will make yourself ill, and I am certain you will not wish to do that, for then we shall have to nurse you, too.'

'I am strong enough, Francis,' she insisted staunchly. 'I shall not break down.' She held out her hands and he took them in his firm clasp. 'But I thank you for your support,' she added. 'I do not believe I could have managed without it.'

'You know you are always welcome to that, Charlotte.'

And he had drawn her to him to place a warm, vital kiss on her forehead. The feel of his lips lingered long after he had left the room. Charlotte stroked the spot with her fingers, wishing he had chosen to kiss her mouth.

Although a nurse had been engaged, Charlotte refused to leave her sister for long, sleeping in snatches during the day between shortened schoolroom hours.

She had taken on the night watch so that the nurse, a stern woman of middle years called Midgeley, who Charlotte suspected would intimidate Rose when her sister was well enough to understand what was going on around her, could take her rest.

By the time Rose's fever did break, and the doctor pronounced her on the road to recovery, Charlotte, while refusing to admit it, was near collapse.

She settled wearily into the chair she used at night, a tired sigh of relief escaping her. She pulled a shawl tightly about her shoulders in an attempt to still the shivering which had suddenly afflicted her limbs. It was almost as though she was suffering from an ague herself. But, although her body felt as though it belonged to someone else, her mind was quiet. Rose had spoken quite rationally before dropping into a deep sleep — laudanum-induced, but healing nevertheless.

After the fevered restlessness and rambling of the past days, to see her sister sleeping so quietly gave Charlotte great happiness. Without the drug, which the nurse had administered before retiring to her own bed, restful sleep would still have been impossible, for Rose's first coherent words had been of complaint at the pain in her hand. At first Charlotte had thought her sister still rambling, until Nurse Midgeley told her this was a common after-effect of an amputation. The patient could still feel the arm or leg although it was not there.

'Lottie, what am I to do?' Rose had cried once they were alone, the tears running down her wan cheeks as she faced the prospect of life crippled by the loss of an arm.

Charlotte had scarcely known how to comfort her sister, but had done her best.

'It is your left,' she pointed out with a bright smile.

'You still have your right. You'll manage very well once you are up and about again, and get used to doing things with one hand.' She did not think Rose was much comforted, but thankfully for them both sleep had claimed the invalid almost immediately.

Her brain having accepted the fact that there was no longer any danger to her sister's life, Charlotte's anxiety lifted. Her subconscious took over to give her overdriven body the rest it so urgently needed. She scarcely stirred when strong arms lifted her from the chair where she sat and carried her to a soft bed. She nestled into the warm cradle of feathers with a contented grunt.

When she did wake she lay for a moment, trying to remember where she was. The room was in darkness apart from the glow from a banked fire and a faint streak of grey light creeping round the edge of the curtain. Everything was in the wrong place. The window was not where it should be.

She stirred, and immediately heard movement in the room.

'Are you awake, Charlotte?'

'Francis! Where am I?'

'In my bed.' Flames flickered and flared as he held a taper to the fire and lit several candles in a sconce on the wall. Then the patterns of light and shadow changed as he reached for the bell-pull then walked towards her. 'Did you sleep well?'

Meanwhile Charlotte had discovered that she had been divested of her dress and crinoline petticoat. She had not been wearing stays for her midnight vigil, but she felt sure that had she been they would have gone too. She would not have slept so restfully encased in tight-fitting and cumbersome clothes, and was glad they had been taken off, but wondered in some embarrassment who had removed them. She pulled the covers up tightly under her chin as Francis approached.

She concentrated on the streaming flame of the guttering candle he carried, the trail of smoke it left behind, and answered him in a breathless rush, 'Thank you, yes. Francis, how did I get here?'

'I found you asleep in your chair, and carried you through.'

'Who removed my clothes?' she demanded in a small voice.

He carefully placed the candlestick down on a table before perching on the edge of the bed. The candle flame stilled. The acrid smoke it had been emitting tickled her nostrils. The mattress shifted under his weight, the bedstead creaked. The white of his shirt — he wore no coat over it — dazzled Charlotte's eyes. One side of his strong face was in shadow, but the candle lit the other, catching the angles of his cheekbone and jaw, the softened line of his mouth. Her breath caught in her throat. She clutched the covers even more tightly.

'Custer and I did, between us,' he informed her easily. 'Don't you remember at all? You stirred a little.'

'I — perhaps.' She frowned. 'I remember something vaguely. I thought it was a dream. . .'

She had not woken because the dream had been delightful and she had known she was safe.

'We thought it best no one else knew where you were, even Hoddy, who might be tempted to gossip. I sat with Rose through the night, and this morning I told Nurse Midgeley you were asleep in your dressing-room and on no account to be disturbed. I locked the door so that she couldn't intrude. I told everyone the same story. You can return to your truckle-bed, and no one will be the wiser.'

She knew that Custer had served in the army with

Francis and his loyalty was unquestionable. She liked him and thought he liked her, though they had not had occasion to speak much. If Francis had told him to be discreet, Custer would die rather than betray his master's confidence. So that was all right. But. . .

'But were you not noticed?' panicked Charlotte. 'And I shall surely be seen in the corridor, and I shall have to walk across my bedroom to reach the dressing-room! Oh, dear! What time is it?'

'Almost time for dinner, but they will not expect us,' he told her dismissively. 'Stop worrying, Charlotte!'

'Have I been asleep all day?' she cried, aghast. 'Rose! How is she? I must go to her at once!'

In her agitation she would have sat up, but he pressed her gently back against the pillows.

'Rose is fine, and quite happy to let you sleep for as long as you need. Hoddy has agreed to sit with her tonight, and will be given time off tomorrow. You were heading for a breakdown, Charlotte, and I could not allow that.'

He paused, but she had nothing to say on that subject. She knew he was right. Jenny would conduct an adequate vigil.

'As for our being seen, I brought you here through the communicating door between our dressing-rooms,' he explained. 'You may return the same way.'

Charlotte's eyes widened. 'You have the key?'

His quirky smile grew, and Charlotte knew he was thoroughly enjoying her consternation. His eyes laughed at her in the flickering light, his face creasing into a deeper, unrepentant smile. She found herself melting impotently under its impact.

'I have a key. Not the one the housekeeper keeps so carefully locked away, but one I found in the back of a drawer when first I arrived here. I had not expected to

use it, but it seemed a useful asset last night.' He
paused. The amusement gave way to another emotion
as he added, 'I have been tempted to use it many times,
Charlotte, for I have longed to have you in my bed.
And now here you are.' His voice had deepened,
echoing the throb pulsing in Charlotte's veins.

Their eyes locked. Francis stretched out a hand to
smooth the tumbled curls from Charlotte's forehead.
She waited, incapable of movement or protest. He
opened his mouth, but before he could say more a
discreet tap on the door announced the arrival of his
man, Custer, bearing a tray of tea and sandwiches. His
short, stocky body sent an elongated shadow before
him as he advanced.

'The young lady is awake, then, Major,' he
remarked, his nut-brown, crumpled face split by a huge
smile.

It was as though he had brought a cold draught into
the room with him. Charlotte felt cheated. He had
interrupted at quite the wrong moment. Francis had
swiftly risen to his feet. 'She is indeed, Custer. Leave
the tray here.' He shifted the candlestick to make room
on the table near the bed. 'I'll ring when I need you
again.'

'Very good, Major.' Custer shared a broad smile
between them, and retreated.

Francis poured a cup of tea and handed it to her,
offering a sandwich. Charlotte sat up carefully, so as
not to dislodge the bedclothes, and accepted both with
shaking hands. She was so strung up she could not force
the food down, but drank her tea in tense silence. Her
emotions were in such chaos that she was incapable of
sensible thought, or she would have been glad of the
interruption.

Francis resumed his place on the edge of the bed and watched.

'Another cup?'

'No, thank you. That was lovely.' She handed back the cup and saucer and sank down in the bed again, but one hand picked at the covers and she avoided his eyes when next she spoke. 'Francis, people are bound to guess that I have slept in here. Custer knows that we are alone. My reputation will be in ruins.'

'I do not think so, my love. You know Custer will not gossip. And it would not matter in any case, for we will simply announce our engagement.'

'Francis?'

The word was little more than a breath. A surge of excitement and joy rushed through her, her senses spun off into a world of delight, of warmth and laughter and exquisite joy. Her whole soul and all the love she felt for him shone from her gold-flecked eyes as she gazed back, dazzled by the blue blaze in his.

Slowly — oh, so slowly! — he bent over her, his eyes softening to tenderness. 'Charlotte,' he breathed. His lips covered hers in a lingering kiss. Her breath stopped from the sheer pleasure and beauty of the sensations provoked as they moved over hers, teasing and exciting, clinging and parting, demanding that she respond. Swamped in a tide of sweet enchantment, she allowed her own lips to part, to cling to his in a wild expression of her love. She forgot her modesty, bringing her arms up to bury her fingers in the crisp softness of his hair, sliding them down to feel the firm shoulder muscles rippling under his shirt.

Soon his lips left hers and moved down to touch the pulse beating like a moth at the base of her throat. Her chemise was quite high in the neck, and had short sleeves. His lips traced its neckline while one of his hands pushed back the bedcovers so that it could cup her breast through the thin material. His thumb brushed its peak and she let out a startled gasp as fire shot through her body.

'Francis!'

'Hush, dear heart; trust me. I'll not harm you, I'll not violate you, though —— ' his voice roughened ' — God knows I want you badly enough. But trust me, my sweet Charlotte.' Now he spoke deeply, soothingly, as his fingers began to untie the ribbons fastening the front of her chemise. 'I have longed to explore your beautiful body, and there can be no harm in that. I believe you want it, too. So trust me,' he breathed yet again.

Charlotte's momentary unease disappeared under the soothing influence of his words and tone, the urgency of her own need. Her newly awakened body clamoured for him, responding to every touch of his lips and hands with soaring abandon. Soon her breasts were free and she shut her eyes, revelling in the knowledge that he found their fullness enchanting, that touching them, kissing them, rousing their peaks to stiffened sensitivity gave him as much pleasure as it did her.

His hand slid down, caressing her bare stomach under the chemise and pantaloons. Charlotte gasped in new alarm as his searching fingers found the secret core of her. Yet she could not stop him, had no desire to. Shafts of fire scorched along her nerves and veins and then something seemed to explode inside her and the world dissolved.

When she came back from wherever she had been it was to find Francis lying quietly beside her, his hand gently stroking her breast, his lips on her temple.

'All right, my love?' he asked quietly.

Charlotte turned her head on the pillow until their

eyes met. 'Oh, Francis! My dearest love! How can you
doubt it? But what happened to me?'

'Something that should always happen when a man
and a woman make love.'

'But it did not happen to you!'

He gave a wry laugh and returned his gaze to the
shadowy, scrolled ceiling. 'No. It will need a little more
action on your part, my sweet, or for us to be truly
united, flesh to flesh, before I can join you in those
realms of delight. But do not doubt that we shall enter
them together once we are wed.'

'Oh, Francis!'

Her wail brought his head round sharply. 'What is
it?'

'I cannot marry you!'

Dreadful reality had overwhelmed Charlotte. She felt
as though she was suffocating beneath a thick, envel-
oping blanket.

Slowly, Francis sat up and resumed his position on
the side of the bed.

'What in the world are you talking about?'

'I cannot marry you, Francis,' Charlotte repeated
miserably.

'I am sorry, but I do not understand. What reason
can there possibly be? I cannot believe that you dislike
the idea!'

'No, but. . .' She hastily sat up and began fastening
her chemise, her colour high. 'Please do not ask further.
I just cannot marry you, that is all.'

Francis stood up and paced away, turned and paced
back. Her refusal shocked him. He had surprised
himself by his declaration — he had not quite meant to
make it — but having done so had been astonished by
the surge of happiness and triumph which followed.

Despite her origins, Charlotte would make him a fine

wife. It dawned on him that he had arrived at this conclusion unawares. Perhaps reluctance to commit himself had blinded him to the truth. All his adult life he had pictured himself wed to some American beauty, a woman who would be a social asset and provide him with heirs. But although he had never met one he liked enough to be tempted into marriage the image had been difficult to erase. A suitable wife had been his goal, there had seemed plenty of time in which to find her and all other considerations had been discounted. He was worldly enough to know that few men found more than tolerable liking within marriage. He had not seriously expected more.

So, despite the undoubted attractions of the seductive witch presently occupying his bed, he had not thought of her as suitable to be his wife.

Yet why not? Charlotte had proved herself deeply loyal, adaptable, shrewd and quick-thinking. Life with her would never be dull — she was full of ideas, and interested in most things — even railways! And beneath her demure exterior lay a latent sexuality he had surely only begun to explore.

And she loved him. He was experienced enough to recognise the signs when a woman found him attractive, and Charlotte did. But he had seen more in her eyes. Her emotions ran deeper than that.

'Charlotte——'

'Please keep your back turned while I dress,' she urged desperately.

He spun away again, restraining a curse, and Charlotte hastily left the bed and reached for her petticoat and gown, which she had spotted on a chair near by. Francis spoke from his position by the mantelpiece, one hand resting on it while he gazed into the depths of the fire.

'Do you want me to ask you on my knees? I will gladly do so, if it will please you.'

'Of course not! Do not be so silly!' She slipped the gown over her head and arranged the pink and grey checked skirts over the crinoline before buttoning the bodice.

'Then what is it? I could understand if I were asking you to become my mistress, but I am asking you to become my wife!'

In his exasperation, Francis turned abruptly, but Charlotte was just fastening the last button. She dropped her hands and stood in helpless silence. What could she say? I am, strictly speaking, a bastard? That would raise other questions she could not answer. Even if he accepted the fact — and he just might, for he undoubtedly desired her, could even have begun to love her, and was in no way strict and stuffy in his morality — even so, she could not admit Sir George to be her father without hurting others.

'I have no wish to live in America,' she told him dully.

Francis drew a deep breath. 'You do not wish to leave your family?' he asked tightly. The disappointment he felt at her refusal alarmed him. He had not realised quite how much she had become an essential part of his life. If she was unwilling to leave home and family to return with him, he could scarcely blame her. But it meant he had been wrong. She did not love him.

Charlotte snatched at the excuse he offered. In a sense he was right, for she was torn by loyalty to her family, but she also knew that such a consideration would have counted for nothing had she been able to follow her heart.

'You must see that I cannot abandon my brothers and sisters simply because my own fortunes have changed,' she said stiffly, while inside unshed tears threatened to drown her in anguish. 'And Rose will need a great deal of help if she is to recover completely,' she pointed out flatly.

'Charlotte!'

Francis's voice held exasperation and a hint of desperation as he took a step towards her, his arms reaching out as though ready to sweep her into an embrace.

Charlotte stepped back quickly, taking refuge behind the chair. 'No, Francis, please! Do not make my choice more difficult than it already is!' Her voice let her down and began to shake. 'My dear, you must know where my heart lies, but I cannot neglect my duty.' Her eyes were wide and glistening with the tears threatening to spill over at any moment.

Francis knew that to press her further at that moment would be of no use. His arms dropped to his sides. He shrugged, as though dismissing the entire matter.

'Very well. You had best return to it. The door is unlocked. You have only to walk through.'

Charlotte straightened, and nodded. Their eyes met for one final instant and Charlotte thought her heart would break anew, for all the brightness had been extinguished from blue eyes which, such a short while ago, had been alight with tender passion.

She walked through his dressing-room, noting his evening clothes laid out in readiness, and passed into her own familiar domain. She closed the communicating door behind her, but did not shift the key to her side of it. Francis would not intrude without invitation, of that she was certain, and she could not insult him by locking the door between them. She waited for him to do so from his side, but he did not. So the way was open should she wish to change her mind.

* * *

Charlotte washed and changed before emerging into the stuffy heat of the sickroom to visit Rose. Nurse Midgeley was there, and Charlotte was glad to see that, despite her rather grim exterior, the nurse had managed to establish a brisk but almost friendly rapport with her patient.

'You had a good long sleep,' she greeted Charlotte. 'Are you feeling better?'

'I was just tired,' responded Charlotte, forcing a smile. 'I have been awake for some time, but had to make myself respectable before I came to see the invalid, or I might have frightened her into a relapse!'

Rose managed to raise a smile in return. Her skin had recovered a more healthy appearance and her eyes something of their old sparkle, but an indefinable shadow lay over her whole appearance.

'I am glad to see my sister looking so much better, Nurse. Would you like to go for your supper now? I will remain with Rose until Jenny Hoddy comes to sit with her — although whether I shall be able to fall asleep again so soon I rather doubt, so perhaps Rose will have two of us to keep her company overnight.'

'You'll drop off soon enough,' predicted the nurse with a decisive nod of her head to bolster her opinion. 'You have a lot of lost sleep to make up. If you need me again, you have only to send someone to fetch me.'

'Thank you, Nurse. I wish you a good night.'

Nurse Midgeley smiled with a certain degree of complacency. 'My room is extremely comfortable; I am most gratified. I will see you in the morning, young lady,' she said to Rose. 'Goodnight, Miss Falconer.'

Once she had departed, Rose turned eagerly to her sister.

'Lottie! I'm so glad you're better. Come and speak to me, do, for although Nurse is most efficient she is not the best companion in the world! She can speak of nothing but other patients she has nursed, and what their gruesome ailments were. I shall have enough medical knowledge to become a nurse myself before she is done!'

In attempting to cheer her sister, Charlotte managed to put aside her own problems for a while. But when she returned to the truckle-bed in her dressing-room they crowded back into her mind, and Nurse Midgeley's prediction was proved quite wrong. For hours Charlotte tossed and turned, reliving those exquisite moments in Francis's arms, wondering what complete union would have been like, longing to experience it, fighting the temptation to open the connecting door and offer herself to him.

He had proposed, but he would take her without marriage if she were willing. She could know the joy of loving him fully. She had only to turn a handle and take a few steps to enter paradise.

'Oh, Ma!' she whispered desperately into the darkness. 'Is this how you felt?'

For the first time, she understood the temptation her mother had faced. Could imagine why she had given herself to the man she loved. It was difficult to visualise her mother and Sir George as lovers — it seemed impossible that older people had once been young like oneself, especially parents. But they had been. She was the living proof of it.

Sam and her mother together she did not wish to envisage. She had abhorred the idea of the act, seeing it as one initiated by the man for his own pleasure and release, endured by the woman and all too often, unfortunately for her, resulting in another pregnancy.

Yet what had occurred between her and Francis was so utterly different from anything she might previously have imagined. It had been a beautiful experience, one she would remember for the remainder of her life. And she would not mind how many babies she bore Francis Langford. Each one would be a joy.

Rose continued to progress well. Charlotte divided her time between the sickroom and the schoolroom. She took her meals with Rose, thus avoiding contact with Francis or, for that matter, anyone in the family apart from Victoria.

She was in no mood for socialising. Concentrating on Vicky's lessons was difficult enough, and it seemed important to hide away until the turmoil inside her had resolved itself into some kind of order. Otherwise the others would surely guess that something was drastically wrong.

Although Rose no longer needed constant supervision and so she was able to take to her truckle-bed each night, she found sleep difficult to find. For one thing she felt bound to keep an ear open in case Rose called. But that on its own would not have kept her awake.

Frankly, she did not know what to do, and lay for hour after hour trying to find an answer to an apparently insoluble problem. She longed to throw herself into Francis's arms. There, she would find comfort and reassurance and infinite joy. But at what cost? Quite apart from the morality of the action, it would spell ruin and heartbreak, for Francis would not take her to America as his mistress, and once the Brixham Branch line was opened he would be taking ship for home.

He was already displaying some impatience at the lengthy wait, for the works would not be finished before the end of the year. Some months earlier he had agreed to attend the opening celebrations and dinner as an honoured guest, and despite the delay could not easily go go back on his commitment without appearing discourteous. In any case, she knew he wanted to see the line in action, to witness the success of the engineering works. His interest had grown rather than diminished over the intervening months of delay and setback. The practical knowledge he was gaining should enable him to invest more knowledgeably in the American railways on his return.

But with Rose's departure for home drawing ever-nearer Charlotte's apprehension grew. She would have no excuse to avoid family occasions, no further reason for refusing to resume her former way of life, the morning rides, the outings in the jingle, the intimate evenings when she sat with her tatting — the results of her industry now admired by everyone — and conversed with her father and Francis, discussing every subject under the sun. Cecily and Felicity seldom joined in except to exclaim over some surprising statement, and Tristram, when he was there, confined himself to clever or sarcastic remarks. Recently, Charlotte had detected an air of excitement under his charming exterior, which worried her. She had caught Sir George watching his son with mounting concern.

Francis had taken to visiting Rose when Charlotte was occupied in the schoolroom. So he was avoiding her just as she was him. Which made life easier, but piqued her just the same — and worried her, for she dreaded his broaching the subject of Rose's supposed relationship to Sir George! Or of Rose saying something which gave him cause to question her position. He was the only member of the household who came close enough to Rose to be a danger.

'Are you two avoiding each other?' demanded Rose one day.

'Of course not,' denied Charlotte, not terribly convincingly.

'If I was you I'd snap him up quick,' Rose had advised. 'I've always thought he was sweet on you, and I'm certain of it now. He's forever talking about you, you know, and he looks pretty unhappy at the moment. He does his best to be cheerful, but I know he's forcing himself.

'You are imagining it!'

'No, I'm not and he makes a better job of it than you do, if I may say so. You're like a wet blanket all the time, Lottie.'

'I am not!'

'You know you are! I can't think why you won't have him, if refusing him makes you so miserable. You can't seem to see your luck when it smacks you in the face. If you ask me, he's got it bad, and you're a fool not to grab him while you can.'

'Well, I'm not asking you!' Charlotte had snapped.

To be told that the man she loved and could not have was as unhappy as she was did not help at all. That just made two of them. She hated to hurt him, yet could see no honourable way out of her dilemma.

'It's not fair,' Rose grumbled, giving voice to her fretting anxiety and resentment at the blow fate had dealt her. 'You could land a rich husband and go to America while I. . .'

Charlotte listened to her sister's grumbles with as much patience and sympathy as she could muster. As Rosie improved physically she seemed to descend deeper into gloom. Charlotte began to think that the sooner she got back to King Street the better. Not only would she have less time to brood, but would not be able to tease with her constant barrage of advice as to how Charlotte should conduct her relationship with

Francis Langford. Of course, Rose did not understand the true circumstances, but her constant harping on the subject was beginning to affect Charlotte's nerves.

When Dr Stone proclaimed her sufficiently recovered to return home Rose surprisingly, since she had envied Charlotte her chance to live at Bradgate Hall, seemed anxious to leave. Homesickness had overcome envy.

Nurse Midgeley departed at once and the following day Charlotte took her sister back to King Street in Sir George's coach.

It was the first time Rose had travelled so stylishly — the journey to the hall did not count; she had been unconscious — and she made the most of the occasion, behaving like an excited child imitating quality.

'Do calm down, Rosie!' pleaded Charlotte, not displeased to see her sister so elated but afraid of the consequences. 'You will tire yourself out and have a relapse.'

At home Rose found herself in the centre of a family bent on making a fuss of her. The younger children's insistence on doing the simplest thing on her behalf was quite touching, but quickly forced Rose to assert her independence. She might bemoan her fate, but it was not in her nature to lie down under misfortune. Backed up by Ada, she immediately began to demonstrate just how well she could manage with one arm.

By the time Charlotte left she was satisfied that Rose was in good hands, that she would soon take up the threads of her life once more, though she would never work at gutting fish again. That could be a blessing in disguise. She had always thought Rose worthy of a more congenial occupation, and there must be plenty of more satisfying things a person could do with one arm. Meanwhile, Aunt Ada would welcome her help.

CHAPTER THIRTEEN

CHARLOTTE walked back to the Hall, for she had not wanted the coach waiting while she made a lengthy visit to her family. She was reminded of her tramp to catch sight of Bradgate Hall, when she had first spoken with Francis, and of her subsequent visit to beg help from her father. How completely her attitude to *him* had changed in the intervening months! She had to admit that she had grown to love Sir George as a father should be loved. Her mother had held him in her heart all through the years. She should have known he would prove a worthy recipient of such devotion.

Gradually, during the course of those sleepless nights, Charlotte had come to an inescapable conclusion. She must leave Bradgate Hall, at least until Francis had departed. To do so, she would need her father's assistance, for she could not return to King Street.

Firstly, she did not want to. It would be an imposition to add to the overcrowded conditions at the cottage, even for a few months. Autumn was already painting the countryside in mellow tones of russet and gold. Perhaps four months stood between her and Francis's departure — possibly six, if storms prevented his sailing until late spring. And, more cogently, were she to live again under the same roof as Sam Falconer they would both constantly be reminded of an incident better forgotten.

Secondly, she would still run the risk of meeting Francis. She had already spent months of her life attempting to dodge him when out and about in the town, and did not relish being forced to repeat the experience.

No, it would be better to do as she had first intended — travel to London. There, she could either lodge somewhere and spend her days exploring the undoubted attractions of the capital, or seek employment with a view to future independence.

She no longer desired this as urgently as she had. Her changing attitude to her father had considerably altered her outlook on a lot of things. Yet if she did not marry, once Victoria no longer had need of her, what was she to do with her life? Besides, without Francis to protect her, she was apprehensive of living at Bradgate Hall with Tristram in residence. Perhaps a spell in London would assist in her search for an answer.

She lost no time in seeking out Sir George, finding him in the library, working at a littered desk. She thought he must have been writing letters, for the taper in his silver inkstand was alight and the smell of sealing-wax hung in the air.

He replaced a quill pen among its fellows and rose to greet her. She told him of her decision and made her request.

An acute observer of all that went on around him, Sir George was not to be fobbed off with weak excuses. He began to question her closely on the reasons for her renewed wish to depart for London.

'Yes, Papa,' she admitted at last, and both were equally astonished at her use of the familiar title so easily used by his other children. It had risen so naturally to her lips. Sir George's face pinkened with pleasure, and Charlotte blushed when she realised what she had said. 'Yes, Papa,' she repeated softly, then went on quickly, before he could comment, 'It is because of Francis. I cannot marry him, for reasons you know only too well, and neither can I become his mistress, since I have ample evidence of what the consequence of such a relationship could be.'

'My dear——' began her father in distress, but Charlotte interrupted him.

'It is all right, Papa, I understand now only too well why you and Mother behaved as you did, but I find I cannot follow the same path.'

'I would not wish you to, my dear. In fact, I would do my best to forbid such a liaison. But Francis is an honourable man; I doubt very much whether he would be satisfied with less than marriage—has he suggested it?'

She nodded. 'And because of that I must absent myself from the house until he returns to America. To remain here together would be unendurable for us both.'

'Is he aware of your intention?'

'No. I am certain he would immediately offer to leave himself, but not only would that hurt dear Lady Bradgate, but I also know how much he wishes to monitor the progress of the railway line. So it is best if he knows nothing of my decision until everything is settled.'

'Do you love him so very much?'

The question took her unawares and colour flooded her pale cheeks. But she did not attempt to evade an answer. 'Yes, Papa,' she told him quietly. 'If I did not, I would not need to escape from him.'

'I see, my dear.' Sir George heaved a sigh. 'Very well,' he agreed reluctantly, 'I will keep you in funds until Francis has returned to America. I anticipate that my aunt, Lady Fielding, will be glad to welcome you to her establishment in Belgravia. She is an elderly lady, but not too old to appreciate a little young company.'

Relief swept over Charlotte. A way of escape was opening before her. She reached up and kissed Sir George on his bristly cheek. 'Thank you, Papa.'

Sir George patted her hand. 'I will dispatch a letter today. I should receive her answer in about a week, unless she herself is away from home. Meanwhile, my dear, you may count on me to smooth your path. We shall have to announce your imminent departure, of course, but not until Aunt Fielding has replied.'

With that, Charlotte had to be content.

The cause of Tristram's secret excitement was made clear a couple of days later. He swept into the drawing-room one evening with a young woman on his arm, and proceeded to introduce her.

'Papa, Stepmama, allow me to present my wife.' He eyed the assembled company with sly triumph, the excitement he had been suppressing for days now evident upon his face. 'Janie, my love, meet your new parents-in-law.'

If Tristram had sought to punish his father for the constant disapproval with which he viewed his son's dubious activities, he had succeeded. Neither Sir George nor Cecily Bradgate even attempted to conceal their dismay. One glance was enough to tell them that the girl was entirely unsuitable, dressed as she was in gaudy finery presumably bought with her new husband's money. To make matters worse, she was unashamedly pregnant.

Charlotte almost swooned with horror. She met Janie Prowse's triumphant smirk with acute distress. Her heart went out to her father and Cecily. Poor Papa! He had been forced into an unwelcome alliance and both the children of that ill-fated union were proving such a trial to him! Was it punishment for the illicit relationship he had enjoyed with her mother? If so, it was far more than his crime deserved. Or was it simply that he had not been able to love these children sufficiently because of the circumstances of their birth? She could find no answer to that question.

Francis's face wore a look of dark anger which boded ill for Tristram, but there was nothing he could reasonably do. He sized up his stepbrother's new wife as she flourished her marriage lines, proof of her new status. Sir George glanced at the document and dismissed it with a wave of his hand.

'I do not imagine you are joking, Tristram, though I could wish you were.'

Charlotte heard the desperate hurt in her father's voice and wanted to rush to comfort him. Instead, she found herself looking to Francis, wondering whether he had come across Janie or her reputation in his contacts with the townsfolk, or whether he was judging purely on appearances. For judging he obviously was. Just for an instant their eyes met. They exchanged glances which spoke volumes before, almost as one, they moved to take their places in support of their stricken parents.

Francis laid his arm across his mother's shoulders. Cecily gave him an uncertain smile, but one full of gratitude.

'Sir,' whispered Charlotte urgently, 'I must beg a private word with you, immediately.'

Sir George straightened his shoulders. He had aged ten years in the past five minutes.

He bowed with stiff courtesy to his son and Janie. 'Excuse us,' he murmured. 'Perhaps you will be good enough to await my return. I shall not be long.'

'Come, Papa! Is this a fit reception for my wife? Janie, my love, it seems we are not welcome company here. Let us retire to my room.'

'Ooh, yes!' giggled Janie with a pert leer. It was the first time she had actually spoken, and her voice grated around the elegant room like an intrusive chain-saw. 'We could do with a lie-down, couldn't we, Trissie, love? Let's go and find that comfy bed you was telling me about.'

'No,' said Sir George brusquely, pulling the bell-rope with unwonted vigour. 'I shall order Parsons to instruct the staff to confine you both to this room until I have decided on my response to your preposterous announcement.' He turned to his wife. 'My dear, will you come with me?'

'Of course.' Cecily was only too glad to escape the awkward confrontation. 'Francis, my love, lend me your arm.'

So the four of them escaped to the library, Sir George lingering long enough to be certain that Parsons had carried out his instructions. Felicity remained behind in the frosty atmosphere of the drawing-room. She appeared stunned by her brother's outrageous behaviour. It would reflect on her and maybe place her own marriage in jeopardy.

'Sir George,' began Charlotte, her agitation so obvious that her father took her hand and began to pat it soothingly, 'I do not know how to tell you this, particularly in front of Lady Bradgate — dear ma'am, I do not wish to shock you — but Janie Prowse has a. . .a certain reputation in Brixham. Why —— ' She swallowed uncomfortably, knowing she had to tell the truth of it, but dreading the pain her information would give. 'Why, even my young brother Danny has lain with Janie Prowse,' she told them uncomfortably. 'There must therefore be grave doubts as to whether the child she carries is Tristram's, though she may have told him it is.'

Cecily gave a small cry of distress. Francis renewed his efforts to comfort her while challenging Charlotte with narrowed eyes.

'God knows, the girl dresses like a loose woman, but are you certain of this? It is not just rumour, gossip? Danny bragging like most young men of something he has not in fact done?'

Charlotte shook her head. 'Unfortunately, no. I only wish it were. But Pa told me Danny had gone with her; it did not worry him, but I wept for my brother's innocence, for we both knew she was no better than the town prostitutes, though she did not do it for money, but simply because she enjoyed her popularity with the lads, and the presents they gave her.'

Silence succeeded these words. At length Sir George spoke.

'There can be no question of the child inheriting Bradgate Hall. The property is not entailed, and even if it were I would take steps to break the entail. Tristram is not worthy to inherit. I have long thought so; now I am convinced. I can do nothing about the title, of course. Pray God the child will be a girl, that the baronetcy will die with him. What a tragic end to an honourable and ancient title!'

He was forced to pause for a moment while he collected himself. No one else spoke, for they did not know what to say.

'But I will not have the slut in this house!' Sir George declared fiercely. 'They must go. I will make Tris an allowance, on condition that he takes himself and his wife as far away from here as possible! Tonight! It will be worth any cost to rid ourselves of their presence.'

'But what of the baby?' agonised Cecily. 'It may be your grandchild, my dearest Bradgate! How can you be certain it is not?'

'I cannot, God help me. And there may be other issue. But I will have no child of that woman inheriting my birthright! The estate shall go elsewhere.'

'Your first wife was a monster of cruelty and ingratitude, by what you have told me, and her children take after her!' declared Cecily indignantly.

'I fear you are right, my love. I suppose,' said Sir George grimly, visibly bracing himself to face an unpleasant episode, 'I must go and inform the happy couple of my decision. I have to confess it will be a relief to have Tristram gone. I have long wished that he would take himself off. He has never shown the slightest interest in the estate. He does not deserve to inherit it,' he reaffirmed vehemently.

He left the room. Francis was still engaged in comforting his mother. Charlotte took the opportunity to return to her own quarters.

The episode had been unpleasant and upsetting, but at least the way was now clear for her to return to Bradgate Hall once Francis had gone. She hoped her father would decide to leave the estate to Vicky, for the child already showed more than a passing interest in its running. And she herself could remain to help her, and perhaps guide the young woman she would become in her choice of a suitable husband. She could be aunt to Vicky's children. The vision of herself growing old in such circumstances held considerable attraction.

Three days passed in relative calm. The newly-weds had departed that same night with a great deal of noisy bluster, but they had gone. Tristram's man was to pack his master's belongings and join him at a hotel in Exeter. The manservant had shown little relish for the proposed change in his circumstances, and Sir George had promised him a position at Bradgate Hall should he wish to leave Tristram's service.

Charlotte knew she could not expect an answer from her father's aunt for several more days yet. She busied herself about the schoolroom and took long, solitary walks in the grounds when she thought she could escape without being observed.

Jenny had been dismissed for the night and Charlotte, wrapped in a thick wool dressing-robe over her flannelette nightdress, bent forward in her chair to poke the embers of the fire into a last reluctant flame. She would have to go to bed soon, but the longer she sat up, the shorter would be the time spent in restless tossing and turning.

In the quietness which had descended upon the house the sound of the communicating door from Francis's dressing-room opening came clearly to her ears. Her heart leapt into her throat. She froze in disbelief liberally laced with apprehension. She had trusted Francis. Had her instinct been at fault?

The door to her dressing-room was pulled to. She watched with bated breath for it to open. It might not be Francis. . .but who else could it be? A gentle tap upon the panel stretched her nerves further. Francis called softly, 'Charlotte, are you awake?' as he entered her room.

'Francis!'

His name was all Charlotte could manage. Francis saw her stricken face in the gleam from a single candle, and smiled somewhat caustically.

'No, Charlotte, I have not lost my self-control, I have no intention of abusing your trust, but we must talk, and you have been avoiding me of late.' He walked towards her, a tall, heart-stopping figure in a tartan dressing-gown. 'May I sit down?'

Charlotte nodded, still unable to find her voice. Francis sought a chair and drew it up to the fire. He sank into it, crossing his long legs and arranging the skirts of his gown with care. Once he was settled he looked across to meet her anxious eyes, his own reassuringly gentle. 'You are proposing to make an extended visit to London,' he observed levelly. 'Yet only days ago you informed me that you could not accept my proposal of marriage because you could not leave your family. That was, quite evidently, merely an excuse. I think I have the right to the truth, Charlotte. So no further prevarication, please, but some honest answers.' He leaned forward, suddenly tense. 'Why will you not marry me?'

Charlotte swallowed. Francis was speaking quietly, yet that edge of steel lurked beneath the surface. She sensed he was exercising immense restraint. He wanted to shout at her, to wring out the answers he sought. She found she was still speechless, so she shook her head helplessly.

He leaned back again, heaving a sigh. For the first time, a hint of uncertainty entered his voice. 'I had believed there to be a strong attraction between us, Charlotte.' He smiled wryly. 'This has been demonstrated on several occasions, I believe. But perhaps you do not love me? Or have you discovered some fault in me that renders the thought of our sharing the remainder of our lives distasteful?'

He paused, waiting for her to respond. She still had not spoken beyond that first strangled gasping of his name, which rendered his task difficult. But her eyes widened and her head shook in instant denial. He went on with more assurance.

'Then why do you continue to deny your true feelings?' he demanded with sudden urgency.

Charlotte tensed anew as he dropped to his knees on the hearthrug and reached for her hand. She wanted to avoid the contact, but the instant his fingers touched hers she found her hand turning in his to take a convulsive grip, as though she were clutching at a lifeline.

'Charlotte?' he husked.

And then her head was buried in his neck. 'I cannot tell you,' she cried. 'The secret is not mine to reveal!'

'Secret?' Suddenly he was alert, quite still, yet intensely tender. 'But there should be no secrets between us, my dearest. Can you not find it in your heart to speak?'

'How can I?' Charlotte lifted her head. Her beautiful eyes brimmed with tears. 'I cannot marry you without telling all, Francis, but to tell you would be to break a confidence, to cause others great unhappiness and. . . and probably make you despise me.' She swallowed and drew a shaky breath. 'You would not wish to marry me if you knew the truth,' she whispered. 'That is why I can never be what I want to be most in all the world!'

'Which is?' he prompted softly.

'Your wife.'

'Oh, my love!'

On the instant she was enfolded in Francis's arms. For long moments she surrendered to the indescribable relief of being where she so longed to be. But gradually the emotional tide receded. She sniffed noisily and fumbled for her handkerchief, to find a large, clean white square pressed into her hand.

She blew her nose and wiped her eyes, crumpling the linen into a ball when she had finished. Despair welled up anew. Why could he not simply accept her word, let her go, cease to torment her with his pleas, his tender concern?

'I could not be certain of your true wishes,' he confessed, with a lop-sided smile that tore at her heart. 'From the first you have seemed so reluctant to allow any closeness to develop between us. I had thought you must hold my intentions or my character in some doubt.'

She returned his smile, a weak ray of sunshine pushing its way through the clouds. 'Not your character, sir,' she teased as lightly as she could, 'but my own strength of will to resist you! Though I must confess that I did suspect your intentions on more than one occasion!'

He had the grace to blush. 'And not without cause! I still remember our encounter in the drive with shame! How could I possibly have thought you so base?'

'I was but a poor girl from the Quay.'

'I am not given to judging a person by the circumstances of their birth,' he informed her sternly. 'My opinion was not based upon that, I can assure you. I suspect it was more a question of jealousy, though I would have died rather than admit it at the time! Even then I wanted you for myself.' Her lips parted in surprise and he laid a silencing finger against them. 'But whatever the mistaken cause of my behaviour I must beg your forgiveness.'

She kissed the restraining finger. 'You have no need, Francis,' she whispered, 'for I forgave you long since!'

That declaration brought its deserved reward. When at last the kiss ended, Francis cupped her face with his hands.

'Nothing you could tell me could prevent my wishing to marry you, my love,' he assured her tenderly.

She could admit to part of the truth, test the sincerity

of his assertion. Did he truly love her? Undoubtedly, he desired her, liked her, felt tenderness for her. Yet she still could not feel certain of his deepest feelings. She longed to know what they were, even though the knowledge could do no good.

'Not even the fact that my birth was. . .not quite what it seems? That Samuel Falconer is not my natural father?' she asked, and waited for his answer with suspended breath.

'No, my love, not even that.'

He did not appear in the least dismayed. His eyes smiled, even twinkled into hers. Charlotte knew then that despite her love for him she had badly underestimated his generosity of spirit. She should not have doubted him. She reached up to touch the scar in his hairline, running a tender finger down his temple and along the roughness of his side-whiskers to his smooth jaw.

As her hand lingered, he turned his head to touch his lips to her palm. 'And unless you have some further obstacle to our marriage the ceremony will take place at St Mary's tomorrow, at noon.'

At her startled gasp he released his hold on her face, leaning back to bring a document from beneath the lapel of his gown. 'I have here a special licence,' he told her blithely, 'obtained from the Bishop in Exeter. You may have remarked my absence from the house last night?'

She had. Knowing his bedroom to be empty, she had felt bereft, a small foretaste of loss to come.

'A special licence?' she repeated stupidly.

'Yes, was it not a fine idea? I have Tris to thank for putting the notion into my head, so his unfortunate marriage served some useful purpose, after all.'

'But I still cannot marry you!' wailed Charlotte,

remembering that the whole story must come out before her conscience would allow her to follow her heart, and such honesty was still quite impossible. Nothing had changed!

'With that statement I fear I must disagree, for I have your father's permission to pay my addresses, and my mother assures me she would welcome you as a daughter-in-law.'

'My. . .father?' murmured Charlotte faintly. Her heart began to thud.

'Sir George Bradgate,' said Francis quietly.

Charlotte paled. 'You know?' she whispered.

'Yes, Charlotte. Your father could not bear to see you so unhappy, so he asked my mother and myself to join him. He told us both of your decision to leave his house. Suspecting your reason after what had passed between us, I informed him of my intention to return to America immediately. My mother, of course, evinced much distress at that. "So you believe yourself to be the cause of Charlotte's departure, do you, my boy?" my stepfather then enquired smugly.' Francis grinned. 'I fear I must describe his attitude as smug. He had, after all, forced me to admit something he had long suspected—that your happiness weighed heavily upon my heart. "I do, sir," I informed him. "I have asked Charlotte to do me the honour of becoming my wife, but she has refused, for reasons she will not reveal. I can therefore fully understand her desire to escape the enforced intimacy of continued residence under the same roof."'

He paused a moment, waiting to see what Charlotte would say.

'I did not wish to precipitate your departure,' she muttered huskily.

'Something your father made plain, my sweet, and

which I appreciate more than I can say.' He squeezed her hands warmly. 'What he told us then will go no further, I promise you. He had come to realise that my mother would not be unduly upset to learn of an episode so remotely set in his past. No one else need ever know the truth; there will be no scandal to disrupt our parents' lives, and your secret is safe. Can you think of further reason to refuse to marry me?'

His voice had turned teasing, but so disarmingly tender. A multitude of emotions threatened to swamp Charlotte completely. For some moments she could do no more than attempt to absorb the fact of the turn of events. A warm tide of gratitude deepened the affection in which she already held her father.

But now it was possible, did she really desire to marry Francis as much as she had thought? It would mean accompanying him to a strange land, far from all she had ever known. That doubt lasted no longer than the blinking of an eye.

Yes! cried her heart. Yes, if he loves me as I love him, I would follow him to the ends of the earth and beyond!

But he had never professed to love her.

'You do not love me,' she said.

The words were out, echoing her thought, and could not be recalled. She watched the astonishment, the gathering anger on his beloved features, and wished them unsaid. Better not to know the bitter truth, but simply to accept the affection and passion he offered and make them enough.

'Do I not?' he demanded fiercely. 'On what do you base your opinion? On my lack of feeling? My lack of consideration? My refusal to despoil you when I could so easily have made you mine?'

Charlotte's distress was evident. She knew exactly

how tender, how considerate he could be. Had she not relied on his strength and integrity more times than she cared to remember? And on his command of self?

She shook her head in rebuttal of his words.

'Then on what, pray, *do* you base your opinion?'

'You have never told me so,' she managed at length.

'Is that it?' His exasperation covered a surge of relief which left him quite weak. This female could turn him to a spineless jellyfish should he not have a care! But the relief was too joyous to be repressed for long. He lifted himself to one knee and placed his hand on his heart, striking an attitude.

'Miss Falconer,' he declaimed, 'I love you, more than life itself. My dear heart, how could you doubt it? Will you do me the honour of accepting my hand in matrimony?'

'Oh, Francis! Do get off your knees, you foolish man!' Charlotte's face reflected her exultant happiness. 'I love you so much I could not bear to think that you did not return my love, that was all! Yes! Yes! Of course I will marry you!'

In a moment they were both on their feet, clasped in an embrace which lasted so long that the clock chimed the quarter and the half-hour before their immediate need to express their love abated.

'I can barely bring myself to wait until tomorrow to make you mine,' breathed Francis. 'My darling, I desire you so much.'

'You do not have to wait, my love,' murmured Charlotte. 'Come.'

She took his hand and led him towards her bed. When he realised where she was taking him he resisted the pull of her fingers.

'No, Charlotte. I know how much you disapproved of your mother's behaviour, how the result on her life left you afraid. I love you too much in every way to take you now. I will not make you fully mine until we are well and truly wed.'

Both were trembling. The strength of Francis's response staggered Charlotte. His harsh, uneven breathing had made his voice sound so ragged.

She drew a sustaining breath. What she was about to do would take all the courage she possessed, but her love would give her strength. In that moment it seemed important that she prove her absolute trust in the man she was promised to marry. He would not let her down. She had doubted his love. Now she must convince him of her unshakeable belief in it. There was only one way to do that.

She tugged him forward; then, greatly daring, pulled at the sash of his gown.

'Come to bed, my dear love,' she urged. 'I want to prove to you that I am no shrinking female, afraid to go to her lover, and demonstrate my absolute conviction that I can rely on you to care for me, now and always.'

This was too much for Francis. How could he refuse such a generous gift? His lips were on hers as he lifted her in his arms and laid her on the bed.

Soon they were blissfully engaged in proving just how much each loved and needed the other, even Charlotte enticed into using hands and lips to express and return the passion Francis had ignited in her.

Francis's touch, his whole approach bespoke his sensitive nature, yet it sparked unimagined pleasure. His lips caressed and teased her sensitised skin, sending shivers of delight to thrill her through and through. She found it impossible not to explore his hard, muscular body, to seek out its secrets as he was seeking those of hers.

He groaned with pleasure, called her his dearest love, his beautiful wife, his darling girl, and so sent the last remnants of her reserve winging into oblivion. How could she remain shy, when her boldness gave him so much pleasure?

Charlotte's own delight far exceeded that of the time in Francis's bed, for then she had been fearful. Now she wanted to give, to prove her love, and her purpose brought its own reward. When their union became complete she cried aloud with exultant joy, her passion rose to meet that of the man to whom she was totally joined, in flesh as well as in heart, mind and spirit. And this time he climbed with her as she scaled the heights of ecstasy.

They lay quietly together in the aftermath of loving, her head nestled into his shoulder.

'I shall never allow you to escape me!' he declared roughly, drawing her supple body closer.

'I cannot imagine that I shall ever wish to!' she answered dreamily.

'We shall not sail to America until the spring; I do not think either of us would wish to miss Mr Wolston's celebrations! But you will be leaving your family behind. Are you sure you will not miss them?'

She paused in her stroking of his broad chest, tugging playfully at a few of the sprinkled hairs. 'Of course I shall. But we shall surely return for visits here? You will wish to see your mother and Vicky?'

He grunted, capturing her teasing fingers. 'You may not be prepared to make the long sea voyage. Quarters are cramped, and it is not a pleasant experience if the weather is rough. You may not wish to repeat it.'

'I am quite hardy enough to survive a couple of months of discomfort, sir!' she told him with spirit. 'Remember my lowly origins, if you please!'

He turned his head to kiss her hair. 'I shall never forget how much at home I felt in your kitchen that night of the storm. It may have been poor by the standards to which I had become used—you have yet to see the mansion I inhabit in America—but it was so welcoming, full of a warmth that money could not buy, for it did not emanate from the range.' He paused to kiss her again. 'That was when I fell in love with you, of course. I had never felt so strongly that I belonged. Belonged to you, my love. My extraordinary feelings were all due to your presence, though I was idiotically slow to appreciate the fact!'

Charlotte had to kiss him for that. But something he had said stirred a doubt in her mind. 'Is your home so very big?' she asked apprehensively. 'I have no experience of running such a household. . .'

'You will manage beautifully, my love, and fill it with the warmth which is peculiarly yours.' He kissed her again, to make sure she believed him. 'I have never been able to imagine any other woman as the mother of my children. But you. . .'

'Oh, Francis!' She clasped him tightly, desperate to show him how much she loved him. 'Knowing the truth about my birth, I was determined not to fall under your spell! I failed dismally, of course. As well attempt to stop iron filings from being attracted to a magnet!'

He chuckled, and stirred languidly. 'I am not entirely certain that I approve of being likened to a magnet, my love. At the moment I feel far too warm and pliable to consider a cold lump of iron a suitable comparison.'

Intoxicated with love and happiness, she could not resist teasing him. 'Would you prefer to be likened to a honey-pot, sir?' she enquired. 'I have no objection to acting the part of a bee.' She began to make a buzzing noise.

'You are the honey-pot,' he informed her, accompanying his words with a throaty chuckle, 'and I have an urgent need to sip again of your sweetness.'

To which she was quite unable to make any reply, since he had already suited his actions to his words.

The other exciting

MASQUERADE
Historical

available this month is:

ALL OF HEAVEN
Petra Nash

Miss Cecilia Avening was determined not to apply to
her grandfather, the Earl of Syreford, even though at 19
her future was uncertain. Required unexpectedly to help
Lord Marcus Inglesham with his three excitable nieces
as they journeyed to London, Cecilia found the children
were not about to let the acquaintance drop, which
meant continued contact with Marcus. But he was
considering the ladylike Miss Chadfield as his future
wife, and a lowly governess surely had no place in such
circumstances?

Look out for the two intriguing

MASQUERADE *Historical*

Romances coming in April

SILK AND SWORD
Pauline Bentley

Lady Eleanor Twyneham's first meeting with the outlaw
Conrad d'Artan was traumatic, but he had eventually acted
with honour. Conrad made no secret of his hatred for the
Twyneham name, nor his all-consuming determination to see
the d'Artan flag flying once again over Highford Castle, his
inheritance, but now Eleanor's prized dowry.

Even so, Eleanor knew that a Lancastrian exile stood little
hope as long as Richard III sat on the throne. Then in that
fateful year of 1485, Henry Tudor defeated Richard, and
Conrad returned in triumph . . . turning Eleanor's world
upside down!

AN UNEXPECTED PASSION
Paula Marshall

Being an account of the courtship and marriage of
Lord Granville and Lady Harriet (Haryo)
Cavendish, daughter to 5th Duke of Devonshire.

Haryo had been childhood friends with Granville, until she
grew old enough to understand that this beautiful young man
was her Aunt Bessborough's lover. In later years that
relationship began to damage Granville's career, and he was
advised to marry. It was Lady Bess herself who suggested
Haryo!

Haryo was intelligent and witty, but plain and poor, while
Granville, needing to marry money, was used to beauty as
well as brains in his lovers. Surely an arranged marriage
doomed to fail?

Also available soon in Large Print

TWO
HISTORICAL ROMANCES

&

TWO
FREE GIFTS!